Works by S.M. Perlow

Vampires and the Life of Erin Rose

Novels
Choosing a Master
Alone
Lion
Hope
War

Short Stories
Alice Stood Up

—

The Grand Crucible

Novels
Golden Dragons, Gilded Age

—

Other Works

Short Stories
The Girl Who Was Always Single

ALONE

VAMPIRES AND THE LIFE OF ERIN ROSE

S.M. Perlow

Bealion Publishing

A Bealion Publishing Book

Editor: Lynn O'Dell, Red Adept Editing Services
Cover design: Streetlight Graphics
Formatting: Polgarus Studio

smperlow.com—updates, social media links, and more information about the story

ISBN: 978-0-9992858-1-7

2.0.5-p1

Prologue

Cold air hit my neck and face, so I pulled my comforter tight under my chin. I buried my head deeper into my thick pillow and enjoyed its clean scent. When I rolled over to lie the other way, my sheets felt just as fresh around my legs. I was far too comfortable to get out of bed over a little cool air. Besides, I didn't have anything to do all day.

Or the next day.

Or ever.

I opened my eyes, sat up, and looked around.

A white desk against the wall opposite the bed had a closed silver laptop on it. To its left, an open door led into a bathroom. Daylight seeped around gray curtains covering a window to my right. A low white dresser was on my left. I didn't recognize any of it, or even the room itself.

The air conditioner turned off, plunging the room into silence. I tried to remember the night before, but came up with nothing.

I couldn't think of any job I had to be at, errands I had to run, or plans to meet up with friends. In fact, I couldn't think of any of my friends' names or faces at all.

What was going on?

The bed sheets and comforter were white. The red digits of a clock on a nightstand to my right read eight fifteen in the morning. I slid out of bed and stood on light gray carpet, then looked down at my clothing—a light blue tank top and matching boxers. I didn't recognize them either.

At the window, I pushed the curtains apart, and a city street bustled far below. To my left, the building curved into view, and it became likely I had woken up on the top floor of an apartment building.

I surveyed the room again and still didn't remember it.

I headed past the desk and cracked open the bedroom door. "Hello?" I asked quietly. My heart started to race, and after a few seconds, I tried again, louder. "Hello?" No one answered.

Through the door, I stood before a kitchen. The space opened to the left into a living room with a black couch, brown coffee table, and a flat-screen television.

I moved past the couch and TV to a large window on the far wall. Pushing aside its curtains, I once again looked down at a city street. I turned around to look back into the apartment. I had no idea where I was.

Near the kitchen, I slowly opened a closet door and peered in—empty. Returning to the bedroom, I cautiously opened the folding door of the wide closet, revealing a pair of sneakers on the floor and a black coat on a hanger. I opened each dresser drawer and found only jeans, some underwear, a few plain t-shirts, and a sweatshirt. None of it was familiar.

Looking down at myself, I didn't see any sign of injury

on my legs, my arms, or my body. I felt around my head for bumps or bruises and didn't notice any. I held some of my brown hair in front of my face—it hit me that I hadn't known it was going to be brown until seeing it.

I rushed to the bathroom and turned on the lights.

The emerald green of my eyes jumped out of the mirror and, like the rest of the girl looking back at me, was completely unexpected.

Who was I?

I couldn't answer the simple question that had crept into my mind, and it started repeating more forcefully.

I didn't know.

Oh, my God.

I looked down at myself and then back in the mirror. The reflection was accurate; it was just of a person I had never seen before.

Chestnut hair reached a few inches past my shoulders, my nose didn't seem too big, and I thought the face in the mirror looked pretty. I was thin and tall. Shades of tan in my light skin gave the impression that it could have been darker, but that I hadn't seen much of the sun recently. My breasts were on the small side.

Leaning close to look at my eyes again, a black mark on my neck caught my attention. I pulled back my hair and saw not one, but two small black circles in a vertical line on the right side of my neck.

A knot formed in my stomach. As unbelievable as the morning had already been, it became even more frightening. The marks looked and felt like scars.

Remembering the laptop and other items on the desk I had rushed past, I went back and found a driver's license, a few cards, a key, some papers, and a small black wallet.

I picked up the license first.

"Erin Rose." The picture matched my reflection.

"Height: 5-09."

"Date of birth: January 7, 1987." Which made Erin… I didn't know.

I didn't know what day it was or even what year. What was wrong with me?

The laptop was powered on, so I opened it and sat down.

The screen flickered to life, and the date in the lower right said September 14, 2007, so Erin was twenty. Or *I* was twenty.

A few tabs were open in the web browser, with a map of Washington, D.C. in the active one.

The second tab held a bank login screen. I replaced the driver's license on the desk and located a red debit card on a piece of paper to its right. The card said, "Erin Rose," and had my picture in the upper right corner. I entered the username and password from the paper on the website, and the account information loaded.

The name on the account read, "Erin Rose," and the balance was one hundred and fifty thousand dollars.

Next to where the debit card had been on the desk were a white and blue credit card and a thin, beige health insurance card. The wallet contained five twenty dollar bills.

A staple held together the bright white pages of a leasing agreement. Just like the map on the laptop showed, it was for an apartment in Northwest Washington, D.C. The lease explicitly listed one occupant: Erin Rose.

All of the evidence pointed to that being my name and the apartment being mine. But I didn't remember anything about myself, Erin Rose or otherwise.

The last piece of paper had only one thing on it, in a very large font:

Sanguan vampires hunt and kill humans. They may do so legally, outdoors, between four a.m. and six a.m. Don't ever be outside between four and six.

The word 'vampires' didn't shock me. I knew they drank human blood to stay alive, but 'Sanguan' meant nothing to me.

The encyclopedia entry on the next tab in the web browser supplied more detail right away.

Vampires are immortal beings that sustain themselves by drinking either synthetic blood (Spectavi) or human blood (Sanguan).

I went to the bathroom mirror, pulled my hair back on the right, and leaned close. The two marks rose a little from the rest of my skin and weren't perfectly round. The scars could definitely have been from a bite.

For a moment, I waited, hoping my memory would be jogged and at least something would come back to me, but nothing did.

I pored over every inch of my body, front and back—it felt like examining a stranger. I checked everywhere, and then checked again, and again. Seeds of relief were planted as I continued to find no signs of injury or abuse other than the scars. Eventually, I headed back to the desk.

"Erin Rose," the license still said. The collection of items in front of me gave the impression that whoever had set it all up didn't expect some other memory to come rushing back to me.

The thought was chilling and swept away most of my newly developed relief. I looked around the room. It wasn't a dream, yet it seemed so unreal.

*What*ever set it up, not whoever. The notion grabbed my attention. The bite mark on my neck had to have something to do with what happened to me, and that meant a vampire.

But why would a vampire have left me here like this? Some person must have. I couldn't think of anyone else I knew in the whole world, but maybe someone saved me from a vampire. Or maybe that wasn't it at all.

I went to the window, opened the curtains completely, and returned to read more.

Vampires are only awake at night and have superhuman strength and speed. In most cases short of decapitation, physical injuries to vampires will heal. Exceptions include extended exposure to the sun and significant silver in their bloodstream, both of which can be lethal.

For whatever reason, that information didn't surprise me. The next bit about the different kinds of vampires, however, was completely new.

Sanguan and Spectavi vampires have been at war since the Dark Ages, though the exact date is unknown. Sanguans do not respect human laws and feel that they should be allowed to do as they please with their abilities. The Spectavi fight them so that humans can be free of Sanguan oppression.

I absorbed as much as possible while reading the rest of it, and then searched for other sources of information on my own. I discovered that Sanguans had always been ruthless killers. Over the centuries, they had ruled countries and enslaved entire populations, though they didn't at present.

Historically, vampires had fought in both epic battles and isolated skirmishes and, thankfully, the Spectavi had won enough that humans had been able to chart their own destiny, mostly free of Sanguan rule. Recently, the battles stayed small because the Spectavi were winning the war decisively nearly everywhere, including in America.

Even so, long lists of Sanguan attacks between four and six in the morning, from all over the United States, were easy to find. In addition, plenty of articles detailed crimes outside that window. The Spectavi acted as a deterrent, but it was hard for them to stop sudden attacks when Sanguans set themselves on killing.

A local search turned up numerous, recent attacks by Sanguans in Washington, D.C. Most were between four and six a.m., making them legal, but more than a few weren't.

After my eyes had been glued to the screen for half an hour, my stomach growled loudly. I ignored it as long as possible before heading back to the kitchen.

I checked the refrigerator and freezer first, but all they had to offer was cubed or crushed ice. One by one, I opened each cabinet and found nothing. I turned to the front door, and two thoughts entered my mind.

First, the idea of going outside to get something to eat terrified me.

Second, it was daytime, so if I ever planned to leave the apartment, it wouldn't get any safer than then.

1

With a new email from work, but no texts or calls, it hardly seemed worth it to have run under the bus stop shelter to check. Still, a few seconds out of the cold rain wasn't the worst thing. My hair was soaked, as were my tights and boots. The rest of me had begun to get wet through my coat, which wasn't meant for such weather, so I was altogether pretty uncomfortable.

I wiped my hair out of my face and listened to the rain pelting loudly on the ceiling. I probably couldn't have heard a voicemail even if I had one.

No one else had taken refuge under the shelter, and beyond its thin plexiglass lay a desolate Washington, D.C. street. The unexpected downpour would only reinforce that, and my phone's weather app said that it would be around for a while. I went online to see if any of my co-workers had posted and couldn't imagine a twenty-two-year-old with a sadder list of friends. I sighed and put my phone away. Out of things to check, it was time to walk the last four blocks to the club. I still wanted to go, but I just hadn't prepared for the sudden change in weather.

I started towards the open entrance of the shelter and, out of the corner of my eye, saw a silver SUV speeding down the road. A black sports car raced toward it from the other direction. The car swerved to the right.

BAM!

The SUV plowed into the driver-side door of the smaller vehicle. Metal twisted and glass flew as the car absorbed the impact. The two vehicles came to rest, and three more SUVs screeched to a halt around the collision. I reached for my phone to call the police, but it slipped out of my hand and fell to the ground as I focused on the unfolding events.

In an instant, the passengers from the SUVs surrounded the crunched vehicle. They wore gray fatigues and brown boots and held assault rifles; some appeared to have swords sheathed across their backs. It was obviously no accident. Across the street and only half a block away, they waited, ready to shoot or do whatever they had come to do.

Two bodies broke through the roof of the sports car and flew into the sky. No human could have done that. Seeing their pressed pants, crisp shirts—both black—and gold jewelry, I figured they had probably been headed to the same club as me. That also meant they were Sanguan. At the club, I would have been careful with them around, but not overly afraid. Aside from being illegal, murdering humans there would be bad for business. People paid a premium for the experience, to be around vampires and maybe drink or dance alongside them; they didn't go to be killed.

But that was at the club. Alone at the bus stop, I fixated on how inhuman the vampires seemed as they rose into the air. I saw powerful animals on the brink of battle and feared what would happen if they saw me.

When shots rang out, I remembered with relief that those animals were also surrounded by men with big guns, presumably loaded with silver bullets. Heading toward the sky, the vampires pulled out handguns and returned fire, but the men on the ground quickly hit their marks. The Sanguans slowed their ascent and, as they started to fall, two more vampires climbed out of the far side of the sports car.

With the men in gray focused on the sky, the two new vampires escaped to hide behind an empty car. They ran, moving faster than anything I had ever seen. In fact, I hardly saw it happen at all. The men in gray turned toward them and, in the same manner, ran to the near side of the empty car. At that moment, I knew those in gray weren't men at all; they were Spectavi. Presumably the Sanguans were being hunted for killing illegally.

I reached to feel the scarred-over bite mark on the right side of my neck. My assumption was that a Sanguan had left it, but, after a lonely year and a half of searching for answers, I still didn't know what had actually happened to me. At first, I held out hope that on any day, at any time, at least a part of my memory would return, or someone would show up and explain that they had left me in that apartment. Neither ever happened. Eventually, it became exhausting and depressing to hold on to those hopes, so I let them go and tried to be proactive.

The police hadn't helped, nor had the Spectavi who worked with them. They all had never seen me before and had never heard of anything like what happened to me. That left the Sanguans.

Lately, when the prospect of more hours, nights and years of wondering about and guessing at who I had been became too much to stand, I would change out of my work clothes and put on something like my current outfit—knee-high black boots with big heels, short skirt, and tank top—to visit Sanguan hangouts with hopes of finding any small clue to follow toward another. In spurts of motivation, anger, and excitement, I convinced myself to be brave.

Sheltered from the rain, I knelt and reached for my phone with my right hand. My left was still at my neck on my scar until I stood back up and finally let it go. Early on, after growing tired of wearing turtlenecks every day, I had covered the black bite mark with a tattoo of a cross. Before that, I couldn't stand the scar in the mirror and felt like it was all anyone else saw when it was exposed.

Shots came from behind the Spectavi, who were focused on those hiding at the car. Two new Sanguans had joined the battle, and some of the Spectavi sped toward them, guns firing. The Sanguans proved elusive. They split up and moved to avoid the bullets coming at them, dancing around the street and onto the surrounding buildings. They fired back when they could and caused their assailants to scatter.

Time seemed to slow as the chaos unfolded at vampire speed. Amidst the stream of bullets, windows were shattered and small pieces of buildings burst upon impact, then crumbled to the ground. The vampires moved so quickly that, in one second, they accomplished more than a human could have in ten. I mostly glimpsed them where they paused before another move and then saw the results of their gunfire.

Finally, one of the Sanguans was hit in the stomach.

The wounded vampire slowed dramatically and, with one hand trying to hold blood inside him, he fired back with his other. His eyes grew wide, and he roared as he shot. I flinched behind my glass as the sound filled the night. He got one of the vampires in gray before a few others hit him. Full of lethal silver, he fell to the ground.

I thought again of the tattooed cross on my neck. Had the vampire just died, or had he already been dead? According to some religions, people died when they became vampires, and their souls died with them, but I wasn't sure. I didn't consider myself Catholic, Protestant, or anything in particular, but I did believe in God and Christ. They knew who I had been before I could remember, and when I woke up, alone, they were who I had to talk to. I chose the cross to remind me of that.

Cold wind blew through the shelter. I regained my composure and saw the Spectavi surrounding the newly arrived Sanguan, who continued to fight back. The combined groups of attackers formed a wide circle and began constricting it around him. He ran out of room and was gunned down all at once, without the parting flair of his companion.

The shots stopped, the block was calm, and time returned to normal for me. I took a deep breath and exhaled, while watching the Spectavi turn and start walking at human speed toward the car and the two vampires left hiding behind it. Guns trained on the Sanguans kept them crouched behind its protective metal.

I remained behind my not-at-all-protective plexiglass. The sound of the rain on the roof of the shelter became deafening, and I considered running while they focused on the car. With mostly Spectavi out there, I was probably safe enough staying put, but there could have been more Sanguans around, and I didn't like feeling trapped. On the other hand, I had just been reminded of how fast vampires were, so I obviously couldn't outrun anyone.

I was fit and good in a fight, at least in class, but face to face with a Sanguan, the small knife in my coat pocket wouldn't do much at all. No, I liked my chances in the shelter best—hidden, or at least ignored.

The rain came down harder, and thunder boomed as the vampires at the car appeared to yell back and forth.

The two Sanguans stood and walked slowly around the car. To my surprise, they weren't shot at as they moved out into the open.

Even through the rain, I could tell the two were different from each other. One was paler than the other, a little leaner, and wore a suit. That one slowly reached inside his coat, knelt, and put a gun on the ground. Then the other vampire did the same.

The paler one motioned to the other to stay back as he walked away from the car. He took off his coat and placed it on the ground, revealing a sword at his side. He turned in my direction.

Lightning lit up the sky and the rain seemed to slow for

a moment. With skin clearly the lightest of the Sanguans from the car, he was probably the oldest, and he looked pensive, not violent.

In that moment, I didn't see an animal in front of me; I saw history. I wondered how old he was, and what he had seen and done over those years. He could have had many human lifetimes' worth of memories and experiences, compared to the meager year and a half I could recall. I couldn't help but marvel at him.

As the lightning faded, he revealed his fangs and drew his sword. His face filled with rage. Thunder crashed, the rain resumed pounding down, and I snapped out of it and saw the animal again. He was old and powerful, and I stepped back until my hands and body were pressed against the rear of the shelter.

One of the Spectavi put down his gun and drew his sword. He moved toward the old vampire and, without hesitation, he attacked. Their swords met, but I couldn't hear the clash over the rain. They didn't move far as they swung again and again. They picked up speed until once more my human eyes could only keep up with some of the action.

Suddenly, the Spectavi swordsman fell to the ground. I hadn't seen the blow, but blood gushed out and mixed with the water around him. The Sanguan stood straight, ready for his next attacker, and paid no attention to the vampire that bled at his feet.

For a few seconds, the old vampire faced forward, and nothing happened. Then, three Spectavi surrounded him and drew their swords. The Sanguan grinned as he lunged at the one in front of him and then engaged all three.

Swords and bodies flew through the night as the vampires battled up and down the street. I had unconsciously moved to the front of the shelter to catch as much as possible. Even in glimpses, the fighting was furious and amazing.

A cut opened in the Sanguan's arm, and he started bleeding. He sliced open the vampire who had done it, forcing him to the ground. The two remaining Spectavi continued their attacks, and one cut the old vampire in the side. He was starting to lose a lot of blood, but managed to take down another of the Spectavi, leaving only one in front of him.

The Sanguan paused and looked around, maybe for a way out. As he did, the other Spectavi who had been watching the fight from afar moved toward him. Two put down their guns and drew swords of their own. The pale Sanguan was surrounded by three attackers once more.

The fighting resumed, and the old vampire proved a match for three yet again, but he was still losing blood. The battle became confined to a smaller space and, when I could discern more of his movements, he must have been slowing down.

Eventually, the Sanguan received a cut high on his leg, then one on his other side, and he slowed even further as blood poured from his wounds. He no longer attacked, becoming completely defensive.

Finally, after another slash to the leg, he went to the ground on one knee. Immediately, he was sliced open across the chest, causing him to fall backward. One of the Spectavi brought his sword high and swung down; the Sanguan's head was separated from his body.

I cringed at the gruesome sight. Thankfully, the other dead Sanguans didn't get the same treatment. The Spectavi left them on the street and loaded up their own fallen kinsmen. They also left the remaining 'living' Sanguan. Unarmed, it seemed they didn't consider him a threat, and their target must have been the old vampire.

The SUVs drove away together, and it was over as fast as it had begun. I had been around vampires plenty, but had never seen anything like that. Part of me wondered what it was all about, especially who the old vampire was, and what he had done to deserve that fate. I debated continuing on to the club to investigate. I hadn't been the cause of any of it, I reasoned. Plus, no one would know just how close I had been.

While I didn't think the battle had anything to do with my past, I was tired of not knowing so much and didn't want to add it to the list of things I spent my days wondering about. I finally decided that I had every right to go to the club.

I put my phone back in my coat pocket and started to step through the entranceway when I noticed the last Sanguan approaching from the right on the sidewalk that ran in front of me. In my eagerness, I had forgotten about him.

I grabbed the glass to my left, and froze there, halfway out of the shelter, but I couldn't stop my long hair from blowing out in front of me.

I held my breath while the vampire walked toward me, growing cold as my face and legs were rained on again and hit by the wind. I stood motionless. I wouldn't stumble out in front of a blood-drinker who had just seen five of his companions killed, and hiding had become impossible, so I waited, hoping to continue to be ignored.

With each step, he came closer and closer. He looked so strong, and I tried not to think about what he could do to me.

Finally, he was in front of me. He stopped, and a chill went down my spine and through my body. He stared straight ahead and breathed heavily through his mouth, revealing his fangs. A gust of wind brought my hair inches from his face.

I had sworn I would never again be bitten by a vampire, and yet, there I was. The Sanguan stood there as my hair blew between us. I still held my breath, but couldn't stop my heart from pounding. Could he hear it pumping blood through my body?

With no change of expression, he resumed walking and passed me. I waited a few seconds before finally exhaling and stepping backward. I tripped and fell into the corner of the shelter. While lying there trying not to make another sound, I considered how close I had been to death.

I couldn't go to the club that night. How could I ever? Reading about vampires and talking to Spectavi was one thing, but those Sanguans and that battle were something else entirely. That world was simply beyond me. I might not remember my past, but I was young and had my whole life ahead of me.

I got up cautiously and, when I didn't see the Sanguan on the street, began marching toward home. The rain soaked me, but it didn't matter. I thought through the events I had just seen over and over and kept coming to the same conclusion—I had to let it all go and move on. I couldn't ask for a better sign, or a closer call, to tell me that. My pace slowed as I calmed down.

I walked back through Chinatown and then another few blocks to reach my building. From outside, I saw the clean, new furniture in the lobby, just like in my apartment. I found my window on the top floor and knew that the place still didn't feel like home.

The rain dripped off of me as I headed through the lobby and into the elevator. I rode up alone, still dripping, and walked down the hallway to my apartment, wondering if it was normal that I didn't know any of my neighbors.

Inside my apartment, I stood on a doormat and unzipped my boots. They came off first and then my tights. It was already comforting to be a little drier. To keep the floor dry, I hung up my coat and finished undressing without leaving the doormat. The water-heavy clothes went directly into the washing machine, and I dried myself with a towel from my bathroom. I put on underwear and a t-shirt before throwing myself onto my bed.

I got under the covers to warm up and stared at the white ceiling. Who was that old vampire, and what had he done to deserve what happened? Was the Sanguan who stopped in front of me planning to attack, or was it something else?

I sat up and looked around the room. I had searched it

high and low for clues to how I ended up there. For countless hours on countless nights, I had lain awake on that bed with tears filling my eyes or streaming down my cheeks, while I struggled to comprehend what had happened. Yet after all that time in that room, still, nothing there felt like my own. Dwelling on it wasn't productive, and I tried not to again, but it was just so frustrating.

And I had new questions, but I had told myself it was time to move on and focus on the future.

Only, I already knew I couldn't.

It had been dangerous, and it would continue to be dangerous, but from the core of who I was, the person I was coming to know, I couldn't get past the fact that someone or something had left me in that apartment one night, to wake up utterly alone.

I lay back down.

It had been a close call with that Sanguan, but I had to keep searching for answers.

2

I finished her hair, put down my pencil, and looked at my notepad. As always, the one on the right had shorter hair than her twin. Aside from that, they were identical, and equally beautiful.

Drawing was one of the few skills I had learned I possessed. I enjoyed it and, during downtime at work, sketching was a welcome break from using my computer.

At the same time, my drawing sometimes added to the mystery I sought to unravel. Over the last year and a half, I had dreamt about the twin sisters only a few times but, after waking up, they quickly faded from memory.

When I drew them, however, it turned my dreams into something more permanent. I hoped to draw something new, something that revealed who they were or what they had to do with me. So far I hadn't, and in the drawings, they always ended up the same—two fair-skinned, light-haired young women smiling back at me.

I wondered if they meant to tell me something or if a forgotten detail would explain more. I made myself stop thinking about them when I had been at it for too long. But eventually, I would draw them again and be right back to searching my mind for answers.

Ding!

Brought back to my office by the soft chime from my computer, I almost laughed out loud reading my friend Kristi's email. I didn't know what she expected it to be like, but she had been begging me to take her to a vampire club since I had first mentioned going myself, and I had finally given in to her persistence. Anyone could go, so I wasn't really taking her, but she wouldn't go without me.

We were headed to Night, the club I had been on my way to two nights before when the pack of Spectavi killed the old Sanguan. I hadn't been able to find anything online or in the news about the battle and was once again firmly of the opinion that the club would be safe and that I wanted to go. Even if it rained, I wouldn't stop and duck under a bus stop shelter.

I had told Kristi the story of that night while we ate microwaved dinners in our office break room the day before, but she hadn't seemed especially moved. To her, it was simple; the Sanguan had broken the law and been punished.

After being so close to it, I hoped to find out for sure. If it was that simple, fine, but if not, I wanted to know what had happened. Kristi was just excited that she could tag along.

The club was within walking distance of my apartment, and the metro station Kristi would use was on my way. I wrote her back and said I would meet her outside the station at midnight, and we would walk over together.

At five after ten, Mr. Oliver was still working, but it didn't really matter. Since we had switched to our crazy hours, he didn't mind if I left at ten o'clock on the dot whether he was there or not, so I headed home to get ready.

I had tried black lipstick on my first trip to a vampire club, but it wasn't me. A little dark, smoky eye shadow was the extent of the gothic makeup I wore that night.

It was a little warmer than last time, but I chose a black turtleneck anyway. While my confidence had returned, covering my cross tattoo and scar seemed prudent considering the circumstances. Also, that night wasn't necessarily about me. If I learned anything about my previous life, great, but focusing on the Sanguan killing would really be enough. After spending so long on the mystery of my own past without finding any answers, it was exciting to worry about a different one for a change.

I added a gray skirt that didn't quite fall to my knees and black boots with lower heels than last time—my favorite pair was still wet. I inspected myself in my full-length mirror.

While a pair of blue jeans was always my first choice of attire, and there wasn't an official dress code at vampire clubs, I did want to fit in with their typical clientele. Plus, I had a nice body and had learned pretty quickly that, just like humans, vampires paid more attention to me when I dressed up.

Of course, I had also learned that a fine line existed between dressing to get vampires' attention and advertising one's self as willing food, so I never went too far.

Satisfied with what I saw, I double-checked the weather on my computer, pulled my hair back into a ponytail, grabbed my coat, and headed out.

———————————

It was a ten-minute walk to the metro station to meet Kristi. From what I had read, fifteen years earlier, it wouldn't have been the best route for a woman to be walking alone after sundown, but of course, I had no memory of then. That night, aside from a few dark areas with no buildings, it seemed safe enough. It was cloudy, but mercifully not raining.

I passed a few people walking by themselves and then saw what was left of Chinatown's nightlife. As always, there were both people and a scattering of vampires on the street and inside the bars and restaurants with big front windows. Most wore the trendy pants, skirts, dresses, tops, and shoes expected for a night out, usually in dark colors, but some provided a little variety by deviating from those norms and wore brighter colors or sneakers and jeans.

Vampires were usually easy to spot, even aside from their generally lighter skin. While they appeared essentially human, with similar attire, vampires often wore the finest fabrics or leather and the newest designer fashions. Both males and females could show off more skin at any time of year because they didn't feel cold.

Night was a Sanguan club where Spectavi weren't welcome, but there were probably both types of vampires in Chinatown. Despite not needing to eat or drink traditional food, they spent time with humans who did.

Most of the vampires out there were young, so I could tell the two types apart with reasonable accuracy by how calmly or aggressively they acted. While that strategy worked well enough for me, the vampires always knew for sure. The Spectavi could smell pure blood in the Sanguans, and the Sanguans couldn't miss hints of the Spectavi's chemical substitute. Occasional altercations arose with them in such close proximity, but for the most part, they wouldn't interact with each other and were civil in that type of setting.

The light crowds were about what I had expected for midnight on a Wednesday and, hopefully, indicated it would be similarly slow at Night.

Kristi stood waiting for me outside the station when I arrived.

People told me I looked very serious all the time and that I should smile more. Usually I was just thinking and didn't have a lot of happiness in my life to think back on. Yet for the second time in the last few hours, Kristi had brought a wide smile to my face. It was her outfit. Whatever she had read, or someone had told her, it was definitely not my fault.

"Well hello, Kristi!"

"Hey, do you think this is too much?" She looked down at herself while opening her coat for me to see. "I didn't know what to wear."

She had on a red strapless top and a short black skirt, which would have been reasonable enough, except they were both made of shiny latex. She was pretty short, so her very high-heeled boots weren't surprising. They were similarly shiny, and reached up over her knees.

Kristi often dressed to draw attention to her chest, and her other outfits had left plenty to see, but she had never dressed quite like that with me around. Maybe she'd learn that it was a bit over the top, even for a vampire club.

"You'll be noticed; there's no doubt about that," I told her while looking her over. Her dark brown hair was down, and her lips were bright red.

She grinned as she rebuttoned her coat. "Well, good. I can't wait. Let's go!"

At least Kristi had a coat over some of her while we walked to the club. She was funny, though, and had become my best friend. I was lucky to have met her.

My thoughts turned to the events of two nights prior. Night was six blocks off the main street of bars in Chinatown. I peered ahead of us to see the bus stop as soon as I could, as if something might have happened to it in the last two days.

The shelter came into view, exactly where it should have been. Either rain or the police had washed the vampires' blood from the street. The crashed car had been removed, and some of the shattered glass had already been replaced.

"There it is." I pointed across the street.

Kristi grabbed my hand and stopped walking, so I stopped with her. She became serious. "Do you miss it?" she asked. "If you need a moment alone with it, I can wait."

I took my hand back and started walking. "Ha, ha, fine. I get it. Let's go."

"I'm just saying, Erin, if you want to hang out at the bus stop again instead of the club, we can do that. Who knows what will happen tonight?"

"I'm the one walking, Kristi; you're just standing there," I called back to her.

"I think I see another bus stop. I'll go to that one, and we can see whose bus comes first. That'll be way more fun than the club!"

I didn't respond, and eventually she caught up, clearly pleased with herself.

———————————

Even with my boots on, the bouncer was taller than me. He was a huge male vampire wearing jeans and a ragged jacket. He didn't check our IDs, which would have been unnecessary anyway because Kristi was my age, but he did turn his head to watch as we went by. Kristi was so excited that I doubted she would have realized it if he had asked her to stop.

We went down a long, narrow hallway typical of the other Sanguan clubs I had been to. The clubs were generally dark, had very few windows, if any at all, and I always felt cut off from the rest of the world when inside one. When we had gone far enough that I was hit with the warm, heavy air that dancing bodies and poor ventilation produced, I took my phone out of my pocket and found it had service.

At first glance, the narrow space of Night met my low expectations for a small club in the city. There was a bar in front of us on the left, and a few people, or vampires—it was too dark to be sure which—danced in the back of the room. A balcony, with small tables set up on it, partially hung over the main floor.

The sound system, on the other hand, did impress me. I could feel the bass from the electronic dance music pounding from the back of the room. Thankfully, it wasn't impossibly loud out front where we were. I didn't have to yell much when asking Kristi, "Want to get a drink?"

Her eyes were wide, taking in the scene for the first time, and she didn't turn to me when responding, "Sure!"

She would have stood there all night, so I took her arm and pulled her toward the bar. Its wood seemed old, as did the bar stools. Keeping with the theme, the stools' fabric looked very worn.

There was plenty of space, so we sat down. While I never drank much, especially not around vampires, one drink wouldn't hurt. The bartender appeared young, which of course didn't mean much. He wore black pants and a tight black t-shirt. Like many vampires, he was muscular, which actually didn't mean much either. I had to remind myself of it often, but their true strength wasn't reflected in their physical appearance.

We hung our coats below the bar, and Kristi's shiny red top stood out like a bright beacon in a sea of blacks and grays.

The bartender came right over, placed his hands wide on the bar, leaned toward us, and asked, "What will it be for you, ladies?"

"Red wine for me," I said. "Kristi?"

She had turned away from the bar to gaze out at the club again. She looked back, and said quickly, "Whatever you get, Erin, just get me one."

"Merlot, cabernet sauvignon, pinot noir? Do you want to see the list?" the bartender asked.

"The house merlot is fine. Two glasses, please." Those places usually had top-notch wine lists. People liked to drink red wine around vampires because of the color, and the vampires had great stores of wine because they lived for so long and could collect it, even though they didn't drink it themselves. House wine was almost always good enough for me.

The bartender poured two big glasses, and I gave him my credit card when he returned with them. I turned to give Kristi a glass. "This one's on me, Kristi." She wasn't there to hear me. As her red top moved toward the dance floor, I smiled. It sure seemed like she was going to have a good time.

"Ms. Erin Rose," the bartender read off my credit card before handing it to me. "It seems your friend has left you alone."

"Should I be worried?" I asked, playing along. I set her glass down next to mine.

"No, Erin, no. What kind of bartender would I be then? I'm Stan." He offered his hand for me to shake.

His grip was strong, and his skin very firm. His face softened a little and, in that moment, he looked like a young man, my age or a few years older. His red hair was shaved in a short crew cut and, if it hadn't been a Sanguan across the bar, I would have guessed army infantryman from Middle America.

"How old are you?" I asked.

"I've been a vampire for more than fifty years."

He went to greet another newcomer, leaving me alone with my wine. I took a sip and found it pretty tasty for a house glass. Stan the Sanguan, well over fifty years old, yet his face and body said twenty-five. He seemed friendly, but it could have been an act. While presumably he wouldn't drink my blood, eventually, he would feed on someone for theirs.

A song I recognized played overhead, and I looked out to the rest of the club. Just as before, the dance floor wasn't crowded. Kristi danced by herself and appeared fine, so I turned back to the bar.

Bottles of liquor and wine lined the wall behind it, but what caught my eye was a small statue tucked behind some of the vodka bottles and rising slightly above them. It was a goat's head on a human body and was probably a little more than a foot tall. Even in the darkness it appeared intricately made and painted.

"Baphomet." Stan had come back over to me. I couldn't have been the first non-vodka drinker to stare in that direction for an inordinate amount of time.

"What is it? Is it the devil?" I asked.

"It's a symbol of Satan, yes."

"It's hideous." Yet, there was something about it. For one thing, I couldn't deny the fine craftsmanship.

"Ha. Well, that's nice. I made it myself." Stan retrieved the statue and set it on the bar directly in front of me. "Is it really so bad?"

Up close, it was both hideous and striking. The intricate

detail of the stone carving and the vivid colors—red, white, and even the black—really brought it to life. The goat head had a pentagram on its forehead, and a pair of wings sprouted from the human body. Instead of feet, the creature had goat hooves. I had to reassure myself it was only a statue.

"Well no, I'm sorry. I've just never seen anything like it." I tried to recover. "I actually think it's really well made."

"Oh, now you're just saying that. But it's all right," Stan said.

"Really, I do." I meant it, but there simply wasn't a lot to say after telling him flat out that it was hideous. But why did he have it behind the bar? I had seen other Sanguans with satanic symbols on their clothing or on their bodies, but had never questioned them about it. That was my chance. "Do you worship him? Satan?"

"Worship? No. I made this when I had only been a vampire for a few years. When I first killed people and drank their blood, I thought I must be an agent of Satan. Back then, I spent a lot of time wondering about it. I don't as much anymore."

"Have you ever seen the devil or spoken to him?"

"No, never. But…" Stan turned to the statue. "… I still feel his work in the world more than anything from some benevolent god. Look around; you're surrounded by immortal vampires who want to feed off your blood. Do you see God in that?"

Stan didn't wait for an answer before going to make another drink. While sitting alone with the statue, I felt very glad to have opted for the turtleneck that didn't advertise as much flesh to the vampires. I wondered if Stan would have minded the cross on my neck if he could see it, then took another sip of wine and hoped Kristi was still all right on the dance floor.

Stan's question wasn't a new one to me. I did wonder where vampires fit into God's grand design. Even beyond all their powers and immortal life, Sanguans were murderers and, until recently, many Spectavi had been as well. As a group, they were the most terrible sinners the world had ever known.

For years, God must have been pleased that the Spectavi fought the Sanguans on behalf of humanity, but they still had to drink human blood to survive. It was possible, however, that living off of synthetic blood had brought them fully back to His good graces.

What was certain was that, since the Spectavi created synthetic blood in 1951, they had strengthened their relationships with many governments all over the world, including America's. According to what I had read, the Spectavi had evolved from a dependable, but feared, ally into their role as an official, if not leading, force for providing public safety from the Sanguans.

I sat there for a while, pondering, occasionally sipping my wine. I tried to ignore the statue, but struggled because it was so lifelike resting only a few feet from me. 'Baphomet.' It even sounded evil. Still, Stan really had done a good job and, while I doubted he cared, I wished I hadn't been so negative about his work.

Eventually, I used getting up to check on Kristi as an

excuse to get away from the statue. I took both of our glasses of wine and made my way through the club. The ever-persistent bass beat stronger, and the electronic music grew louder as I neared the dance floor. Unlike the bar, that part of the club had become reasonably crowded, so I couldn't find Kristi right away. I leaned against the wall on the edge of the dance floor to listen and watch.

Club music wasn't my favorite, but I didn't hate it and couldn't deny that it fit the scene. A strobe light flashed occasionally in spurts, penetrating the surrounding darkness. The young crowd, mostly eighteen to thirty years old, I thought, was a collection of scantily dressed people, some in groups and some in pairs. Slightly more women than men danced, and artificially pale faces and dark makeup abounded, but the look wasn't universal.

Vampires danced, as well. A muscular male Sanguan reminded me of Stan and the others I had seen in the battle, but a few were a little thinner and shorter. Some wore makeup against their light skin. Except for one pair, they all appeared to focus on the music while dancing alone, with humans surrounding them.

In the pair of dancing vampires, the female's tiny skirt and top left little to the imagination. The male wore dark gray pants and an extremely tight, lighter gray t-shirt. They both looked to be in spectacular physical shape. The two held each other while moving to the music in what seemed like perfect unison. Her hair was loose and wild and, occasionally, they opened their mouths to reveal their fangs; I wasn't sure if it was to each other or to the people around them. I had never paid close enough attention to that part of clubs in the past to notice such raw emotion between two vampires.

I watched them until the shiny red of Kristi's top caught my eye, and I saw her dancing among a group of humans. While her outfit wasn't nearly as absurd as I had expected it would be, the bright color did make her stand out. Lost in the music like most everyone else, she appeared to be having a great time. I felt pleased with myself for finally bringing her with me.

When I turned and started back to the bar, Baphomet waited for me, right where he had been before. Once seated again, I put our drinks down and pushed the statue at its base to move it away. Stan must have noticed because he came over and returned it to its place behind the vodka bottles.

"Stan, were you working here two nights ago?" I asked while he faced away from me. He had been in a talkative mood earlier, so I figured I might as well get him back to it.

He turned around with a stern expression. "Yes, why?"

"I was on my way here, actually, and I saw something. I, um, wonder if you know more about it."

Stan stood in front of me, right up against his side of the bar. "What did you see?" With my left heel hooked over the bottom rung of the bar stool for balance, I leaned back to create a little more space between us. Clearly, the subject was more serious than our choice of drinks or the statue, and I didn't know how the Sanguan would react.

I told him how I had stopped at the bus stop to get out

of the rain. I explained that it had been hard to make out many details or hear anything useful, but that I definitely saw five Sanguans killed by Spectavi, and that one of the Sanguans appeared very old. And then I described the sixth Sanguan who had walked up to me and paused before walking away.

Stan listened intently and never interrupted my story. At the end, I asked, "Do you know what happened?"

Stan glanced at the bar. "The old vampire must have done something wrong to be killed like that."

"What do you mean, 'must have'?"

"Well, the Spectavi wouldn't have killed him for no reason; would they?"

"No, I don't think so."

"Well then, Francis must have done something to get himself killed." He walked away to clean some glasses below the bar.

I sipped my half-finished wine and mulled over what he had said for a few moments. Stan came back as if he knew I was ready to ask more questions.

"You don't think he did anything to deserve what he got?" I asked.

"I don't know, I really don't. I didn't know Francis well, to be honest, but he didn't seem like the type to all of a sudden break a law and get himself killed."

"Who was the vampire who walked up to me at the end? Do you know him?"

"His name is Grant. I know him a little. He came in here after the attack and sat at the end of the bar, but he didn't say much except that Francis had been killed. I put together what I could after the fact, and now from your story."

Based on that, it didn't seem like Stan knew much more. "Do you know how to reach Grant? I'd like to meet him and ask him about that night."

Stan thought for a moment. "If he comes here, I'll tell him you're looking for him. But one piece of advice: meet him somewhere public. You just never know."

I would have done that regardless, but it was good advice, even if one Sanguan warning me about another seemed a little strange. I left Stan my phone number and asked him to only give it to Grant. If necessary, getting a new number would be easy, I reasoned, and it wasn't like I had a long list of friends to update if it came to that.

I didn't talk to Stan much more. When I finished my wine, it was two thirty in the morning, and Kristi's full glass still sat on the bar. I didn't want to be outside anywhere near four o'clock, so I decided to go find her so we could leave.

I settled my bill, took my coat, and thanked Stan. I told him again that the statue he had made was really well-crafted. He responded politely, but briefly, and I guessed he wasn't terribly concerned with my opinion of it. Realizing that, I wished I hadn't bothered thinking about the monstrous thing again.

The dance floor had grown even more crowded. Apparently, no one else was in as big a hurry to get home. Standing on the edge, I couldn't see Kristi, but knew her red top would give her away eventually.

After a few minutes of waiting, I walked around the

outside of the dance floor, peering through the crowd. I couldn't find her, so I went back to the wall and leaned on it to wait some more. We had a little time; she could just have been in the restroom or taking a break.

The vampire couple from earlier was gone, but other vampires danced among the people. There were also pairs made up of vampires and humans and, while they didn't move together quite like the two vampires had, I sensed real passion between them. The powerful vampires weren't faking it as I assumed they might have.

I pondered how it would end for the mortals among them, and if the dancing would lead to something more.

A boy bumped me on his way to the dance floor. He turned and apologized. He was clearly drunk or on some drug. It was time to get Kristi.

I went out onto the dance floor, but couldn't find her. I crisscrossed it a few times, doing my best to brush against as few people as possible, but still, no Kristi. I was getting a little worried before remembering the tables upstairs. She had to be there.

After finding the narrow staircase, I had to wait for three people to come down before there was room to go up. At the top, she wasn't at any of the four high tables. I surveyed the club from the balcony, and the place looked even smaller from that vantage point. Stan leaned over the bar, talking to a girl sitting where I had been. I still didn't see Kristi anywhere, and my concern grew into fear.

I didn't find her downstairs in the women's restroom. I checked my phone and didn't have any messages, but did notice that it was already three o'clock. I tried calling her and got her voicemail, then texted her, telling her to call me.

I went to Stan and his new customer. "I'm sorry to interrupt, but have you seen my friend Kristi?"

"No, I'm sorry. It's getting late, you know." He smiled at the girl in front of him. "It's getting late for you, too."

She giggled, but she wasn't my concern. "Stan, do you think you could check the men's restroom? I can't think of anywhere else she could be."

"Sure," he said to me, and then, "I'll be right back," to the girl. She just giggled again.

Stan scanned the scene near the bar before leaving it. I followed him, in part because I didn't want anything to do with the giggling girl.

He came out of the restroom after a few seconds. "No, I'm sorry. I didn't see her."

"Her coat's still here. Is there anywhere else she could be?"

He pointed to the balcony. "Did you check upstairs?"

I nodded.

"Then not really, no. Maybe she left?"

"Maybe," I said skeptically. "If you see her tonight, call me please? She's wearing a red top and a black skirt. I'm going to keep looking."

"Sure thing. I remember her. But don't stay out too late. She probably left with someone, possibly a vampire. Don't get yourself in trouble over this." Thankfully, he had put aside his act with the new girl at the bar.

"Right." I moved quickly to check the dance floor again.

It wasn't like her to leave without saying anything. She hadn't touched her wine, so she wasn't drunk, unless someone else had bought her drinks, or perhaps something stronger than a drink. Anything was possible.

I wished I hadn't brought her in the first place. And leaving her alone for so long had been dumb. But she really had seemed fine. I ran upstairs again and found nothing. It was a quarter after three, and I had no idea where Kristi was.

Other people started to leave, finally, and I tried calling her again, but it went straight to voicemail. I texted her, saying I was going home and that she should call me whenever she got my message.

When I passed the bar, Stan was talking with the giggling girl, who seemed to be in no hurry to get up from her stool.

Back in the long hallway that led out to the street, I couldn't believe Kristi wasn't with me. That I would have left without her had never once crossed my mind.

Outside, people scattered away from the club, many stumbling more than walking. The handful of taxis were already full. A few people waited for more, but that could be a dangerous game. Taxi drivers had to be indoors by four o'clock like everyone else, so there was no guarantee more would show up.

I put on my coat, checked my phone, and begrudgingly began to walk around the block to see if Kristi was nearby. While cutting it closer than I should, I felt I had an obligation to do all I could to find her.

A concrete sidewalk ran against the building, and dim bulbs hung on the brick wall providing minimal light.

Hearing the conversations of those leaving the club reassured me at first. Unfortunately, as I went farther, their voices faded until they were eventually gone. All I could hear was low bass from the music inside the club and my boots clicking against the ground with each step. Numerous light bulbs were out or missing, and I knew I shouldn't have been alone there at night, especially not so late.

I pushed my hands into my coat pockets and kept going. It wasn't four yet; the law said I should have been safe. After a few more steps, I turned the corner at the rear of the club, then stopped. Two people, or vampires, stood under a bright light half a block away. They paused their conversation when they noticed me, and I saw fangs when one smiled before I turned away.

I walked as fast as I could up the block toward the club entrance. I turned back and didn't see them following, but kept going quickly. When the voices in front of the club returned, I checked behind me once more and still didn't see anyone. I didn't slow down until reaching the front of the building.

It was three thirty, time for me to get home.

3

The rest of the walk home was stressful. I checked behind me repeatedly to be sure nobody or no*thing* followed me. The vampires outside the club were probably waiting for people to leave late, people they could legally kill and drink from. Considering all the dancing after three, I had a hunch they wouldn't be going hungry.

It had become close enough to four that, while I walked, I looked out in front of me as well. It occurred to me how unwise it would be to rely on precision in the timing of the law.

I had learned that some Sanguans fed from humans without killing them, often carrying on consensual relationships for months or years. For Sanguans who weren't interested in such arrangements, the set time they were allowed to hunt was designed to keep them happy. Any people out at that time were fools, so while they might not necessarily deserve to die, they had been warned. Everyone knew the laws.

When I finally got home, my phone said ten minutes until four. Even so, that just about made me a fool, too.

And what about Kristi? Was she out there somewhere? She hadn't contacted me on my way home and didn't appear to be online. I glanced at the crucifix I had hung on my wall and said a prayer for her. Except for calling her over and over, I couldn't think of anything else to do.

Dawn's light filled the sky when I finally fell asleep with my phone next to my bed.

My alarm woke me at eleven in the morning, but my usual run wasn't going to happen. Kristi hadn't called or texted, and I stayed in bed worrying about her until noon, before finally showering and then throwing on black pants and a green shirt for work.

Commuting to get in by one o'clock was a major improvement over rush hour. Getting a train home after ten o'clock could take a while, but I preferred it to dealing with big crowds. Working and living on the red subway line helped in any case, because there were typically more trains than on some of the other lines.

That day's commute seemed to take forever. I checked my phone repeatedly for any word from Kristi while waiting in the tunnel for eleven minutes for a train. If she was at work when I got there, I'd be mad at her, but of course would also be hugely relieved that she had survived the night. It was a harsh reality that, even with the Spectavi's help, as soon as anyone went missing, death was always a realistic possibility.

Only two stops separated my home and work, and it

seemed like the train waited extra long at both before moving on.

Finally, we arrived at Dupont Circle, and I walked up the long escalator to the street as usual. Outside the metro station, people enjoyed their lunch on the sunny, warm spring day. I often envied them for being half done with their workday when mine just started, but on that occasion, Kristi's fate dominated my attention.

I headed to our office, showed my ID to the security guard, and took the stairs up to the fourth floor. Kristi's cubicle was my first stop—empty. I continued to my desk and saw her idle on our office instant messenger program. That wasn't good, but she still had a few minutes to show up before being late.

Brian Oliver, my boss, already sat in the office behind my cubicle. He said he came in whenever he woke up because he couldn't stay home doing nothing. I didn't have the same problem and was relieved he let me stick to the one-to-ten workdays we had switched to after Eure had bought our company, two months earlier.

Eure Global, named after a river in France, was a huge company run by Spectavi vampires. The company was old and private, and seemed to have an interest in everything from manufacturing to medicine to technology. Their customers ran the spectrum, as well, from consumers to other businesses to governments—including the United States. I hadn't figured out why specifically they had bought our little company.

Before the acquisition, we had been Snap Safe Software.

We made the software that controlled the small cameras on every streetlight in Washington, D.C. If someone went through a yellow light too late, our cameras snapped a picture of their license plate, and they got a ticket in the mail. While the cameras weren't a huge hit with everyone, the statistics said that they did reduce accidents. Less controversially, our software also monitored turning lanes for how much traffic waited.

My boss ran the company until the change in ownership, and I was his secretary. We had shifted our workday to accommodate the vampires from Eure. It was strange at first, seeing Spectavi come in at night to meet with our managers, and there hadn't been any big welcome speech from the vampires. One day, we changed our schedule, they showed up, and that was it.

After the acquisition, hearing that there would be almost no staff changes and, most importantly, that my job was safe, had been a huge relief. For someone with my experience, or lack thereof, it had been hard enough for me to get the job in the first place.

When I woke up with no memory, I grew bored of doing nothing almost immediately, so I took a job as a waitress. As it turned out, I found being a waitress almost as boring, and eventually got tired of dealing with the customers. I made myself a fake resume and began applying for administrative jobs.

Mr. Oliver's last secretary had left abruptly, and he seemed desperate during my interview. I couldn't figure out why else he would have hired someone with so little experience. Aside from the fact that my resume consisted of lies, there simply wasn't a lot to it. At twenty-two, I could only include so much.

When I started, Kristi had been a lifesaver. I met her on my first day and went to her with lots of questions. She had always been happy to help.

Before long, however, I picked up more and more on my own, so I ended up not having to bother her anymore and being good at the job. I had just been lucky to get it before knowing that would be the case.

I remembered those days while sitting, literally on the edge of my seat, staring at my computer, hoping for a sign of life from Kristi. I knew a few people from my last job, and talked to a few others at my new one sometimes, but Kristi was the only one I would come close to calling a friend. I felt so powerless and kept switching from my email to my contact list hoping her icon would change to green.

"Erin, did you see that email I sent?"

I turned to Mr. Oliver, who stood behind me. Even as he asked, he had a kind face, as he always did when talking to me. He was older, close to sixty, and had a bit of white hair left. He was a little heavy and appeared very much the grandfather he was. While he said I could call him Brian, I never did.

"I did, I mean, I will. Sorry."

"That's okay, but please get to it quickly. You'll see it's for a meeting soon."

"Okay." I found his email. He needed financial information turned into a few slides, which wouldn't take me very long. Kristi still showed as 'away' on my contact list, so I started working for the distraction.

After the second slide, my attention drifted back. Once again I wished I hadn't brought her with me or had paid more attention to her after I had. I tried to figure out how her disappearance could possibly have anything to do with me, but came up with nothing. Maybe Stan was involved somehow, and I had been too quick to trust the Sanguan.

A square message alert from Kristi showed up in the lower right of my monitor. Thank God!

I'm soooo sorry!

I sat back in my chair and took a deep breath before typing, *What happened?*

I was dancing with some people, and then I started dancing with a vampire named Christopher and I left with him.

What? Are you OK?

I'm fine! I left my phone at the club. I'll tell you about it later, I have some work I need to get done first.

Wow. She went home with a vampire. A Sanguan! At least she was alive. I couldn't wait to tell her how mad I was at her.

I had enough work that the afternoon went by quickly. Mr. Oliver had the first meeting that the slides were for, and afterward another one with a few Spectavi and our chief programmer, Todd, that we had to prepare for.

Todd was only a few years older than me, but he wrote the most complicated parts of our software. He had started Snap Safe by himself after college and brought Mr. Oliver on board later to run the business side of things and lend some credibility to the company.

Todd had asked me out a few weeks back, but I said no. He was handsome, and I had been tempted, but I didn't really know him that well. Plus, I didn't know how it would look at work if we went out. I lied and claimed to be uninterested, thinking I might reconsider in a few months or a year.

Coffee? Kristi messaged.

Sure.

She stood in the lobby wearing a purple turtleneck dress. It was hard to be certain, but she looked paler than normal.

"I'm so sorry," Kristi said.

I shook my head. "You can't leave me worrying like that, Kristi. I had no idea what happened to you. I was almost out past four looking for you."

"I know, I know. It just happened so fast, and then I didn't have my phone."

I sighed. "It's all right. Let's get some coffee." We walked outside and headed for the coffee shop. "So what happened, anyway?"

"Well, like I said, I was dancing with a bunch of people, and then Christopher, the vampire, came up and started dancing with me more than anyone else. I was shocked. We danced for a while, and it got pretty intense, and then he asked if I wanted to go somewhere with him. I didn't know what to say, so I said yes.

"I knew it was wrong, stupid even, but when I looked into his eyes, I couldn't stop myself. He was so kind and sincere. He had a car waiting at the back of the club, and he acted like a perfect gentleman. The next thing I knew we were in an apartment on the couch kissing, and then…" She paused.

"And then what?" I asked. We had arrived outside the coffee shop, and Kristi was about to walk in. "And then what?" I asked again, before she did.

"Well, he bit me."

"Oh, my God! Are you okay?"

"Yeah, I mean, I think so. It was incredible, Erin. Have you ever been bitten?"

I pointed to the bite mark scar on my neck.

Kristi inhaled sharply. "Sorry… I mean that you can remember."

"No," I answered, and let us walk into the shop.

We ordered our coffees and sat down. Kristi stared out the window to the street. She definitely looked pale.

"So, you're okay?" I asked again.

She returned to our conversation. "I'm more than okay. It was amazing. He drank from me slowly, and it was like my whole body was tingling. It's hard to explain exactly."

My stomach churned as she described it. I pointed to my scar again. "You know, Kristi, I think a vampire, probably a Sanguan, did this to me."

"I know, I know, but look, I think the mark is getting smaller already." She rolled down her collar to show me her neck. "I don't think it's going to scar."

"I don't mean the scar. Well, I do, but I mean they took my memory, remember?"

"I don't think Christopher would do that. I've never heard of *any* vampire doing that, except with you."

"I know, me neither." She was right, but still, she had been so reckless. "How much do you know about Christopher?"

"Not much, I guess. He was gone when I woke up today, of course, but he seemed so nice. He was so gentle. I hope he calls tonight."

We talked for a little while longer, and I reminded her how dangerous Sanguans could be. I told her that she looked pale and that a night off wouldn't be the worst thing. While she didn't agree to that, she did promise to be careful.

I told her about my conversation with Stan, and about Grant, but she seemed distracted.

While we talked, I couldn't help being a little jealous of Kristi. I didn't want anything to do with a vampire and imagining being bitten, however she described it, really did sicken me. But I had been alone for a long time, and Kristi spared no detail describing her excitement about Christopher, and her eagerness for it to become a serious relationship.

I had gone on a few dates with one guy almost a year before then, mostly to break up the monotony of my nights and weekends spent investigating in vain, or at home on my own. But I had never mentioned my missing memory, and upon realizing I wasn't ready to do that, I broke things off with him. Todd came to mind while Kristi went on and on, but I shook the idea out of my head.

We headed back to the office to finish the day, but we didn't talk on the way.

4

That night, Kristi texted to say she was going out with Christopher. She sent me his picture, and his shaggy blond hair and square jaw jumped out at me right away. He looked fine, but I really never thought of vampires that way.

They were going to another club, and she asked if I wanted to go. I couldn't tell if she was being polite, or if she didn't understand that I went to those places for very different reasons. Either way, I declined her invitation.

I did make her give me the username and password to her phone, though, to use in an app to track her location in case anything went wrong. The app's real use was to find your phone if you lost it, but people also used it for other things. I promised not to spy on her and said that if she planned on going out with Christopher regularly and didn't want me to give her a hard time about it, that was the compromise. She likened me to her mother, but didn't argue much.

After setting that up, I finally had a chance to focus on what Stan had said at Night. I didn't believe his suggestion that Francis could have done nothing wrong. The Spectavi just didn't work that way. Still, I had become even more curious. His crime could have been out of the ordinary somehow.

Grant came to mind, too, and Stan's warning to meet him in public. I assumed Stan wouldn't set me up with him if he was dangerous, and if Grant had wanted to hurt me, he could have at the bus stop. Unfortunately, I really had no idea what Grant had been thinking. Five of his companions had been killed, and he had never had a chance to fight back.

I didn't even know if Grant would be willing to meet with me.

The next day, after a good night's sleep, I went for a jog.

I could never have outrun a vampire if one chased me, but staying in shape still felt like the right thing to do to be prepared. Beyond that, I thought clearly when running. Focusing on the workout, instead of my past, vampires, or work, seemed to give the rest of my mind a chance to come up with new ideas related to those things I normally dwelled on. I didn't understand why it worked, yet it consistently did.

My usual route took me around the National Mall. On one hand, running by the Washington Monument and Capitol building offered nice scenery. The problem was, that time of year it meant avoiding hordes of tourists there to see the same things. I made a mental note to make a new route, but realized I would probably get lazy and not bother.

When not dodging tourists, I again went through my

decision to stay in the city and investigate my past. I could have been anywhere in the world before being left in that apartment, but since I spoke English, and based on my lack of another obvious regional accent, my best guess was that I grew up near D.C.

That aside, I couldn't search everywhere and had to hope someone had left me where they had for a reason. If not, I had a very long search ahead of me—perhaps impossibly long.

I finished the run, still confident in that reasoning.

Back at work, Kristi didn't show up until almost one thirty, but the wait wasn't nearly as nerve-racking the second time. I went to her desk, and she said her night had been wonderful, even better than the night before. She looked pale and seemed tired, but otherwise fine. I worried about her, but there wasn't much I could do other than remind her to be careful. If she liked Christopher, she liked Christopher. Lots of people had relationships with vampires, both Sanguans and Spectavi, in one way or another.

Todd came by my desk later, and we chatted about the new software he was writing, something about trying to take a picture of the driver as well as the license plate when a car ran a light. The details and technical hurdles he described went a little over my head. Or maybe I just ignored them while wondering if he'd ever ask me out again, and what I would say if he did.

At nine thirty, I got a text message:

It's Grant. Let's meet at Night? 11:30?

Apparently, he was willing to meet me, and meeting at

Night sounded good. Not that I loved the club, but I had been there before and, with a little luck, Stan would be working, so I would know someone there, as well.

I texted Grant that I'd see him there.

I didn't get any work done the rest of the night wondering what Grant would say. I briefly questioned the wisdom of going to meet a Sanguan, but reminded myself that a vampire club was a place of business and should actually be relatively safe. Frankly, the genuine prospect of some answers was so exciting that I would have met him almost anywhere.

I debated what to wear for most of the commute home before eventually deciding on something like what I had worn when first crossing paths with Grant. On the off chance I had stirred a memory of his from the past that I couldn't remember, I hoped to stir it again. Thankfully, my boots from that night were finally dry.

Going with a tank top also meant my tattooed cross would be visible. I hoped he wouldn't mind, and hoped Stan wouldn't either, but Grant's reaction to my scar could be important. I did take a coat for the walk.

I didn't mention that trip to Night to Kristi. It was going to be all business for me, and I didn't think I could handle her palpable excitement for vampires.

My brisk pace made me warm, so I had taken off my coat by the time I got to Night. I arrived a few minutes early, and when the big bouncer asked for my ID, I fumbled through my coat pockets to find it.

Once inside, I walked down the long, dark hallway toward the main room. The muggy, sweat-filled air was unavoidable, and the electronic music got louder with each step. It was Friday, so I had to push through a crowd at the end of the hall to get out into the room. Perhaps we hadn't chosen the best location after all.

Another crowd surrounded the bar, and I strained to see over it. Just as I spotted two bartenders behind the bar, someone grabbed me and lifted me off my feet.

"Mmm!" I tried to yell, but a hand covered my mouth and jaw. My coat fell as I tried to break free of the grip, but it was like my upper body had been wrapped in iron. I kicked out my legs while being carried, but the people I hit ignored me. To them, the bumps were probably just another person trying to squeeze toward the bar or the dance floor.

"Mmmmm!" I kept trying to yell while being moved, but couldn't. Conversations continued, music blasted, and despite my efforts, no one had any idea what was happening to me.

Finally, a door swung open, and I was carried into the men's restroom. I saw the short, scrawny vampire who held me in a long mirror that hung over two sinks. His clothes were tattered, and his large, crooked fangs protruded from a mouth and face that might have been burnt in permanent disfigurement. He threw me toward the wall.

I started to cry out, my mouth finally free from his hand, but after my body hit the hard wall, my neck snapped back to it, and I only whimpered while falling to the floor.

Instinctively, I got to my feet and tried to think of

something from my self-defense class. In an instant, the vampire pressed against me with his fangs out at the level of my neck.

"What is this cross on your neck, girl?" He held his hand tight over my mouth and jaw again. "It looks like you've been bitten before."

His small, but powerful body pinned me against the wall, and I fought for the short breaths that were all I could manage. He reeked of sweat that overpowered the foul odor of the restroom itself. I was woozy from hitting my head, but conscious enough to dread what he'd do while he had me alone. Would he kill me quickly or do something worse first? I feared what his bite would feel like more than anything else.

With his free hand, he reached for my left hand and brought it up between our faces. "You hide the mark of a vampire behind the mark of Christ? Let's see where your god is now, shall we?"

In my mind, I pleaded to Jesus for His help. The vampire's eyes moved to the hand he held and he took hold of my pinky. With a flick of his fingers—*snap*! Pain shot through my whole hand.

"Mmm!" I tried to yell again, but he still held my mouth closed. My breaths came even more rapidly, tears streamed down my face, and I closed my eyes.

"Watch!" he said. "Watch to see if your god comes!" He clutched my ring finger.

I opened my eyes—*snap*! "Mmmmm!" The whole side of my hand throbbed in agony. I didn't want to die, but if that was how the attack would end, I wanted him to get right to it. Every second with his bite still looming was torture.

He let go of my hand and pressed his dirty fingers hard into my cross tattoo. "It looks like it's just you and me, doesn't it? Do you think one of the next eight will do the trick? Let's see."

Please, God, help me, I thought.

I mustered all of my remaining energy and pushed out with my arms and legs, but against his strength, the effort proved futile. Defeated, I stared at my hand, waiting for him to break my middle finger.

Behind him, the door flew open. Stan and another vampire—Grant—rushed through it. The vampire who held me let go, turned to them, and gathered himself to fight, but they quickly grabbed him. He was no match for their combined strength, and they dragged him out of the room while he struggled.

Holding my left hand with my right, I leaned against the wall and took a few deeper breaths. The left side of my hand had already turned purple. I moved my ring finger with my right hand and almost screamed out in pain. The fingers had definitely been broken.

Stan and Grant returned to the restroom. I noticed a crowd gathering outside before Grant closed the door and locked it. Maybe God had heard my prayer, or maybe they had just seen the commotion.

"Are you okay?" Stan came near me.

I felt the back of my head; it seemed to be in one piece. "Yes, I think so. Well, except this." I held up my purple hand.

"Can you walk?" Stan asked.

I stood up straight, away from the wall. "I think so, yes." I wiped my face with the back of my right hand and realized the music outside the restroom had stopped. Night seemed like a very different place without pounding bass.

Grant came forward and spoke for the first time. "Do you still want to talk? If not, I can take you home."

Grant was as I remembered, one of the big, solidly-built Sanguans who had been with Francis before he was killed. His skin was dark for a vampire, and he looked almost as intense as he had at the bus stop. Like then, I saw him after a fight.

He had short black hair and the same color stubble on his face. He wore a brown leather jacket and jeans.

"I'll stay." Then I thought for another second and wasn't as sure. Getting out of Night didn't seem like the worst thing. "Actually, can we go somewhere else to talk?"

Grant responded, "We can if you want, but here might be a safer place than some. We can go upstairs. I'll be with you, and Stan can keep watch from below."

It seemed to make sense. "All right."

I straightened my skirt as best I could with a hand and a half, quickly washed my hands and face, then followed Grant out of the restroom with Stan walking behind me. The whole club had stopped to watch, and the crowd parted in front of Grant. I held my left hand with my right to keep from bumping my broken fingers and causing any more pain.

When we got upstairs, all of the high tables were empty.

We sat down at one and pushed the glasses on it aside. Two men came by and collected their drinks and, almost simultaneously, the music played again. The conversations started back up, and surely the dancing did, as well. The show was over.

"Stan's going to bring something for your hand," Grant said.

I nodded, and we sat and waited while my hand throbbed on the table. If they weren't vampires, I would have been sure Grant was older than Stan. He didn't appear drastically older, just more mature, like he had been through much more as a human.

My body had started to get sore all over, but with Grant's brown eyes on me, I sat up straight on my barstool anyway. A chair with a back would have been preferable, but I didn't know that there was one anywhere in the club.

Stan returned with my coat, which he placed on a third stool at our table, a plastic bag full of ice, and a glass of red wine. "I thought some merlot might help, too."

"Thanks." I put the bag over my hand and finally felt some relief as the throbbing became less intense. Stan looked me over for a moment before putting the wine on the table and going downstairs.

When it was just Grant and me again, he finally spoke. "Can I see your hand?"

I held it out, and he moved my pinky finger gently, but it still hurt quite a bit. I flinched and pulled it back. "We can get splints for those when we leave if you want," Grant said. "That's all a doctor would do for them."

"Are you sure?"

"I was a doctor before becoming a vampire. A hand surgeon," he said.

"Really?" What were the odds?

Grant smiled, in stark contrast to the intensity that had been on his face. "No, not really."

I couldn't help but smile a little. "Great, thanks." He had successfully lightened the mood.

"I've seen plenty of broken fingers before, though. The good news is that it's the bones at the end of each finger. If it were the others, closer to your wrist, it would be worse. Splints are all you need."

I nodded again and put my hand down flat with the ice on top of it. My head hurt, but it was bearable. I figured wine would help dull the pain, so I took a drink while considering what had just happened. I needed even more answers.

"Who was that who attacked me?" I asked.

Grant shook his head. "Snake. I don't know his real name. He's an evil creature."

"Do you know why he attacked me? Was it something I did?"

"It could have been the cross on your neck. It's dangerous to flaunt it like that around some vampires. Or it could have been nothing at all, totally random. He's attacked people like this before. I don't know."

I understood the cross could be dangerous in the wrong situations. When I first got it, I had imagined it might actually deter vampires, that they would fear God's power when they saw me with it. But soon, the foolishness of that idea became obvious. I was just a girl with a tattoo, and they were immortal vampires. Even so, I didn't regret picking it and greatly preferred it to the scar it covered.

"What will happen to him?" I asked.

"What do you mean?"

"Snake, what will happen to him?"

"Nothing."

"Nothing?"

"He may not be allowed in the club for a while, a few years maybe, but aside from that, nothing." Grant became stone-faced. "The only thing he did wrong was attack you in this club. Outside, he can hunt who he wants."

"But it wasn't after four." As soon as the last word left my lips, I guessed what the gist of Grant's response would be.

"That's not our law, Erin. Others might punish him for breaking that law, but not us." His face softened. "He shouldn't have attacked you here, and I wish he hadn't hurt you like he did."

Of course, Grant was right. The peace we had with the vampires seemed stable enough, yet on an individual level, it was hard to be sure of much. Carrying around a gun full of silver bullets helped some, but even then, vampires moved so fast that if they wanted you dead, it was almost impossible to stop them.

"Will he attack me again?"

"I don't know. I don't think so. I told him I'd kill him if he did, so hopefully he forgets about you and moves on."

"Would you really kill him?"

"Yes, he's been warned."

That was something at least. I shifted in my seat for the first time since we started talking and took the ice off my hand that had gotten very cold. "So, what did you really do before you were a vampire?"

He thought for a moment. It was a bit direct, but I didn't want to talk about Snake anymore.

"Not much, actually," he finally responded. "Or at least, not much worth mentioning. I was in some gangs, I stole to get by. It wasn't much of a life."

"I see. Where did you live? Around here?"

"New York City mostly," he said. "How about you? What do you do?"

"I work at a software company here in D.C. I'm a secretary. Our company was just bought by Eure, actually." Talking to a vampire, it seemed like a relevant detail, so I added it, but didn't really want to discuss work either. "Who was Francis?"

Grant's face grew grave. "He was my maker. For thirty-three years, he was like a father to me. He was everything my real father had never been."

That was unexpected. "I'm sorry." I meant it, but in spite of that, and my physical pain, I was getting excited. I couldn't help it. Finally, I had an answer to one question, and I assumed more must be on the way.

"And they killed him for *nothing*," Grant said.

"What do you mean? Why would they kill him for nothing?"

"He was a teacher, a historian. They killed him because he was old."

"Old? I don't get it."

"We get more powerful as we get older. The Spectavi don't want us to be able to fight back, so they kill old vampires if they can."

That didn't sound like the Spectavi at all. "How old was he?"

"More than a hundred and fifty years old, and they killed him."

I remembered Francis's face in the rain that had appeared old and full of history. He had also been full of rage and power, and had fought ferociously. Still, if Grant was telling the truth, that wasn't right.

"Surely the police wouldn't allow the Spectavi to do that if they knew. Have you gone to them?"

"The police are no help to us; neither is the government. They'll always side with the Spectavi. They work together now," Grant said. "This war has been raging for centuries. It's ours to fight, as it always has been."

While not convinced of his story, I understood his pain and anger. It would be wrong, but very logical, for the Spectavi to be killing old Sanguans. It obviously would help them keep the upper hand in the war. As for Francis, perhaps Grant was telling the truth, and he had done nothing wrong. But Francis could easily have kept secrets from Grant, and it didn't shock me that Grant would be loyal to his maker. His loyalty could have blinded him to aspects of Francis's life that had led to what happened.

"Why did you want to talk to me tonight?" I asked.

"*You* wanted to talk to *me*."

"Well, why did you agree to talk to me?"

"Mostly, I wanted to be sure you didn't have anything to do with Francis's death. I was curious how you came to be the only mortal on the street that night."

"I was headed here, actually."

"Why? To dance with these people? Maybe meet a vampire?" He obviously thought I was just another human there to party.

I became nervous as soon as the conversation had shifted to be about me and caught myself brushing my hair aside with my good hand. "I hoped to talk to a vampire, any vampire, who might be able to help me. I'm trying to learn about my past." While a quick lie would have felt drastically more comfortable, it wouldn't have led to any answers.

"What do you mean?"

I put the ice back over my hand. "I have no memory before a year and a half ago. I woke up alone in an apartment with no memory of my past. I didn't know who I was or where I was." While always unpleasant to think about, it did get easier each time I recited the story. "I found a driver's license and a credit card on my desk when I got out of bed. They both said 'Erin Rose,' so that's my name, I guess. There was a laptop and some clothes in the drawers and closets, and that was it. No friends, no family."

I could never decide if that was the worst part. Other people struggled through their lives with siblings and parents to lean on, and I had neither.

"Oh, and the scar. I added the tattoo later, but when I woke up, there was a deep scar from a bite mark on my neck. I assume that has something to do with what happened to me, who or what did this to me, but I don't really know. A doctor said I was perfectly healthy, yet they couldn't explain what had happened to make me forget. I spoke to some Spectavi at a few police stations, but they didn't know anything about me. None of them had ever heard of this happening to anyone either. Now I've started asking Sanguans; though, in retrospect, maybe that's not the best approach." I glanced down at my hand and adjusted it below the bag of ice. "You've never seen me before, have you?" I asked only half-jokingly.

"No, I'm sorry, I haven't," Grant said. "That must be terrible for you."

"It is, but at least I wasn't killed by whatever did it to me." It was my weak attempt to stay positive.

Grant must have seen through it. "I can ask around, if you want. I can take your picture and show it to some others. I know a few older vampires. It might be safer than you going out alone, talking to vampires you don't know."

He had a point, but it didn't feel right. "I couldn't impose on you to do that. Thank you, but I just couldn't. This is my problem to deal with."

"Erin, I insist. After you were attacked meeting me here, it's the least I can do. And maybe something good can come from Francis's death. He'd want me to do what I could to help you." Grant took out his phone and pointed it toward me.

I smiled out of habit as he snapped the picture. Even after talking with him, the kind gesture came unexpectedly. I could imagine him in a gang on the streets of New York City, and he seemed to me more of a fighter than someone who would offer to help a person they had just met.

"It's getting late. Let me take you home?" he asked.

It wasn't actually that late, but my head had started to hurt more, and I could feel a bruise forming. I hardly knew him, but I couldn't go back out there alone with Snake possibly around. And as surprising as it had been initially, Grant having my picture was like someone else working on my mystery. Home and rest sounded good and going with him seemed like the safest way to get there.

"Sure." I took another sip of wine before leaving the mostly full glass on the table.

My left hand was cold enough that it didn't hurt that much when I carefully slid it through my coat sleeve. I stopped at the bar and thanked Stan for his help and the ice.

Outside, I immediately scanned from left to right for Snake. He was nowhere in sight, but I stayed close to Grant while he walked to his motorcycle anyway. It was a big bike, black and silver with wide handlebars, and there was definitely room for two. I had never ridden a motorcycle, and I didn't see how I could in my skirt. The bike started loudly.

"There's a taxi coming for you, Erin. I'll ride behind it to make sure you get home safe."

"Thanks," I said over the noise.

A yellow taxi drove up, I got in, and we began the short drive home.

5

The twin girls sang. My view zoomed out wider, and they were part of a church choir, or something like one. It was an angelic sound, and the twins were the stars of the show.

They stood outside in a field, and the sun shined above them. It was warm, and the high grass moved in a soft breeze. Their voices soared through the air. I couldn't make out any specific words, but it was joyful to hear regardless.

I woke up lying on my side, wondering where they had gone, before realizing I was in my bed in my apartment. That dream had been a new one. Who were they? I tried to recall everything I could, but the dream left me quickly. No details that seemed important came to mind, just twin sisters, singing in a choir in a field.

I rolled onto my back, but even resting on my pillow, my head hurt where it had hit the wall. I inspected my broken fingers, which were covered in metal caps over blue padding. We had stopped at a drug store, and Grant set my bones straight before taping the splints around my fingers. It hurt when he set them, but the splints were doing their job.

Grant had offered to stay for a few hours to be sure I was safe, but we agreed it was unlikely that Snake had followed us after Grant's threat and with both of us on the lookout on the way home. I thanked him, but declined his offer.

After Grant had left, I remained wide awake. I could hear Snake's threats and feel his filth and the filth of the restroom where he had attacked me. A long, hot shower helped calm me down, but, even after that, I wasn't tired. I poured a glass of cheap wine from an open bottle in my refrigerator and sat down at my laptop.

I searched online, and it appeared Grant was right: splinting was all a doctor would have done for my fingers. He had left out anything about painkillers, presumably because they were useless on him and his wounds would heal quickly on their own.

I, on the other hand, had needed painkillers and, thankfully, I had some to take.

I searched for more about the theory Grant had mentioned regarding the Spectavi killing old Sanguans for no reason. I found entire websites devoted to his claim, but they presented their cases like conspiracy theories on disorganized pages.

Many more sites laid out evidence to the contrary, that the Spectavi were keeping people safe in the face of horrible crimes Sanguans committed. I had seen many of those sites before, and the crimes disturbed me as always, yet the websites were well-organized, presented logical facts and statistics, and generally seemed much more credible.

Eventually, I went to bed, very much doubting Grant's story.

Looking at my hand, I knew it could have been worse. Broken fingers on my right hand would have made living and working harder. And if Grant and Stan had been even a minute later, well, it could have been a lot worse. I drove the image of Snake out of my head and turned to the clock on my nightstand. It was almost noon. Living on that schedule still felt weird.

I got up and moved to the couch planning to watch TV. A lazy Saturday seemed like a fine idea to me. However, instead of the remote control, I picked up a notebook and pencil from the coffee table, once again glad my right hand hadn't been hurt.

Carefully, I sketched the images from my dream. The twins looked like they always did. The faces of the others in the choir were blurred. I didn't draw the field in much detail either; it was all about the sisters. Again, I came up short of anything more revealing and put my notebook down, frustrated as usual.

I checked my refrigerator. It was mostly empty, and I would have to go out to eat anything other than one of the microwavable meals I typically had at work. That prospect didn't excite me, so my lazy day in the apartment didn't last very long at all. With some luck, though, I'd be back quickly and would resume doing very little.

Pulling jeans over my legs and slipping on sneakers felt great. Between work and my focused nightlife of going to vampire clubs, I hardly got to wear them anymore. I headed for a salad place a few blocks away and was ultimately happy that my fridge had been empty. Not unlike my dream, the weather was almost perfect. The bright sun warmed my arms. It wasn't humid and might have been a little too warm if not for a light breeze that blew occasionally.

The large crowd at the salad shop disappointed me, but I wasn't in a hurry, so I got in line. I took out my phone to check the news and pass the time.

"Erin?"

I looked around, but didn't see anyone I knew.

"Hey, Erin." Todd came up next to me with a mostly empty tray. He had already eaten.

"Oh, hey, Todd."

"What happened to your fingers?"

"Oh, I… I was helping a friend move their old TV, and it slipped and fell on my hand."

"Ouch." He made a face.

"Yeah, 'ouch' is right." He had no idea how painful it had been.

"Well, it's nice to see you, but I have to run to work, unfortunately."

"On Saturday?"

"Yeah, but just for a little while, I hope."

"Well, good luck getting out of there soon; it'd be a shame to be inside all day."

"Thanks, we'll see." He turned to walk away, but turned back, and added, "I hope you feel better."

After I ordered my salad, I sat down still thinking about Todd. He was really handsome and a few inches taller than me, which I liked. His athletic body was not at all what I had expected when first hearing he was a computer programmer. It had been nice to see him, if only briefly.

Grant's accusation about the Spectavi came to mind. Eure Global was run by the Spectavi, and they had just bought Todd's company. I wondered what Todd thought about both groups.

I headed straight home after lunch. The salad had hit the spot, and it was a gorgeous day, but my body ached from Snake's attack even more than when I had woken up. I decided I deserved a short nap.

———————————

My ringing phone woke me. I had forgotten to put it on silent. It was Todd... peculiar.

"Hi, Todd."

"Hi, Erin, how are you doing?"

I almost said groggy, sore, and broken, but didn't. "I'm fine. How are you?"

"Good, good. So, it was nice to see you earlier, but I had to leave so quickly, and... well, do you have any plans tonight? I thought we could get a drink later or something."

"Oh..." What could I say? What did I want to say? "Sure, yeah, why not?"

"Great! I'll come by around eight?"

"Sure."

"Okay, I'll see you then. Bye, Erin."

"Bye, Todd."

It had happened so fast that I didn't know how I felt

about the development. Even before the whole Spectavi story from Grant, Todd had been on my mind, and after seeing Grant, I had something to ask him. The idea of going out with a higher-up at work still made me nervous, but it was basically his company, aside from Eure, so if it was all right with him, maybe it should have been with me.

I thought of Snake and the attack. I wished Todd was coming earlier, when the sun would be up for hours longer, but I hadn't put that together during the call.

I had been waking up, too. Todd might have been lucky to catch me under those circumstances to get his 'yes.' Still, I really did want to hear his opinion of the Spectavi, and Snake might not have been after me at all. Plus, it was just a drink.

I had a nicer pair of jeans, so I went with those. Intent on not dressing for going to a vampire club, I added a light blue shirt with a v-neck and black flat shoes. I was nearly set, but still in my bathroom fixing my hair when my phone rang. Todd was early and at the call-up box outside my apartment.

"Hi, Todd. I'll be down in a minute."

My hair was down, so that would to have to do. I glanced at my metal-covered fingers and was disappointed for a moment, and then I grabbed my keys and purse and headed downstairs.

"Hey, Todd," I said.

"Hey, Erin. You look great."

"Oh, thanks." Todd looked good in his jeans and button-down shirt. While he didn't wear the glasses he did at work, his short brown hair was neat, as usual. He was only twenty-six years old, but since he had founded a successful company, always seemed older to me.

"How does Smith's sound?" he asked.

"Good with me," I replied, and we started walking. Smith's was a nice bar, but we wouldn't be out of place in our jeans. It was cooler because the sun had set, and I kept a watch for anything out of the ordinary as we walked.

We made it to Smith's and sat down at the bar. Everything looked newer and fancier than Night had been. The wood on the bar had a fresh finish. The upholstery on the furniture was clean and a deep green. The whole room was much brighter, and there was no pounding music.

Todd ordered a beer, and I went with a gin and tonic. My first sip reminded me of why I preferred wine, but I was continuing my anti-vampire theme for the day, so I vowed to persevere and not switch drinks.

We talked about work for a while, and even so, it was really fun to see Todd outside the office. Like at work, he seemed a little shy and a little unsure of himself. But I sensed his confidence growing as the conversation continued. It turned out he was a big sports fan and loved fine wine. Slowly, I became more relaxed about being out with him, too.

"So, why did you sell your company to Eure?" I asked when the moment seemed right.

Todd was about to respond, but the bartender came over to us and our nearly empty glasses. "Would you like another drink?" Todd asked.

"Sure." My drink had gotten more bearable, so I could manage another one.

"Why did I sell? Well, money mostly," Todd said.

"Makes sense," I said, and it did.

"Well no, I mean, yes. It was money, which is great, but not just for me. There's also more money for the company." He had become more animated, and clearly meant what he was saying. "We have some really exciting things we want to do with our cameras, and Eure has the resources and connections to make them happen."

"Like what?"

"Facial recognition, for one thing. As you probably know, when we take a picture of a license plate after a car runs a red light, we have to give the ticket to the owner of the car, and they don't get any points on their license. We see a lot of the same cars running lights over and over, but we can't tie them to the driver.

"Our cameras are good enough to get a shot of the front of the car, and with Eure's help, we can tap into a database of drivers. It may sound like a small difference, but the cameras already help reduce accidents as it is and, if we could ticket the people and not the cars, they would be even more effective."

"That makes sense; I get it," I said. "I had no idea Eure was that big." I lied about Eure in hopes of leading him on.

"Oh yeah, they're huge. Did you know they're the largest company run by vampires in the world? They're old, and they have connections everywhere. Business, government, you name it. I met their CEO, Edmond Duchart. I knew right away he was a very old vampire, but I was a little surprised that he was as smart as he was. He isn't a software person, and yet he seemed to know all about our business and our products."

"Why did they want your company?" I asked.

"Diversification and talent mostly, from what I can tell. We have a nice, steady revenue stream. For them, acquiring us was a drop in the bucket, but it did make financial sense. They don't have another company quite like us, so we give them exposure to something new."

"What did you mean by *talent*?"

"Oh, well I'm not saying it to brag, really, but Edmond told me he had some other projects he wanted me, specifically, to work on. It was flattering coming from someone like him."

It was all really interesting, but I hadn't learned much about the Spectavi yet, except that Edmond knew how to flatter Todd. Edmond was no figurehead CEO.

I took my new drink from the bartender. "What has it been like working for vampires? I don't see much of them except when they walk by my desk."

Todd swallowed some beer. "It was strange at first. I didn't know what to expect. But actually, it's like working for the smartest managers in the world. They let me do my thing with the software, but for strategic decisions, they've literally seen everything before. I almost always have to defer to their decisions, but really, they know what they're talking about. They have a ton of experience."

"Have they ever done anything totally unexpected or weird?" I asked.

He looked confused. "What do you mean?"

I didn't know what I meant actually. "I don't know, just strange actions or decisions. They *are* vampires."

"No, nothing comes to mind. They're Spectavi after all. They're just so old and experienced. I'm learning so much."

I sipped on my drink. It didn't seem like the conversation would yield anything out of the ordinary about the Spectavi. And Todd remained thrilled with his decision to sell, which was something else I had been curious about.

"Do you mind if I ask a personal question?" Todd asked.

"Oh, probably not. What is it?" Of course, it absolutely mattered what he asked.

"Why the cross? Are you very religious?"

With Grant, I had jumped right into the truth, but I had a reason to. He needed to know the truth if he was going to be able to help me. That wasn't the case with Todd, who I was just getting to know.

"A little, yes, but I got it to cover a scar."

He leaned closer to my neck. "Oh, you were bitten by a vampire?"

"A long time ago. I don't really like to talk about it." Part of the truth would have to be enough for him.

"I'm sorry, I didn't mean—"

I stopped him. "No, no, it's fine, really. But like I said, I'd just rather not talk about it right now."

"No problem."

"Actually, it's getting late. I should be going." I couldn't help feeling a little uncomfortable.

"Oh, okay… but for us, this is only the end of the work

day normally. We could do something else if you want. They have darts and pool downstairs. Play a quick game at least?"

"I'm not really good at either," I said.

"Neither am I, but come on, let's play." He really wanted to extend the… date.

"Okay, sure," I said with a little fake enthusiasm. I was bad at pool and had never played darts. Todd paid our bill, and we brought our drinks downstairs with us.

The basement had another bar and a few tables with chairs to go along with two pool tables and two dartboards. The walls were dark brick, but lights scattered throughout the room gave enough light. We stopped at the bottom of the stairs, and two men squeezed past us into the room.

"Sorry," Todd said to them, and then he said to me, "Looks like everything's being used."

"Well, it might be for the best," I said. "I'm bad at pool, and I've never played darts."

A couple left one of the dartboards.

"Perfect," Todd announced.

We headed for the board, and as we did, the two men who had come downstairs after us did too. They looked to be roughly Todd's age.

"We were waiting to play. Sorry," one said.

"What do you mean? You got here after us," Todd said.

The other man spoke up, "We were here earlier. We just left to get a drink."

Todd pointed to the bar. "There's a bar down here. Why didn't you go there?"

"Look, we're playing. You can wait for the other one. Sorry," the first man said.

"It's fine, Todd. We can just get another drink," I said.

Todd turned away from the dartboards and the two men, but then turned back. "Let's shoot for it at least. Give us a fair chance."

The two men grinned at each other, and the first one spoke. "One shot each, most points gets the board?"

"Fine," Todd agreed.

While I didn't want to be near a fistfight over the board, the contest seemed reasonable enough. Perhaps Todd had been being modest and actually was good at darts.

Todd took a dart from the ledge on the wall, walked to a line on the floor, and threw. He hit the board, but I had no idea what it meant.

Todd walked back to me, and said quietly, "I got eighteen, which isn't terrible, but I bet they get twenty." I nodded.

The man who had spoken second picked up a dart, stepped up to the line, and threw.

When it hit the board, his friend said, "Well, it's good enough."

Todd threw up his hands and said calmly, "The board's yours, guys."

"Wait," I said loudly enough for all three of them to hear me. "What happened?"

"They got twenty. I got eighteen. They won," Todd explained.

Since we were competing, I didn't like us losing. "Oh, well, can I shoot? I thought it was one shot each."

"I meant it was one per team," the man who hadn't thrown said. "But why not? Go for it."

I took Todd with me over to the ledge with the third dart on it. "What am I aiming for?"

He looked perplexed. "What do you mean?"

"I told you, I've never played before. What do I need to hit?"

"Oh, well, a bull's-eye—right in the middle—would be good, but I don't think you'll hit that on your first throw. You see where his dart is? Right below that there's a little area in red. He was aiming for that. It would be triple twenty, sixty points. So aim for that, but, well, it's not easy to hit."

I grabbed the dart with my healthy hand and found the line on the floor. The two men grinned widely. I focused on where Todd had said to hit, set my feet, brought my arm back, and took aim. I let the dart go, and it hit the board with a solid *thunk*.

"Wow!" Todd said. I had hit the triple twenty.

The two men looked stunned. The one who hadn't shot yet took the three darts out of the board and came back. He shot, but hit in the black just above where I had, so it was only another single twenty.

"Lucky," the other man said, and they both walked away.

"Wow," Todd said again. "You've really never played before?"

I smiled. "Not that I can remember, no."

We played the rest of the game and discovered it hadn't been a lucky shot. While every throw wasn't perfect, I hit most things I aimed for and won quickly. By the end, the people at the board next to us had stopped their own game to watch me. The attention was embarrassing, and I missed some on purpose, badly, to support my claim that it was my first time playing.

I didn't tell Todd, but my confidence had grown with each shot, and I assumed darts was something I had been good at before my memory loss. I had simply never tried it before.

Todd wanted to keep playing, but I persuaded him to leave after that game. As exciting as it was to be so good at something, it also scared me. Learning more reminded me of how much I didn't know about myself, and, as always, that weighed on me.

Outside in the dark, I couldn't keep from thinking of Snake. Was he looking for me, or had I been a random victim that he had since forgotten? While I believed Grant would get him if he did anything to me, that would be after the fact, and by then, I would probably be dead. I hoped Grant's threat proved enough of a deterrent to keep me alive.

As we walked to my apartment, I moved close to Todd, and he put his arm around me. He wasn't Grant, but if Snake was out there, I would stand a better chance with him than without him.

6

Snake didn't show up, thank God. I waited up for a while in case Grant called, but he never did. All in all, it had been a fun night with Todd. While I hadn't learned much about the Spectavi, I was satisfied to have followed up on the lead. Monday would be interesting in the office, though. Hopefully, I hadn't made a big mistake by going out with him.

Then, much to my surprise, after getting home from a run on Sunday, I had a voicemail from him. Todd wanted to take me to a baseball game that day. I didn't know how to respond. It was nice out again, and having never been to a game, trying something new sounded exciting. On the other hand, I feared it was too much too fast.

I wrestled with the decision for almost half an hour before finally calling him back and saying yes. I had nothing else to do except wait for night to come and possibly some word from Grant. Being out in the sun sounded like a fun way to pass the time, and there would be no Snake to worry about there.

At the stadium, our seats were amazing. We sat right

against the first base line. Looking out, I pictured what the view was like from the seats high above. Of course, I didn't want to trade and was thrilled Todd could afford for us to sit so close.

"Let's go get you a baseball cap," he said after the third inning.

"Oh, no, that's okay, but thank you."

"I insist. Come on." He got up, and I followed him to the concourse.

We got in a line that mostly consisted of children.

"Really, Todd, I've made it this long not having a baseball hat, I think I'll be fine without one."

"Nonsense, this is your first game, and everyone needs at least one," Todd said. "What color, red or pink?"

I crossed my arms and faked as much anger as I could. "Not pink."

I wore my red hat the rest of the day. Todd strongly suggested trying my first ballpark hot dog, so I did. The Nationals lost, but Todd said that was normal for them. More than anything, I enjoyed being out in the sun for the afternoon, not worrying about vampires for a change. For the second day in row, that had been the case for the most part, and I felt more relaxed than I had in a long time.

Later, outside my apartment, Todd kissed me. He caught me off guard, or just out of practice, because I didn't return the kiss very strongly. I think at least he could tell that I was glad he had done it.

Grant never contacted me, so I devoted the night to watching TV and thinking about the events of the last week—it was a lot to process.

I concluded that I probably knew all I ever would about Francis. Grant had his story about him, and I had my doubts, but what else could I hope to learn? More importantly, Grant had my picture to show around, even if I had been overly eager in expecting results right away.

I spent a lot of time thinking about Todd. Everything else I worried about was the past and a mystery. Todd could be a future. We had just started going out, or whatever we were doing, but I had fun with him. My broken fingers, splinted with metal, reminded me that I did not have fun with vampires. At best, it was frustrating work, searching for answers that always proved elusive, and at worst, it was dangerous to my health. First, there had been the close call with Grant at the bus stop—I still didn't know what his true intentions were at the time—and then Snake's attack.

Snake was out there somewhere and, while I wished it weren't so, I could remember the attack in detail. If I let them, his foul stench and awful words filled my mind. I could see him inches from my face and clearly recall flying through the air and crashing into the wall after he threw me like a rag doll.

I kept thinking how lucky I was that things hadn't gone even worse.

———————

By Monday, the bruise on my head had gotten a lot better and didn't hurt much to touch. My fingers remained splinted and would be for a while. I sat at my desk and tried to get used to typing without using them. It was going to be harder, but I could get my work done, just a little more slowly.

I gave Mr. Oliver the same excuse about my fingers that I had given Todd, and he bought it, not that there was any reason for him to doubt me. Kristi came over to my desk and listened to my story, but she obviously didn't believe it. I sent her an instant message as soon as she left, saying that I would tell her the truth later. She still looked pale, but seemed happy and otherwise unhurt.

A few hours went by, and I was relieved not to have heard from Todd. I really hoped things wouldn't be weird at the office.

Kristi and I had dinner in the break room. No one else was around, so we talked quietly about our weekends.

"Christopher and I went to two new clubs; it was so much fun," she said.

Clubbing was their thing, apparently. "Cool," I said. "Were they like Night?"

"Oh, much better than Night. I mean, Night was fine, but these were bigger and fancier places. A lot more upscale. It's a good thing Christopher was paying."

I smiled.

"You know what else?" Kristi asked.

"What?"

She leaned over and looked around before she whispered, "He bites me more often, and drinks just a little blood each time. He does it when we dance sometimes, too. It's unbelievable, Erin. I think I love him."

"Listen to yourself. He's a vampire! You just met him!"

For some reason, hearing her say it didn't shock me. I was afraid for her and unsure if she really understood what she was getting herself into. She'd had nothing but good times with Christopher; I just worried they might not last.

"I know, but still, I think I do," she said. "I thought I'd miss the fact that we can't have sex, but the bites are so amazing. They're different. In some ways, they're better."

It was well documented that vampires couldn't have sex, but that their bites were extremely pleasurable. While it could have been a single bite, more likely many contributed to the scar on my neck, and how they might have felt always scared me. I assumed I had hated it, and the idea of being bitten repeatedly sickened me.

Unfortunately, I didn't know what I had been like before, so my assumptions were nothing more than guesses, or hopes, really. Nevertheless, I had a hard time believing that I had ever enjoyed being food for vampires.

"You haven't drunk from him, have you?" I hadn't considered that with the two of them before.

"No," she said.

Good, I thought.

She continued. "Not yet anyway, but maybe someday. Can you imagine living forever? Never growing old?"

She was really thinking about it already. Most people fantasized about becoming a vampire at some point, but it was a romanticized fantasy that only included the good parts. At first, no one thought about watching their family and friends grow old while they didn't, not being able to have human children anymore, never spending a day in the sun again, or having to drink the blood of real, live people to survive—unless they were Spectavi, of course.

When people considered those things, most realized it wasn't for them. Those left had to think about the spiritual consequences—including what would happen to their soul if they became a vampire. The major religions all had vampire-run factions, but most human religious leaders called vampires evil and said their souls could never get to Heaven, however each religion's version of Heaven was defined. Most people couldn't get past that. Even if no one was sure of the truth, it was a heck of a thing to take a chance on.

Still, some would take that chance, or they simply didn't care. For those people who really did want to become vampires, the hardest part was usually finding a vampire that would make you one of them. They had to drain most of your blood and then let you drink from them. It was believed they couldn't do it very often, so they chose their offspring carefully.

It seemed Kristi might have already taken care of the most elusive aspect of becoming a vampire, before coming to terms with the others.

"Be careful, Kristi. There's no going back, you know."

"Oh, I will. I'm not about to become a vampire. Don't worry. So anything fun on your weekend?"

"Well, I ran into Todd, and then we went out for a few drinks." It sounded so plain compared to her story, and yet I found myself proud to say it.

"Wait, *this* Todd?"

"Uh huh."

"Whoa! That's huge."

"I guess, I don't know, it might have been nothing." Kristi rarely seemed so interested in my news, but since it was about Todd, discussing it there suddenly felt wrong. "I need to get back."

"Well, you have to tell me all about it soon!"

I promised and went back to my desk. Todd had emailed. He said he was busy that night, but hoped we could hang out after work the following day. A night off for us seemed right, but I also looked forward to seeing him, so that was a fine plan.

The next night, we went out for drinks again because getting off work at ten o'clock didn't leave many other options. Unlike before, I didn't have an agenda, and we just had a good time talking. Todd asked if I wanted to play darts, but I declined. We did laugh remembering the guys' faces when I had hit the triple twenty.

Todd began visiting my desk at work occasionally and, after some initial apprehension, it became a welcome occurrence. We kept the conversations brief and infrequent, and he seemed to understand how awkward things could get if we weren't careful.

That weekend, I still hadn't heard from Grant, and Kristi asked me to go to a club with her and Christopher. While my first instinct was to go and get back to work searching for answers about my past on my own, I didn't know if I really wanted to return to that world. My fingers weren't healed, but that wasn't the whole issue.

I declined and called Todd instead. We hung out at his apartment in Penn Quarter. It was a nice area, and it felt good to be in a home with real meaning for a few hours. Todd's place had pictures of his friends and family, old books he had read, and souvenirs from trips he had gone on. His apartment was much warmer than my mostly empty one.

Todd and I went out most nights after work the next week, taking turns picking restaurants, bars, and movies. While we always had a good time wherever we went, I was both amused and relieved that the places I picked tended to turn out better. Online reviews seemed to be a fine substitute for a lifetime of experiences, at least in that regard.

"How'd you find out about this place again?" Todd asked that Thursday. We were at a sports bar known for their pizza.

"I found it online. I subscribed to some alerts for deals." Finding places for us to go had become my new favorite thing to do during downtime at work, and it was two-for-one pizza night.

"And you've never been here?" he asked.

"Nope."

"Well it's great, well done," he said. "We'll have to come back."

"Absolutely." We were less than halfway finished, and I had already reached that same conclusion.

"What's your favorite color?" Todd asked, as I bit into a new slice.

"What?" I asked with a full mouth.

"You never talk about yourself, Erin. I'm just curious."

I immediately became uncomfortable. I had successfully deflected such questions so far, yet Todd's warmth made me want to come out of my shell a little. Or at least try.

I had time to think while chewing the pizza and, after swallowing, said, "I don't know, green, I guess."

"Me, too!" Todd's face lit up. "It's kind of silly, but I like the green grass on a field at the start of a season or a ballgame. I hate artificial turf, and real, green grass is getting so rare."

"That's not silly at all." It was cute. "For me, it's one of the first things I remember, my green eyes." I vividly recalled the first time I saw myself in a mirror.

"I think your eyes are amazing," Todd said.

I came back to the conversation and couldn't help smiling. "Thanks."

"What's your favorite food?"

"I don't know. I've never really thought about it."

"There must be something," he prodded.

It had never been important for me to consider. "Steak, maybe? I eat a lot of salads, but I don't think they're my favorite. I don't eat a lot of steak, but I can't remember ever really disliking one."

"Nice," Todd said. "I'd have to go with a good hamburger, so we're actually close there, too. Favorite TV show?"

"Oh… I don't know…" The questions were getting harder. "I don't really have one."

"Was there anything you watched growing up, or in college, all the time?" Todd asked.

"No, not really." I was letting him down, but feared a follow-up discussion if I made something up. "I don't watch much TV."

"Oh, okay." He might have noticed my difficulty with the last question because he didn't ask another one like it.

I tried to get over it, but felt bad for the rest of the meal. It pained me that there wasn't any more to tell him. I watched a little TV, but nothing regularly. There was no favorite movie, either. While there would be someday, presumably, I had a lot of catching up to do first.

He changed the subject, we went on eating our pizza, and I realized how much I really liked his light blue eyes. Unfortunately, I had missed my earlier opportunity to tell him. I was so bad at dating. At least I picked good places for us to go out.

Kristi asked me to check out a new club with her and Christopher that Friday. I said no right away. I would meet her vampire eventually, but just wasn't in the mood at that moment. I doubted Kristi really cared.

Another week had gone by with no word from Grant. I thought about it less and less each night, though, and began to accept the fact that I might never hear from him again. At least I hadn't seen Snake, either, and I worried about him a lot less, as well.

I woke up in bed with Todd at his apartment on Saturday. His arm was around me, and I rolled under the sheets toward him while he slept. I never imagined such a thing could have happened so quickly, but I really liked being with him. It was the first time I had ever felt that way about anybody, at least that I could remember.

I was glad he held me that morning.

That night, we had reservations at a fancy new sushi restaurant that had received a glowing write up. When I suggested it to Todd, he was able to get us a table on short notice.

When Todd woke up, we tested my healing fingers. They were stiff to move, but didn't hurt anymore. We agreed that since I wouldn't be playing sports or anything like that, I would probably be all right with them loose. It was exciting to finally be free of the splints. Aside from their restrictiveness, I had gotten very tired of looking at them.

Everything would be easier with all my fingers, and getting them back was a great way to start the day.

Holding my phone in my left hand comfortably for a change, I unlocked it and found a missed call and a text message. Both were from Grant from late the previous night. He said an older vampire named James might have recognized my picture and wanted to meet me at a Sanguan club that night.

7

I told Todd the truth about my past, or lack of a past, and why I had to cancel on our dinner plans. I cared about him and our relationship and making up a lie about that part of my life felt like the wrong thing to do. Not lying also meant letting him in on my most personal secret, which actually felt right. I hoped it would bring us closer together. He guessed the truth about Night on his own.

"A vampire broke your fingers, didn't they?" he asked.

We were sitting up in his bed while we talked. "Yes, but that was different. It was just a random attack, that's all."

"A random attack? Is the vampire still out there?"

"Yes, but it's been weeks since that happened."

"He could have killed you, Erin!"

"I know, but he didn't. A vampire could kill me anytime I go out at night. Or one could kill you. I'm not going to live in fear of him."

"Did you go to the police?" he asked. "The Spectavi could help you if you did."

"No, it happened at a club; another Sanguan took care of it." I thought of my earlier visits to the police and the

Spectavi. "The police have never been able to help me."

Todd got out of bed. "What do you mean, 'another Sanguan took care of it?' The police could help with this, Erin."

I faced forward instead of looking at him. We had never argued like we were. "Grant said he'd kill Snake if he did anything else to me, and I haven't seen Snake since then."

"But Snake is still out there, and you're going back to another club? That's crazy. How well do you know Grant, anyway? He's just another Sanguan."

I *had* just met him, but he didn't seem like just another Sanguan. I turned to Todd. "I know Grant saved me from Snake, and I know he said he'd help me. He seemed like he really meant it. Maybe it's a mistake; I don't know. Maybe you're right, and I shouldn't go, but you don't know what it's like not to know who you are or what happened to you to make you like you are. I have to meet him tonight and see what he's found."

A large part of me didn't want to go and wanted to go to the restaurant with Todd. I really didn't want to mess up our relationship, and already things had changed since we started arguing.

And I didn't think he'd be so upset about me going. I was an adult and could take care of myself. It had just been two broken fingers, and I would be with Grant.

"Then I'll go with you." He had clearly become more worried than anything else.

It was sweet of him to offer, but I couldn't let him. "No, Todd, I have to go alone."

"Why?"

I got out of bed and found my jeans on the dresser. "I just do, I'm sorry." I almost said, "You wouldn't be safe," but didn't think that would go over well.

Todd had never been to a place like that and taking him to a club I had never been to either seemed unwise. I figured Grant could protect me if anything happened, but didn't want him to have to worry about Todd, too.

I finished getting dressed and walked over to him. "I'll call you tomorrow." I tried to give him a kiss, but he turned away, so I kissed him quickly on the cheek, then left his apartment.

I walked in the nice weather instead of taking the subway home. Grant's message said he'd send a car at eleven o'clock, so I had plenty of time. It hurt to have left Todd's like that, but he didn't understand. He *couldn't* understand why I had to go.

I commuted to work every day and saw families on the subway and wondered if my family was out there somewhere. They might even have been searching for me. Kristi told me stories about her friends from college and, while they didn't all sound like my idea of a good time, at least she had the friends and the stories. Mr. Oliver had his children and grandchildren.

Being with Todd had turned my attention to the future, but it had also shown me another person with a full life of family and friends, and I couldn't help being jealous of him. While I was truly happy for him and hoped to meet all those people and become a bigger part of his life, I also longed to know if I had ever had a life like that of my own.

Meeting James, perhaps I could get that life back, or at least learn about it. For the first time, someone might have recognized me. That it was a vampire made perfect sense.

My excitement and curiosity grew and yet, as I got farther from Todd's, I also had a nagging feeling that I was walking away from a good future with someone who cared for me, and it might be a mistake. I couldn't make the idea go away completely, but I pushed it into the corner of my mind. I had to go to the club. I called Kristi to ask if she knew which one I might be headed to.

––––––––––––––––

Grant had said he'd send a car and nothing more than that. Kristi agreed that probably meant we were going to a club outside D.C., in Virginia or Maryland. She couldn't hide her excitement when describing a club Christopher had taken her to in Maryland that she said blew Night away. It was bigger, louder, and much fancier, and we assumed my destination would be similar.

I didn't get into it with Kristi, but it also made sense to me that an old Sanguan wouldn't want to come into D.C. if they didn't have to. If Grant was telling the truth, the more crowded city would make it easier to be ambushed and harder to get away if things went badly.

I couldn't ignore the irony—people were always as vulnerable as the old vampire claimed to be, except they could do even less to defend themselves.

I wondered what James would be like. I had seen Francis

from afar before he was killed, but had never actually met a Sanguan I knew to be very old.

At ten forty, I was ready to go, but decided it was a bit early to go outside. I poured myself a small glass of wine and sat on my couch. The weeks old sketch of the twins remained on the front of my notebook. Their image still didn't make any sense to me, so I turned the page over and put the notebook down.

I flexed my fingers, which were already much less stiff than they had been in the morning. Grant would be with me, I reassured myself. And it was the right thing to do. I had to know if someone had really recognized me. After a year and a half of searching, it was by far the best lead I had ever had. Todd would understand eventually.

I was warm, so I took off my coat while waiting and sipping my wine. In addition to my dark eye shadow, Kristi had convinced me to wear something a little nicer to the club, so I chose a short black dress, sheer black tights, and black suede pumps with heels a few inches high. At first, the tights weren't part of the outfit, but I decided too much of my skin was showing for the vampires without them. I didn't want to tempt them. The dress had a high, rounded neck, and I wore my hair down to cover my cross tattoo some. I didn't want to antagonize them, either.

I hadn't gotten so dressed up for anything with Todd yet, so it felt strange to be sitting like that to go to a vampire club, but Kristi had assured me the place would be classy, and I had to be certain to get in to meet the old vampire. At least with my coat on, I was well covered.

After finishing the last drop of my wine, my nerves weren't calmed, but more didn't seem like a good idea. It was ten minutes until eleven anyway, close enough. I put my coat back on, checked that my keys, wallet, and phone were in the pocket, and headed downstairs.

There was no car in front of my apartment, so I stood at the circular driveway. The night was warm, but a breeze kept me comfortable. I had seven minutes to wait.

Eventually, a couple I didn't know approached, holding hands. They smiled at me before walking past and going inside. Presumably, their night was ending while mine hadn't quite begun.

My feet started hurting a little, and I considered running upstairs to change into a more comfortable pair of shoes. I checked my phone again—ten fifty-seven—I probably didn't have time. It was okay, though, I'd manage. I just wanted to get going.

Finally, a black limousine with dark tinted windows turned into the driveway. It pulled up next to me, and the rear window opened a few inches. A female voice came from behind it.

"Please get in, Erin."

It had all been drastically simpler in my head. It was just another vampire club with Grant, who I had already met. I hadn't thought through getting into a limo with someone else.

"Where's Grant?" It seemed a reasonable question.

"He's going to meet us there." The voice came from the far side of the limo. "Please get in. We have a long drive."

I opened the door in front of me and sat down. The inside lights were on, and another gray leather bench seat faced me. I closed the door without taking my eyes off of the vampire to my left, and we drove away.

"I'm Zhilan, a friend of Grant's." She smiled and extended her hand.

Her skin was firm, but smooth, and significantly lighter in color than Grant's, which meant she was probably older than him. She wore a short, red dress that made the top Kristi had worn to Night seem juvenile and plain. Zhilan's dress was tight, fine silk or satin, and embroidered with gold designs. She wore bright red lipstick to match. The contrast of the red against her pale skin was striking.

"Your eyes might be greener than mine, Erin." She caught me, entranced with hers.

I finally let go of her hand. "I'm sorry."

Her jet-black hair was up tightly behind her head, and she looked like a young Chinese woman, perhaps a few years younger than me. She had only a slight accent, and I wondered how old she really was. I slowly scooted closer to my side door.

"It's all right. We have an hour drive. Would you like a drink?"

"No, thanks." Inquiring about her age felt rude, so instead I asked, "Where are we going?"

"A club called Fire and Ice, in Virginia. We're going to meet James; he won't come into the city anymore."

The club's name confused me, because vampires usually didn't like fire, but I assumed it would make sense later.

"Why won't he come into D.C.?" I wanted to hear her version.

Zhilan grew serious. "Grant said you saw Francis's murder?" I nodded. "Another old vampire was killed last night. It isn't safe for James."

"The Spectavi?" I asked.

"Yes, it was them." I couldn't tell if she was angry. Vampires' emotions could be hard to read. "But don't worry, we'll be safe where we're going."

"And Grant's going to meet us there?"

"Yes, he will."

Zhilan turned off the inside lights, yet her skin and bright dress continued to stand out from the darkness.

For a while we didn't talk, and the limo was silent except for the sound of the engine and the tires on the road. I wondered why Grant hadn't come himself, but decided I'd rather ask him. And as young as she appeared, Zhilan's assurance that we'd be safe at the club was impossible to doubt. She sat very still, with a very slight smile, exuding confidence.

There was little traffic as we left the city and got on the highway. I didn't travel far from D.C. often, so I watched the landscape in the darkness while we drove. I couldn't see much, but black-tinted glass blocked my view out the front windshield, and I couldn't stare at Zhilan to my left the whole time, so there was nowhere else to look.

We drove west into Virginia. When I took my phone out of my coat pocket, I saw that we had been driving for forty minutes.

"Erin, we're almost there. You should put this on." Zhilan's slight smile was gone. She turned on the light and held out a metal collar.

I stared at it in disbelief. "What is that?"

"It will let everyone at the club know that you are with Grant."

I had never heard of anything like that. "Do I have to wear it? I don't want to."

"You won't be safe if you don't wear it. Fire and Ice will be full of vampires. Hungry vampires. But they will respect the collar in the club."

I felt sick to my stomach. I had finally started to relax during the drive and, for some reason, Zhilan had seemed trustworthy to me right away, but the steel collar was not in my plan for the night.

She leaned over and put her hand on my shoulder. "I wouldn't go into the club without it on, Erin." She moved toward me and turned me so my back was to her. She collected my hair and pulled it up.

"I thought it would be best with my hair down." I almost explained that my bare neck might be tempting to all the vampires before deciding she probably didn't need the reminder. Then I realized what she was doing might be tempting *her*. I had quickly considered her a friend since she claimed to know Grant, but I didn't really know anything about her. In fact, Grant might not have been coming at all. She could have killed him, taken his phone, and set everything up herself.

But it seemed like a lot to do to me. I didn't see the point of going through all the trouble, instead of killing me at my apartment, or perhaps a few miles outside D.C.

"It would be better for everyone to know right away that you're spoken for." She put in a few pins, and my hair was up, leaving my neck bare. "And the collar will cover most of this cross."

I couldn't believe what I had gotten myself into—the club was so full of hungry vampires that the only way I would be safe was by covering my neck and cross with a metal collar?

She brought the collar around my neck and closed it in the back. I gulped. It was tight, but I could swallow without trouble. Rubber coated the inside against my neck and, while not light, the collar wasn't as uncomfortable as I had feared.

There was a loud *click*, and then there was added weight at the back of my neck. Zhilan had locked the collar. It made sense—the collar would be pointless if easy to remove.

I turned toward her, ashamed. I hadn't done anything wrong, but there I sat with a metal collar locked on me. I felt owned, even if I trusted Grant and Zhilan. But what if I was wrong about them? Todd might have been right. At least he wouldn't see me with the collar.

Zhilan's youthful smile returned. "Don't worry, Erin. Grant just wants you to be safe. Only he has the key."

I tried to fake a smile of my own, but didn't think I succeeded. I reminded myself that she could have had my blood already. Despite the pit in my stomach, I still trusted her.

I leaned back on the seat and was startled when the padlock on the collar prevented my neck from resting against it. Wearing it felt so wrong, but there was nothing I could do about it; Zhilan didn't even have the key. I wondered if she or another vampire was strong enough to break it off.

I kept my head forward and used the front camera on my phone to see the collar. Most of my cross tattoo was covered, as Zhilan had expected. The steel was about two inches wide, and the rubber lining the inside was black.

On the front was the head of Baphomet, which I recognized from Stan's statue behind the bar. It was the same ugly goat head with horns, though it wasn't colored-in like his had been; it was just an etching. It was harder to see the sides, but I made out a pentagram on the left and an upside down pentagram on the right. As much as I didn't like them, a few satanic symbols around my neck were the least of my worries.

I pulled my coat close around me, crossed my arms, and gently rested my neck against the seat. I reminded myself why I was going, and then Zhilan handed me a glass of wine that she had poured while I had been inspecting my collar. "This might help," she said.

8

We were a few miles off the highway, and I stared into the sky outside the window. It was partly cloudy, but many more stars shone than in the city. They were a welcome distraction from what lay ahead.

We turned onto a dirt road that cut through a field, and I figured we were getting close. I finished my wine and looked for the club, but only saw low shrubs, or possibly grapevines.

Finally, a small house with its porch lights on came into view on a hill to the right. As we approached, I saw a parking lot with a few other cars and motorcycles. The building looked old, with faded yellow paint, and it seemed too small and rundown to be the club.

We pulled directly in front of the house and stopped. Unfortunately, I didn't spot Grant's motorcycle. The limo door to Zhilan's left opened, and she stepped out. I put down my glass, slid over on the seat, and followed her. We stood on a narrow marble path that led to the old house.

The limousine driver was an old man.

"Thanks, Bill," Zhilan said and started down the path

towards the house. Her dress clung to her thin body and was even more impressive when she stood. I didn't think she was quite as tall as me, but her black high heels were much higher than mine, so she was definitely taller than me then. She turned to me, and said, "Come, Erin."

I nodded to Bill and followed after Zhilan. The quiet night, filled with sounds of insects I couldn't see, reminded me of how far out of the city we had come. The lock on my neck rattled against the collar with each step, and I worked hard not to think about the humiliating noise. I tried to remind myself that I had been to vampire clubs before, but Fire and Ice was going to be different, and I knew it.

Eventually, I reached the porch where Zhilan waited. She opened the old door, and two vampires dressed in all black clothes holding big guns stood in front of a silver elevator door. The guards glanced at me and my collar.

Zhilan said something to them I didn't understand, and the door opened behind them. They stepped aside, and I followed Zhilan into the elevator. The door closed behind us, and we started down. I hadn't seen anyone press a button.

"This place isn't so much hidden as it is protected," Zhilan explained. "The Spectavi know it exists, but it would be hard for them to get to us here."

"Two vampires?" I asked.

"There's a lot more than that. Don't worry." She formed a slight grin, and added, "Besides, you're with me."

The ride was longer and quieter than I expected, until eventually we came to a stop. The doors opened, and instantly, the electronic notes of dance music from down a long hallway hit me. It was even louder than at Night, but at least it was a familiar sound.

"I'll take your coat, girl," a middle-aged man in a black button-down shirt said from behind a counter, as soon as we stepped out of the elevator. He made no effort to hide the numerous bite marks littering his neck.

"Oh, no, thanks, I'll keep it," I said.

"Another first timer..." The man sighed. "We insist. Your coat, please."

My eyes asked Zhilan for help, but she didn't give any. I took off my coat, handed it to the man, and waited for a ticket or something in return.

"I'll remember you. Don't worry," he said.

On the drive, I had decided to leave my coat on as long as possible. Without it and with my hair up, I had become much more exposed than planned. In spite of what Zhilan had said, I fought a strong urge to let my hair back down. Once again, I couldn't believe I had put myself in a situation where it was an issue.

Zhilan headed down the hall, so I followed. Like at Night, the music got louder with each step. Orange and red lights flickered in front of me. Yellow mixed in, and I realized I saw bursts of fire.

I said a prayer, at the same time wondering how much it could help me, all the way down there.

We stepped into the main room, and I stopped. The club was drastically bigger than Night in every dimension and appeared to have side rooms off the huge main one as well.

Balconies of varying sizes jutted out of the very high walls and plenty of bars were spread all over. In spite of its size, souring vocals and pulsing beats sounded crisp and clear and had no trouble filling the room completely.

Then I saw the fire more closely.

Scattered throughout the dance floors, columns of narrow fire burned and occasionally grew wider and brighter for a few seconds. The flames had thin metal poles at their centers where the fire came from and were perhaps ten or fifteen feet tall. It was already warm where I stood, then waves of intense heat reached me as nearby fires flared.

There must have been a predictable pattern because vampires and humans danced around them just far enough back to avoid being hit with the flames when they grew. The expanding fires made it easier to survey the action around the room. Crowds of vampires and people danced in groups and pairs like at Night, but the similarities to the smaller club ended there.

Everything from the dark gray walls to the black and gray bar stools and booths looked new and modern and, even though the air was warm, it was unexpectedly clean. From where I stood, at least, there was no overpowering stench of sweat.

While there were plenty of young people, like in the city clubs, there were definitely more older ones as well. Everyone wore much finer clothing, like Zhilan, or else had covered themselves in leather, rubber, or latex. There were short dresses and long gowns, suits and tight pants, and corsets and bare bodies. Kristi had been right to insist I dress up a little.

There were other collars like mine, along with handcuffs, masks, and chains, on plenty of people. I had seen such things in other clubs, but never on that scale. While I didn't like the collar locked on me, I certainly fit in with it.

Plenty of dark, gothic faces filled my view, yet a significant number of people hadn't chosen that style. Rationalizing it seemed heartless, but it made sense that some vampires preferred their food to look more classically human.

Scanning the room, I noticed that some groups of dancers moved from flame to flame as the bursts came and went. It wasn't everyone in the club, but it was impressive to watch them crisscross the room as giant waves of bodies. I had never seen a party of such size or splendor in person.

A male vampire's hard body bumped me, and then a man he pulled on a leash did, too. I still stood in the opening to the hallway and tried to find Zhilan. She must have gone ahead. I took a few more steps into the room and spun in a circle, but didn't see her in the darkness around me.

"Erin." Her voice came from somewhere to my left.

A flame shot bright and revealed her red dress and light skin. She wasn't far, thank God. I walked over to her.

"Grant will be here soon," she said. "Do you want to dance?"

No way. I never danced at those places, or hardly ever at all. "Um, no, can I just sit somewhere and wait?"

"If you'd like. Follow me."

On the side of the main room, we found a small booth with a black half-circle bench and the name 'Zhilan' on a little white card lying on the table.

"I'll be dancing. If you want a drink, a waiter will come around, or you can go to a bar. Grant has an account here," she said.

I thanked her, and she walked away, disappearing into the darkness once again. I sat down in the middle of the table with my right leg crossed over my left and my arms down at my sides. I felt very small gazing out at the expansive scene and didn't notice anyone else sitting alone. Everyone was dancing, drinking, or at least talking with someone.

A flame lit up a new corner of the room. A big male vampire held a small girl against the wall with his mouth at her neck. I sat back in my seat.

The girl wore almost nothing, yet I couldn't see much of her because the vampire's shirt was off and the bulging white muscles of his chest and arms enveloped her tan skin. Red slid down her neck from where he was biting. She didn't struggle and opened her eyes while he fed. Her mouth opened very gradually, and I shuddered at the thought, but she clearly enjoyed it.

The fire went dim, and they were gone.

My fingers touched the protective steel at my neck. If I had been like that girl some time in my past, voluntarily or not, I didn't want to be again. But where was Grant? If he would show up, I could meet James, then get the detestable thing off of me.

Cold hit my shoulders and my neck where it wasn't covered, and I turned to check why. A clear sheet of ice covered the blue wall behind me, and air blew over it and onto my back. Once I figured that out, I noticed the walls behind the bars were the same. While the ice fit the club's name and was an interesting juxtaposition to the fire, I didn't understand its purpose.

It was cold, though, and I was glad to have worn tights for another reason. I felt for the pins in my hair and wanted to rip them out and be warmer, but managed to stop myself.

An explanation for the ice came to mind—it made people cold so they would want to get up and not sit around. It seemed too simple, but I was shivering, so if that was the idea, it was working.

I thought of checking my phone, but remembered that it was back by the elevator with my coat. In addition to being very cold, I was also very alone. I wished Grant would show up.

After a few minutes of shivering with music blaring, I couldn't sit there anymore. I decided that a glass of wine might warm me some. I made sure Zhilan's name card was visible on the table, then headed for the closest bar I could see in the occasional light.

I made my way through the crowd as quickly and carefully as possible, hoping that if I didn't bump into anyone, I would be ignored. The trip progressed as planned until a pair of wildly dancing girls came near me.

I shuffled my feet and jumped to my right to avoid them, and found myself before a big male vampire sipping from a wine glass. He lowered his drink and grinned at me. It took a few more quick steps to get past him. When I looked back, he still watched me, so I moved faster.

As I neared the crowded bar, I turned back once more and

didn't see him. Slightly relieved, I found a place to walk all the way up to the bar, but the bartenders were busy. While I waited, a female vampire in a black dress caught my attention.

The dress was shiny and skintight, but there were plenty like that there. What I couldn't ignore was the way she sucked gently on a young man's wrist that she held to her mouth. They both sat on barstools, and she had to hold him up on his while slowly sipping his blood. Both the vampire and the man seemed to be enjoying it immensely.

"What would you like, girl?" a young-looking vampire called over all the noise. Apparently 'girl' was going to be my name among the staff.

"Merlot." Trusty merlot, it would be a small comfort compared to the chaos I had gotten myself into. I could take it and head back to the relative calm of Zhilan's booth.

"Let me see, then," he said.

"What?"

"Turn around, girl."

I did, and he took hold of the padlock at my neck. He pulled me toward him slightly, and I heard a beep. He must have scanned something.

"No, I'm sorry, you can't order for yourself, girl. Don't waste my time again." He walked away.

Turning to him, I almost protested and said that Zhilan had told me I could order from Grant's account. He must have forgotten to set it up or something, though I had no idea how things really worked. I touched the collar on my neck and felt like dirt, like a slave.

I headed back to the table, but no longer had the energy

to avoid the mess around me. Sweaty bodies brushed against me while I walked. One man bumped me so hard it almost knocked me to the floor. Near the table, I got tangled in rope a vampire used to pull a woman around the room.

I freed myself, sat down, and brushed a tear from my cheek. I wanted to meet James and then go back to Todd's. I tried to find comfort in the bit of warmth that had come from the walk, but I knew it wouldn't last.

I caught a glimpse of Zhilan in a burst of firelight. She was unmistakable in her red dress dancing with a female vampire who wore a deep-yellow dress. I didn't often see vampires in yellow, and the color contrasted vividly with Zhilan's red while they moved. The light faded, yet I kept looking at where they had been.

Another flame burst, and a third vampire had joined them. It was a male who wore tight black pants and, with no shirt on, could have been the one I had seen feeding earlier. The three of them danced in the fleeting light, sometimes holding each other, and sometimes alone. It looked beautiful and powerful, the first positive thing I had seen all evening.

The light faded, and I couldn't help waiting for the next flame and then the one after that to see as much of it as I could. Humans came near and danced around them. The waves of the crowd moved toward them, but parted to pass. None dared get in their way.

I couldn't tell the songs apart, but must have watched them for three or four before Grant finally sat down next to me. "Erin," he said. "I'm sorry I'm late. You look nice. Sorry about the collar."

"Zhilan said it was necessary, so, it's fine, I guess." I hated it, but they were right that I needed it. Grant was dressed like before, jeans and a leather jacket over a t-shirt. It seemed there was no strict dress code after all. Once again, it must have been a few days since he had last shaved.

"Yes, it is, and you can trust Zhilan."

"Who is she?"

"A friend, someone I trust."

I nodded, then asked, "So where were you?"

"I… I had something to take care of." I had never known a vampire to stammer like that.

"What do you mean?"

"It's not important. Don't worry about it."

He looked agitated, but was obviously being evasive, so I pressed on. "Look, I want to know why you sent a car and a vampire I had never met before to bring me here. While she's been out there, I've been sitting here alone, trying not to be eaten by one of your friends. Is it too much to ask why?"

He hadn't expected my outburst. "I had to feed."

And I hadn't expected that. Since meeting him at Night, I hadn't once thought of Grant with his teeth at the neck of a human like I had seen across the dance floor. I thought of him as a friend, or a protector of some kind, but of course, that was nonsense. Suddenly, I wanted to know more about the creature sitting across from me holding the key to the steel collar around my neck.

"Oh. Well, who was it?"

"What?" Grant obviously wasn't used to be interrogated, as he looked uncomfortable or maybe even angry.

"Who did you feed on?"

He shook his head a little and spoke louder. "I'm a *vampire*; I need to *feed*. That's all *you* need to know."

"How can I trust you if you won't tell me? I don't really know why I trust you at all. Can't you give me this little detail? I'm not going to tell anyone, if that's what you're worried about."

"Erin, let it go."

"No, tell me!"

His expression became stern. "Fine," he said. Then, he smirked. "She was a girl about your age; Alice was her name." The details I had begged for stunned me, and Grant apparently knew it. "I picked her because she reminded me of you. I had to feed so I wouldn't be tempted to feed on you."

He had caught me completely off guard. I managed to ask, "Why did you pause next to me outside the bus stop the night Francis died?"

The Sanguan seemed to revel in my fear. "I thought about holding you and biting your neck, then each of your breasts under your little coat. I wanted to know what your blood tasted like. I think you're beautiful."

As it had that night, a chill went down my spine. Unlike before, it hadn't quite paralyzed me. I started to move across the bench to leave, but Grant grabbed my arm. I glanced down to reassure myself that my dress covered my chest before looking at him.

His face softened immediately. "Erin, wait."

"Let me go, please." I'd find a way to get home,

somehow. I could get the collar cut off me. I tried to move my arm, but it was hopeless against his strength.

"I won't hurt you, I swear. You wanted to know, so I told you. Please, calm down. I'm a vampire; I need to feed, and my food is humans. That's just the way it is." I stared at him while he held me. "I don't kill when I feed, but I'm no fool. I didn't want to be tempted by you; that's why I sent Zhilan. You can trust me."

He loosened his grip, and I didn't run off. I was with a Sanguan who planned his meals ahead, but since he had to, I found his claim of not killing hard to believe. He disgusted me.

Two Sanguans like the ones who had been at the door of the elevator came up to our table.

"Come with us," one of them said.

"Follow me, Erin." Grant let go of me and got up. "Please, meet with James."

I debated my options and strongly considered leaving, but I had been through too much to say no. I slid out of the booth and followed him and the two others. Some people glanced at us as we went by, but less than I expected. We went into a side room off the main dance floor where the music was a little quieter. As we made our way through the room, Sanguans drank from at least a dozen humans and seeing them brought me back to Grant's description of what he had almost done to me.

How could I trust him?

Two vampires drinking from each other caught my eye. Grotesque as it was, it appeared they loved what they were doing even more than those I had seen feeding on humans.

One of the Sanguans we followed punched a code into a keypad on the wall to open a door, then led us through. Dim overhead lights lit the small room. When the door closed behind us, the music from the club became very soft.

"Come here," one of the Sanguans said.

I took a few steps toward him, and he let his gun hang around his neck. He grabbed my arms and brought them above my head, toward a pair of black straps connected by a chain over a ceiling beam.

"Wait." I tried to break free. "What are you doing?"

The Sanguan wrapped a strap around each of my wrists.

"Grant, please do something!" I called out.

The straps were pulled tight and locks securing both clicked closed.

Grant was in front of me, but stayed a few feet away. "Don't worry, Erin. Trust me, please."

I stared at him, shocked. My body stretched with my arms stuck high above me, and I would have had to stand on my toes if I hadn't been wearing high heels.

When I had walked into the club, I still had some illusion of freedom, but even that had been taken from me. What were they going to do to me next?

The lights went out, and I screamed into the blackness. "Grant!"

He didn't answer. I tried to move my feet in all directions, but was so stretched out that it strained my body to be anywhere except directly below where my wrists were held.

Visions and feelings of Snake's attack rushed back to me all at once.

I pulled down on my wrists, but there was no give in the chain, and the straps held too tightly for my hands to fit through them. I pulled again, and the straps creaked while I tried twisting my arms and wrists. I let all of my weight rest on my wrists and arms and pulled down until lifting myself off the floor. I finally stopped without accomplishing anything.

The dim lights flickered on.

"Erin Rose, is it?" a vampire standing in front of me asked. I assumed he must have been James.

He came closer, and his very light skin told me he was an old vampire. He had gray hair and looked old as well. He must have become a vampire late in life.

He wore a light gray suit with a white shirt and dark blue tie. He took off his coat and put it on a black couch that I hadn't noticed before, then came close to me again.

"Erin Rose," he repeated, but I still didn't respond. "Erin Rose, what do you think of Grant?"

"What do you mean?"

"What do you think of him, of what he does to stay alive, that he drinks the blood of your kind?"

My eyes went to Grant, and I thought of what Zhilan had said, that at the club my steel collar would be respected. James could bite me anywhere, but perhaps its mere presence would deter him.

"Speak, Erin, please," James said.

"Well, he has to feed to stay alive. I don't have a problem with that."

"You don't have a problem knowing that he mostly feeds on girls about your age? Did he tell you that? And did he tell you that some welcome his bite, while others do not?"

Grant looked down at the floor. A year and a half of extensive research told me his crimes were akin to administering a powerful drug and not rape, but in my current predicament, I had a hard time appreciating the difference.

I looked up at my hands locked to the beam, and then back to James. "I guess he can feed on who he wants, but…"

"Yes, but?" James appeared very interested.

"Well, I just hope it isn't me."

He smiled. "All right, Erin, now tell me about Edmond."

"Edmond?"

"Yes, Edmond, the head of Eure, the lord of the Spectavi. The one who hunts us. Tell me what you know about him."

"I don't know anything!" Could it all be about work somehow? "Well, I do know he runs Eure Global; they recently bought the company I work at. People say he's a good businessman."

"And?"

"And nothing, that's all I know about him, I swear."

James paced for a moment. "Okay, Erin Rose. Perhaps I do believe you. It looks like you are telling the truth. But I don't know how it could have happened, so I can't really believe you yet. Grant, would you please?"

"How what happened?" I asked. No one answered. Grant took a key from a chain around his neck and unlocked my collar.

I saw the pentagram on its side as he walked away with it. I tried to think of something to say, but all I could do was wish the metal was back around my neck. I felt naked without it and with my hair up.

James's firm body pressed against me. He had moved too fast for my eyes. He put one hand on my back and another around half of my neck. "Erin, do you believe this cross will protect you from me if you're lying?"

"Lying?" I asked quietly, my voice almost inaudible.

"Yes, lying about what you know." He opened his mouth and brought his fangs near my cross tattoo.

"Wait," I said, just as softly.

"Yes, is there something more you want to tell me?" He was still right up against my neck.

A little more loudly, I managed, "I already have a scar; please don't give me a new one."

I felt him grin, then there were two pricks in my neck. They hurt tremendously for an instant as the skin was broken, and then there was no more pain.

I closed my eyes, and my legs became weak, but James held me so there wasn't any pressure on my arms.

Every inch of me grew warm, starting from where he had bitten. I could feel James sucking at my neck and, as blood flowed over his fangs, I felt the most incredible thing I had ever experienced. It was wonderful. It was as if I could feel each drop brushing against his teeth, leaving my body and entering his.

I wanted to fight him and fight how good it felt, and I thought I might have been able to, but the same sensation worked its way from his bite out to the rest of my body. Like the warmth, it radiated to my head, out to my arms and fingers, and down to my toes.

It felt too good. I tried to resist it, but gradually lost control of my emotions, and then I forgot what was happening altogether.

All I could comprehend was the pleasure.

James's fangs released my neck, and he moved away. My arms caught my weight until my legs remembered they had to stand. I opened my eyes, and his mouth was bright red with my blood while his shirt and tie were as neat and clean as they had been. He took a white handkerchief from his pocket and cleaned his face.

Todd came to mind first, and then Kristi. Sanguans were her world, not mine. Todd had been right; I should never have come.

I glanced at Grant, who had betrayed me. He had saved me from Snake only to bring me to a different animal.

If I could just be with Todd once more, I would tell him he was right and I wouldn't see Grant or any of those vampires ever again. If only I had listened to him.

"She wasn't lying," James announced. Grant came over and unlocked the cuffs around my wrists. I tried to push him away, but couldn't. I became lightheaded, so I let Grant help me to the small couch. I slumped into a corner of it, reached for my neck, and then brought my fingers around to see my blood on them.

It had happened. I had sworn it never would, but it had. Another vampire had drunk from me. I almost put my head down and sobbed, but was slowly regaining my strength. I decided that since they had taken my blood, I didn't want to give them my tears, too.

"I'm sorry, Erin, but we had to be sure." James walked over to me. My instincts told me to run, but it obviously would have been a futile gesture. He offered me the handkerchief he had used on himself, but even as I felt fresh blood running down my neck, I shook my head in refusal.

He took a photograph from his pocket, unfolded it, and left it next to me. "Do you recognize that girl?"

I picked up the photo and held it close to my face. It was bright enough in the room that I knew what they were thinking right away. Three people, two men, or vampires, and a woman stood in front of what appeared to be a white office building. The woman had long brown hair, and I couldn't tell for sure, but the woman's eyes might have been green. She looked like me.

The woman in the photo wore a white lab coat and appeared to be talking with the two others. One of them wore a lab coat, while the other wore a dark gray suit and had his back to the camera.

"The suit is Edmond, and the other vampire is William, one of his scientists," James said. "We think the girl is you."

"Me?"

"Her name was Vera. She was close with Edmond, and we think she was his chief chemist."

"Was?"

"We have this picture of her, and a few others, but none of them are recent. She disappeared, and we thought she had probably been killed. Then Grant showed me your picture."

I examined the photo again. The girl appeared human and did look similar to me, but her hair seemed lighter than mine, and the eyes could have been more blue than green. The picture was zoomed out too far to be certain.

I looked over the vampires in the room. One had drunk from me, which I was struggling to come to terms with. Grant wanted to drink from me and, if not, from another girl like me. The other two were henchmen with guns, and I had no doubt they would suck my blood if given the chance.

"If this was me, why would they have sent me away, and why don't I remember?" I asked.

"We don't know. I took your blood to read your thoughts, but you're telling the truth. There's nothing there but Erin Rose. I've never seen or heard of anything like your memory loss. Edmond is a very powerful vampire, so who knows what he's capable of or his true motivations?"

"What do you want from me?" I asked.

"You could get close to Edmond at Eure and let us know what he's planning. You could help us fight back."

"What does Eure have to do with this?"

"Eure is the Spectavi. The business funds them, and it legitimizes their cooperation with governments. Edmond runs Eure and the Spectavi. It's all one big organization bent on wiping out any vampires who won't join them."

I didn't have the energy to be as defiant as I would have liked, but I tried. "You want me to help you? Why should I trust you? You have no answers for me. All you have is a picture of a girl with brown hair." I put the picture down and managed to stand while leaning on the couch for balance. "You tied me up and drank my blood. You're all evil. This place is evil."

James shook his head. "Erin, Edmond is having us killed unjustly. We are who we are; we drink because it's in our nature, but we don't all kill when we drink. We don't all deserve to die as he would have it."

"They drink synthetic blood," I argued.

"Presently, yes, but it wasn't always so," James replied.

"I want to go home."

"Erin, listen…" Grant started, but James put up his hand to stop him.

"I know it's not an easy thing to see, Erin. Please understand that you came to hear what I knew, and I had to know if I could trust you. But you may go, you aren't our prisoner. Grant will ride with you."

Grant sickened me. "I don't want to go with him."

"You'd be safer—"

"I'll go with Zhilan."

James motioned to one of the Sanguans in black. "He'll get Zhilan, and I'll walk you out."

I took the pins out of my hair, and it fell—finally covering my neck. I threw the pins on the couch, then turned to Grant. He seemed to want to say something, but remained silent. The vampire in black had already left the room. After James put his suit coat on, I followed after him.

While still woozy, I walked more confidently than I had

before as we made our way through the club. I had survived, after all, and was leaving.

The collar was off my neck, the bursts of flame didn't amaze me as they had before, and the walk down the hallway out of the main room didn't seem as long or as dark. The sound system was loud, but it played the same dance music I could hear anywhere. Fire and Ice wasn't the same club to me that it had been on the way in.

Outside the elevator, the man at the counter went back to get my coat as soon as he saw us.

James moved in front of me. "Please think about it. I do think the girl in the picture is you, but I understand it may be startling to see."

The man returned, and I reached around James for my coat and put it on.

James continued, "You know, many of us did not choose to become vampires, but that's what we are. You believe in God and Jesus, and there's no mention of us in the Bible, yet here we are. Whatever you think their grand plan is, we exist, and it's in our nature to drink human blood."

"The Spectavi don't drink our blood," I said. "Maybe that's God's new plan."

"Maybe it is, but I don't think so," James said. "For centuries, the Spectavi fed on mortals just like we do. Now they drink the fake blood Edmond created and kill us as he commands. No, our war is about more than what we feed on. It always has been. Do you think synthetic blood is going to satisfy those at this club?" I didn't answer. "Grant, Zhilan, and I don't kill when we drink, Erin. And we aren't the only ones."

The elevator opened, and I stepped in. I turned to James and the club behind him.

"Think about it. We can help each other," he said, as the doors closed.

I rose to ground level and, once outside, the cool air was welcome. Bill stood next to the limousine with the door open. I walked on the thin marble path, got inside, and he shut the door behind me. I kicked off my shoes, closed my eyes, and curled into the corner against the door.

A few minutes later, the door on the other side of the limo opened, and Zhilan sat down where she had been before. She smiled, but didn't say anything. I couldn't help noticing that she appeared as elegant as earlier, like she was ready to start a night out, not that she had just left one.

As we drove away, I checked my phone. I had missed a call and a text message from Todd. He wanted to meet me at my apartment. I responded that I was fine, but would see him the next day, then asked God to please get me all the way home so that I really would.

Todd had been right; I shouldn't have gone. I thought of him until falling asleep.

I woke up as we pulled into the driveway outside my apartment building. Zhilan had put a blanket over me and faced straight ahead as we came to a stop. I took off the blanket, picked up my shoes, and opened the door without waiting for Bill. Once inside the lobby, I thanked God for seeing me through the night.

I checked my phone while taking the elevator up to my apartment. It was almost three o'clock in the morning. Grant had texted, *I'm sorry if I scared you. I'm a vampire, and you wanted the truth. Think about what James said. Think about the picture.*

My hallway was quiet, as usual so late. Todd sat against the wall outside my apartment door.

"I'm sorry, I couldn't wait," he said, as he stood.

I hugged him. "It's okay. I'm glad you're here."

"Your neck. Are you all right?" He looked so concerned.

"I'm fine; I'm just tired. Can we talk in the morning?"

"Sure, sure."

I unlocked my apartment door and went straight to the bathroom mirror. Dried blood crusted around the fang marks and trailed down to the top of my dress, but they were the same marks I had before. James had listened to me; I wouldn't have a new scar.

9

"You have to call the police, Erin. If you don't, I will." Todd stood in my kitchen after I had told him most of the story the next morning.

I sat on my couch and put my coffee cup down on the table. "And say what? That I voluntarily followed Sanguans to a club and came home unharmed?"

"Unharmed? They bit you!"

"They had to; they had to know what I knew." I hated how they had gone about it, but I understood their motivation. "And I'll be fine."

Todd didn't appear convinced.

"Todd, really, I'm fine." I held up my left hand and flexed my fingers. "They all still work."

"Do you believe them?" he asked.

"Believe what?"

"The photo, do you think it was you?"

"No… I don't know. I guess it could have been, but I don't think it was. The hair was wrong, and I'm no scientist."

"I think they're trying to use you. I think they're losing

their war, or whatever they call it, and they're desperate. You might look like that girl, but it's not you." He made some sense.

"Yeah, maybe," I said, and took a sip of coffee.

Todd and I spent the afternoon in my apartment watching TV and discussing Fire and Ice. It had been the most disturbing night of the life I could remember, and I was grateful not to be alone like the morning after Snake attacked me.

Todd was furious at their treatment of me and also clearly relieved that I hadn't been hurt further. He never said, 'I told you so,' and I appreciated that very much.

Kristi insisted that we meet for dinner because she had to know what had happened the night before. I agreed only if she'd meet before nightfall and without Christopher. I couldn't take any more Sanguans. She accepted my terms reluctantly and, with Todd at my side, I told her the same story I had told him: everything that had happened minus the names of the vampires in the picture. I didn't want Todd getting involved somehow through work.

Kristi wanted details about the club more than anything else. She said she had worn a collar like I had when she went out with Christopher, but that she actually liked it. She excitedly described how wearing it had made her feel safe and close to Christopher. Kristi was a very different girl than me.

She asked about James's bite, as well. I didn't say much about it, but she knew that I understood what it was like when Christopher bit her. I didn't tell them, but my biggest relief was that I didn't feel raped. I hated being forced to do anything against my will, and the bite was intense, but it really was like a shot of a powerful drug, as I had read it would be.

I couldn't let those Sanguans do it again, but Kristi did agree that there was nothing to go to the police about, and it was helpful that Todd saw it wasn't only my opinion.

Todd and I went to his place after dinner. We went to bed early, and he fell asleep first. During the day, I had put on a brave face to reassure Todd that I was fine, but I hadn't really had time alone to focus on thinking through it all. With his arm over me, I lay in bed, finally able to do that.

The whole thing still sickened me more than anything else. One of the first things I remembered deciding was that I wouldn't let myself be drunk from by a vampire again. I promised it to myself. But James had done just that; Grant and even Zhilan had led me to him.

Grant, who I had thought would protect me, also craved my blood. The vivid details were unforgettable: how he had wanted me before, outside the bus stop, and how he hunted other young women so the sight of me wouldn't tempt him. It was monstrous, even if he claimed he didn't kill.

Zhilan... well, she had only done what Grant had asked. I couldn't think of another specific reason to hate her at that moment. Her dancing was the one bright spot all night.

And the photograph... could it really have been me? I couldn't rule it out, but it made no sense to me why, if I had been a great scientist, the Spectavi would have sent me away. James had offered no explanation, perhaps assuming I'd be so desperate that the picture was all they needed to convince me. As Todd had suggested, they could have been trying to use me. And James could even have been using Grant and Zhilan to get to me. He might have orchestrated things without telling the other two.

I searched for information about Edmond on my phone. The name wasn't new to me, nor was his picture, but I had never given either much thought. As I scrolled through images, I had a tiny hope that I might recall working with him from some saved part of my memory, but I didn't.

Edmond Duchart was the public CEO of Eure Global and the more private leader of the Spectavi. I learned that he had moved the French company's headquarters to the United States in 1919 after the devastation of World War I in Europe.

Edmond was the subject of countless websites dealing with vampire history. On them, there were plenty of rumors about how long his life had been and his role in major historical events. However, aside from indications he had been active during the French Revolution in the eighteenth century, most rumors either conflicted or were unsubstantiated, so I found it hard to separate fact from fiction. He was an old vampire, but it wasn't even clear how old.

I turned to Todd and snuggled close. I decided to be done with Grant, Zhilan, and James. While they claimed not to kill humans, they had already drunk from me and avoiding them was the only way to ensure it didn't happen again. I'd keep the picture in mind and continue investigating on my own.

Work was actually a welcome occurrence on Monday, helping me think more easily about something other than Fire and Ice.

Unfortunately, I couldn't quite leave that night behind completely, as I was back to wearing turtlenecks for a few days while my bite mark faded from fresh red to black. The days were getting hotter, so I got strange looks for wearing them, and I almost didn't bother.

One of my initial reactions after being bitten had been that my cross tattoo had caused more harm than good recently. It hadn't deterred anyone, and just like Snake, James had made a point about it and how powerless the god that it symbolized was.

Yet even as they mocked me and my cross, I had survived both attacks. My fingers healed, and my blood would be replenished. Vampires were a reality, but I had survived, and my fresh bite could be a badge of honor for both me and God.

Of course, that wasn't how others in my office would see it. People who walked around with bite marks exposed were seen as willing food for vampires, not survivors—even Kristi hid hers. I certainly wasn't one of those people and didn't want that reputation.

The turtlenecks were annoying, but it would just be easiest to keep my neck covered.

As the weeks went by, Todd and I talked about vampires less and less until the subject rarely came up at all. I was happy, and he was the reason why. We went out and tried new restaurants and new things I had never done before, and I had a great time meeting some of his friends. Once Todd knew about my lack of a history, he became eager to help me create one.

I went ice skating and played mini-golf for the first time. We took a boat cruise on the Potomac. I wasn't as good at anything else as darts, but we both had fun wondering if I would be. While I didn't regret spending so much time before meeting Todd trying to solve the mystery of what had happened to me, being with him, I couldn't help but enjoy the rest of life while ignoring it.

Kristi saw Christopher almost every night, and I worried about her, but she kept coming back to work every day in one piece, if a little tired and distracted. It wasn't my place to say anything; she was happy. I did keep her in my prayers, just in case.

I considered the photograph occasionally, though I didn't tell Todd. It still seemed unlikely that the Spectavi would have sent away a great scientist, but if they had to for some reason, killing her would have been a much simpler solution. And if I had been Vera, why wouldn't any of the Spectavi I had talked to since losing my memory have recognized me? If Vera had been an important player in their system, I should have been well known to them. On top of all that, James had said he had never heard of a vampire taking memories. Surely at some point, it would have happened before me.

I concluded it was almost impossible that James's story was true.

Todd started working more and more. I asked him about

it, and he vaguely mentioned a new project with the street cameras. I didn't press him on it. I didn't want him to feel like he owed me every last detail about work because we were dating.

I spent almost every night at Todd's apartment, but went home after work one day to change before we went out. When I got to his place, he was leaning over the counter in the kitchen with his back to me, talking very loudly on the phone.

"But you said... Look, I know... Yes. But... Yes. Fine. We'll talk tomorrow."

"Who was that?" I asked as soon as he took the phone from his ear.

He turned to me, looking defeated. "Just work."

"What's wrong?"

"Oh, the people... well, the vampires from Eure want us to do something with our cameras that I'm not so thrilled about."

"Like what?"

"We had planned to start taking snapshots of drivers when we caught them running lights, I think I mentioned that. Now Eure is talking to the government about leaving the cameras on all the time and taking snapshots of everyone who travels through the city."

"Wow, that would be pretty crazy," I said.

"Yeah, I mean, the idea would be to catch fugitives, or deter them from coming into the city, so it makes some sense," Todd explained.

"Right."

"But what happens next? The scale and real-time capabilities would be far beyond the cameras they currently use. With access to all that data, who else would they track?"

"Yeah, that could be pretty bad."

"It's not even the Spectavi, or Eure, I'm worried about," Todd said. "Everyone knows they've been perfect partners with humans recently. I trust them. I don't trust the U.S. government with all of that data, though. I can't believe anyone would trust them with it. Anyway, it's my work; it's not your problem. Let's not worry about it."

We dropped the subject, but it clearly wore on Todd. After that, he didn't come by my desk as much at work, and his emails became shorter and less frequent. He stayed after normal hours and worked more weekends. I was busy doing things for Mr. Oliver related to the same deal with the government but, for me, it was merely a job. The company—and the software even more than that—was Todd's baby. He had created it from nothing and grown it over many years, and suddenly he didn't agree with where it was heading.

I didn't blame him. For the most part, I shared his trust in the Spectavi, but the United States government? No, thank you. I had no interest in living in a city where someone was always watching me and tracking me.

"I just don't know why they think the government wouldn't abuse the power they want to give them." Todd and I were out at a bar, and he couldn't seem to stop talking about work.

"Yeah, I can't see there not being issues."

"They might have the right intentions, but I see this getting rolled into some secret agency with no oversight. The NSA, or the CIA, or something we don't even know about."

"You know I agree with you, Todd."

"I know; I'm sorry. Edmond is coming to the office tomorrow night, and I'm afraid he'll end the discussion, and it won't go our way."

"Edmond is coming to the office?"

"Yeah, I was surprised, too. We're just a tiny part of Eure. Apparently, he cares about this a lot for some reason. Their headquarters is so close that I guess it's not that big a deal for him to come into the city for a meeting."

Their headquarters was nearby in Virginia, but like Todd, I never imagined Edmond would pay our little office a visit.

"What if we moved away from D.C.?" Todd asked suddenly.

"What?"

"Not now, not today or tomorrow, but if things go badly with Eure, I might not want to be a part of it."

"Wow. Well, where would we go?"

"I don't know. I hadn't thought about it before. The west coast, maybe? I have a few friends from school out there working on interesting things."

I considered it before answering. "I don't know. It's a big question, Todd."

"Okay, okay," he said. "I know. Don't freak out. No

pressure, and I wouldn't go without you, but it could be fun to get a change of scenery."

We spent the rest of the night considering where we might go. It was an unexpected idea for both of us, and for Todd, it seemed a very exciting one. For me, while I did enjoy discussing it, I really didn't know if I could do something so drastic, so soon.

The long conversation made me realize just how much Todd doubted he'd convince Edmond to turn away from his plan.

———————

It was a quarter after eight, Edmond was coming at nine, and the minutes were dragging by at my desk. Mr. Oliver didn't need anything from me, Kristi had left early to get ready for a big night with Christopher, and Todd was getting ready for his meeting, so I had nothing to do.

I hadn't given the photo much serious consideration in a while, but suddenly, I couldn't stop thinking about it. What if James had been right? Edmond couldn't expect to run into me at Snap Safe.

James had said Vera and Edmond were *close*. I should have asked what that meant.

Mr. Oliver had suggested we all wear suits for Edmond's visit. While it made sense, I had never been comfortable in a suit, and that occasion was no different.

To pass the time, I read the news online over and over, until thinking I had read it all. I played solitaire and found a crossword puzzle website that kept me busy.

Finally, I heard Todd's voice at the end of the room. My computer clock said eight fifty-three. I stood to get a look at them.

Todd, wearing a gray suit, appeared hopeful while they walked and talked. The two vampires with him also wore gray suits, but theirs were much darker or at least seemed so against their very light skin. They came closer, and I couldn't believe how white their skin was. They looked like ghosts, and seeing Todd interact with them so confidently made me proud.

I recognized William from the picture of Vera. He was the leaner and taller of the two vampires. He was bald and had a narrow face. I didn't know why a scientist was needed at the meeting, but figured after enough years, he could have taken on many roles at Eure beyond that one.

Edmond was tall, too. He had broad shoulders and a full head of black hair. He talked energetically, and it was clear he would be driving the conversation. I remembered the rumors I had read that put Edmond in the middle of epic military battles, yet he appeared the consummate businessman.

As old as they must have been, I found both of their faces unexpectedly friendly. Edmond's was the more inviting and kind of the two, but William's had the same qualities to a lesser extent. If they had been humans, I would have guessed thirty-five for Edmond and a bit older for William.

"Edmond, this is Erin. She works with Mr. Oliver," Todd said. I was still standing, and they had made it all the way to my desk. I stopped looking into Edmond's brown eyes.

"Hello, Erin." Edmond put out his hand. He appeared distinctly French, yet had no accent I could hear. He was very handsome.

"And this is William," Todd added.

I didn't say anything, but shook Edmond's hand and then shook William's, and then they all headed for the conference room and resumed their conversation as if they had never stopped.

I sat back down in my chair and stared at my monitor without actually seeing anything on it. Their skin had felt like smooth stone, and while we had mutually shook hands, in truth, their strength had done all the shaking. They could have crushed my fingers in their grip even more easily than Snake, Grant, Zhilan, or James.

Edmond hadn't flinched when he saw me, and I hadn't recognized him. To my great disappointment, no hidden memory had stirred. It would have meant so much to me if one had.

Still, I couldn't conclude anything, one way or the other, and I might see him again on the way out. I would wait for them until almost eleven. After that, it would be inexplicable that I remained at work.

At only ten after nine, Edmond and William walked past my desk in silence as they left the office. Todd followed them and then came back to my desk.

He looked tired and rundown, but I caught some optimism when he forced a smile and asked, "So, San Francisco?"

10

"What do you mean you have to do this?" Todd asked. We were arguing in his apartment the next morning, but it wasn't as heated as last time. "Last night we were talking about San Francisco, we went to bed, now you're going to infiltrate Eure, or whatever they want you do."

"Last night I told you I would think about going to San Francisco," I answered. "Today I'm saying I don't think I can. I really like you, Todd; it's just a lot for me really fast. I'm sorry. Stay here with me. Give me a few months, and we'll see."

He shook his head. "And you'll be at Eure in the meantime or something?"

"I'll be working there, yes, but I don't know exactly what I'll be doing. I have to talk to James again."

"James is the one who bit you, right? After he tied you to the ceiling?"

"You know he is, and you know I hated that. But they had to do it. They had to know what I really knew."

"What if they do it again? Or worse? How can you possibly trust them?"

I didn't know if I could trust them and feared another bite more than Todd would ever know, but I had spent all night thinking it over and convinced myself that succumbing to that fear wouldn't have led to any answers. "Grant or Zhilan could have drunk from me if they wanted to, and James could have done worse than he did. They could have come after me since then, too, but they haven't. They're fiendish creatures, and I didn't want to ever see them again, but everything changed last night when I saw Edmond. I shook his hand. He's real, and he could be the one who did this to me. I can't ignore the picture anymore. I tried, but I can't."

"Why didn't you tell me Edmond was in the picture in the first place? I could have asked him about it myself."

"That's why I didn't tell you!" I said. "Do you think he would admit what he did because you asked him nicely? I don't think you know what these vampires are capable of."

"He's Spectavi, Erin, not a Sanguan. He doesn't do the things that you're accusing him of."

"I'm not accusing him of anything! I'm saying I want to investigate it. I don't think it was me in that picture, but I have to know. And if he's nothing to worry about, then there's nothing to worry about at Eure, right?"

"I don't know," Todd said. He must have known convincing me not to do it was a long shot from the start, but the complete hopelessness of the task seemed to have set in.

"Look, I'm not even sure what James wants me to do, and I don't know how long it will take, but I'll see you after work every day. What's so bad about that?"

"I guess, if it will put your mind at ease."

"It will." Then I had a new idea. "And what if I move in here with you now? San Francisco is a long way, but I could live here."

Todd looked relieved for the first time since we started talking. "Well, that might work." He walked over and hugged me. "But... I want more."

I leaned back from him. "More?"

"Let's get away for a bit. San Francisco can wait until you're ready, unless we think of somewhere better, but I'm leaving my job, and I need to get away from D.C. for a while. Would you go with me to the beach for a week?"

"Absolutely."

———————

I was going to reach out to Grant right away, but Todd convinced me to wait a night so we could celebrate our new plans. It didn't seem like too much to ask, and it did mean one more night without Sanguans, so I agreed happily.

After we talked about it more, I was surprised that Todd wasn't devastated to be leaving his company. For one thing, they paid out all of his stock options even though his contract didn't say they had to. That wasn't really it, though. He seemed burnt out after working on the same software for so many years. Inventing something, getting people to use it, building a company, selling it, and working with new owners had taken its toll.

He had expected Eure to open new doors for him.

Instead, they took his company in a direction he couldn't go along with. It was a miscalculation owners must have made all the time and, in Todd's case, one he made only after making a lot of money from selling the company. He seemed content to have accomplished what he had and eager for both a break and whatever he came up with next.

Discussing his plans only made me more hopeful that things would continue to go well with Todd. I had already begun to think that, once I had closure about the photograph, we could both start fresh in a new city.

Todd still had work to do that night when I finished mine, so I went home to start packing the few boxes I would need to bring to his place. Kristi called when she got home from work.

"Where are you going again? Which island? And when?" she asked.

"St. Lucia, it's one of the eastern islands, in a week." Todd was eager to go right away, and we were fortunate to be able to afford a trip to the Caribbean on such short notice.

"What's it like?" Kristi sounded in need of a vacation herself.

"How should I know? I've never been there. I suspect there will be sand and water. And a hotel, most likely."

"You'll have to tell me all about it when you get back. And we have to go out before you go, okay?"

"I will, and sure," I said.

"All right, I have to get going." She added playfully, "Have a good night celebrating with Todd."

"Have a good night doing whatever you do with Christopher." I would miss her dearly if we moved away.

———————————

Later, at Todd's, I walked out of the bedroom to where he was sitting. "What do you think?" I wore a blue bikini I planned to bring on our trip.

"Wow, you look amazing. Stunning. You're already tan, and we're still in D.C. I can't believe I have to go back to work now." He came close, put his arms around my waist, and gave me a kiss. "I can't wait for the beach."

"Me, neither," I said.

He stepped back and looked me over from head to toe. "Blah, I do have to go, though. I'm sorry, but I'll be back soon, and we can find something to do. We're still celebrating tonight!"

"Definitely," I said eagerly, and then Todd left. It was almost midnight, and Todd had just gotten home, but there had been an issue with some cameras and our software. It seemed under control; Todd was going to confirm that. It put a damper on our plans for the night, but he wanted to leave the company in good shape, so it did seem like the right thing to do.

I changed into pajama pants and a t-shirt and lay down on his couch to watch TV and wait.

———————————

The twins were flying through a clear blue sky. They joined hands and smiled at each other briefly. A dark dot on the horizon must have been their destination. They flew toward it, and their blond hair blew in the wind. The one on the right's hair was a little shorter, but other than that, they were identical. The dot grew until it looked like a building, and then a big building. They were almost there, and it might have been a light gray castle in the distance.

Ringing from my coat at the kitchen table woke me up. Todd must not have come home, and I had fallen asleep on the couch. I got up slowly and searched through the pockets for my phone. Eventually, I found the right one and saw that it was Kristi, but by the time I answered it, the call had already gone to voicemail. It was almost three o'clock. What did she want? And where was Todd? He should have been home already. I waited a minute before checking my voicemail.

The call began, but remained quiet. Finally, I heard a whisper. "Erin, he's killing me. Please help me. Erin—" I heard a commotion, then Kristi screamed, and the call cut off.

Oh, my God. I assumed the 'he' was Christopher, but what was going on? I finished waking up that instant. I tried to call her back, but she didn't answer. I left a message and told her to call me if she could, but I didn't hold out much hope.

I remembered the app I had installed on my phone that could locate Kristi's with her username and password. Things had seemed to be going so well with Christopher.

Kristi raved about how he treated her and how she loved being with him. The app was supposed to be peace of mind for me, but to need to use it had become unthinkable.

I entered her information in the app and waited while it found her. How long would it take? It just said, *Locating, Locating,* until finally, it showed her in a building on the waterfront in Georgetown. At that time of night, it was only a ten-minute cab ride, but it was close to four o'clock. I wouldn't have gone for anyone other than Kristi.

First, I called the police and gave them her location. They said they would send a car. I hoped they'd send more than one.

I called Grant. I had always only texted him, but it was an emergency. He didn't answer.

I threw on jeans and a black fleece, put my small knife in my pocket, and headed out to find a taxi.

Finding a cab so late was lucky, and there was almost no traffic, as expected. It was after three, and every minute counted for me, let alone Kristi. I didn't even know what I would do when I got there.

I hadn't carried my folding knife since the night Francis had been killed because, after seeing the power of the Sanguans first hand, it seemed like a futile gesture. It was the only weapon I had, though.

I called Todd, but got no answer. He was surely at work, safe with the Spectavi. I was the one about to be in danger.

As we drove down M Street toward Georgetown, I said a

prayer for Kristi and added myself to it, too. When I finished, I questioned if God could, or even wanted to, help with vampires involved. James's words came back to me.

No vampires existed in the pages of the Bible, yet they rose from their coffins into God's world each night. Alone, humans were helpless against their power, and Kristi certainly had no chance of fighting them off if they meant to kill her. If God's plan did include the Sanguans and the Spectavi, I couldn't imagine why.

A police car with its lights on sat at the entrance to the waterfront, with the driver still inside. I got out, and my cab drove away immediately.

The police officer was speaking quickly into his radio when I walked up to the car. He wasn't a small man, but he looked nervous. He noticed me and lowered his window. "You should move along, it's not safe here right now."

"My friend is down there. I called the police," I said. "Did someone else go after her already?"

"No, it's just me. I'm waiting."

"For what?"

"Vampires. Spectavi. I'm not going in there; they will."

"Are they almost here? Kristi could be dying!"

"I don't know," he said.

He disgusted me. "You're a cop!"

He didn't respond.

"Which building is it?"

The officer pointed as he spoke, "All the way down by the water, on the left. But I wouldn't—"

"I'm not just going to sit here and wait." I started off on

a walkway between two sets of low brown buildings. A large moon illuminated the quiet night. Bars and restaurants lined the path on both sides, but they had closed and emptied by then. The river in front of me sounded peaceful.

It was warm and very muggy, so I didn't need my fleece, but I didn't want to take it off, either. I wiped sweat off my forehead with its sleeve and then ensured the blade of my knife was locked open. I held it down to my side.

Ahead, a fountain sprayed water into the air, and I went down a set of stairs toward it. When I had almost reached the apartment the officer had pointed out, I heard voices behind me. I turned to see a silver SUV like the ones I had seen the night Francis was killed. Thank God.

Two Spectavi dressed in gray fatigues spoke to the police officer through his car window. They left him behind and ran at vampire speed until stopping next to me.

"We'll take care of this, Miss," one said. They both held big rifles and had pistols on their hips, but no swords. They wore mirrored goggles which hid most of their faces, and each had a dark blue cross patch on their shoulder. I would have liked there to have been more, but two Spectavi were a lot better than none.

"My friend's up there; I have to go." I did consider staying behind and out of harm's way. But what if something went wrong? I couldn't leave Kristi, whether she was still alive or not.

"It's too dangerous for you," the same one said.

"I have to go in there."

The two Spectavi glanced at each other, and then the one

who had done all the speaking said, "Stay far behind us." They jogged toward the apartment building at human speed so I could follow. I checked my watch—three twenty. If things went quickly, I might be back inside by four.

One of the Spectavi waved an electronic key at the wall of the building, and the door opened. We all walked into the empty lobby.

"Top floor," he said.

That meant the fifth, by my count. We started climbing the stairs, and I stayed a few steps behind the Spectavi with my knife out. We went cautiously up each of the alternating sections between floors until reaching the top. The Spectavi moved out into the hall. I waited a few seconds then followed them.

The hallway was empty, and it seemed the Spectavi knew where to go because they went directly to a door at the other end. They paused outside an apartment, and I held my breath a few feet away with my back against the same wall as the door.

Jesus, please let Kristi be alive on the other side of that door.

One of the Spectavi kicked down the door, and the other rushed in. The one who had kicked followed after him. Gunshots rang out and vampires roared, but no girl screamed. She could be fine, I told myself, and resumed breathing.

The shots continued in spurts and then slowed until I heard only one or two every few seconds.

I heard loud *thuds*, which I hoped were Sanguans hitting the floor, and then it became quiet.

I took a few more breaths, then turned and carefully walked through the half-open door into the apartment. Moonlight filled the large room, so it wasn't as dark as I had expected it to be. I heard the soft sounds of river water from outside.

A body, cratered by bullet holes, lay motionless on the floor. It wasn't a Spectavi, so I assumed it was a Sanguan.

The apartment was a mess with disorganized furniture. Seeing a bathroom next to me, I guessed the partially open doors on both sides led to two bedrooms. Most of the moonlight came from two large doors in the back that opened onto a balcony. With the doors wide open, it felt just as warm and muggy as it had outside.

I crept toward the bedroom on my right and peered in, scared of what I'd find. A body on the bed was a large man, or vampire, not Kristi. Blood and gunshot holes covered the body, the furniture, and the walls. Though he held a gun, he was probably dead, too.

Turning to the main room, I moved toward the bedroom on the left side of it. I was only a few steps away when one of the Spectavi came out carrying a body. It was Kristi; her eyes were wide open, but unmoving.

"She's gone; I'm sorry," the vampire said.

I turned my head away and started to cry. I looked back at her and saw fang marks and blood on her neck, arms, and where her ripped dress should have covered her.

There wasn't time to see more because a vampire burst through the open balcony doors and was at the Spectavi's neck before he could put Kristi down and reach his gun. I moved back against a low wall that separated the kitchen from the main room and made myself stop crying. I clutched my knife, unsure what to do.

The Spectavi struggled while the Sanguan sucked his vampire blood out of him. It was a gruesome sight.

I was still deciding where to stab, when the Spectavi dropped to the floor. The Sanguan took Kristi's body from him as he did and, when they moved away, I saw another body in gray fatigues lying motionless in the doorway to the bedroom. Both of the Spectavi were dead.

The Sanguan brought Kristi's body to the couch and laid it down. He knelt next to her and sobbed. It was Christopher. I recognized him from Kristi's picture. He wore a long, brown leather coat and a light-colored shirt. He wasn't quite as big as Grant.

"How did this happen? I'm so sorry, Kristi," I heard him say. "I'm so sorry."

He wept next to her, and then he held her. I didn't know what to think. Tears slid down my cheeks once more.

"Christopher." I took a step forward with my knife at my side.

Still holding Kristi, he turned to me and was clearly miserable.

"Christopher…" I started. His eyes grew wide.

The next instant, his body pinned mine against the low wall behind me.

I stabbed into his side with my knife and, from his facial expression, I obviously hurt him, yet he easily pulled out the blade and threw it across the room.

"Christopher…" I said again. He pushed on my shoulders, and my upper back arched over the wall. I tried to move my feet out toward him to relive the pressure, but his legs were against mine. I thought my spine would snap if he kept pushing. "Stop, please."

"Why should I stop?" he asked.

"I'm Erin…" He held me there, bent too far. "I'm… I'm Kristi's friend."

"Not anymore, you aren't."

He showed me his fangs, then turned his head to bring them to my neck. Two gunshots came from behind me. One hit Christopher's side, and he let me go and moved back. He looked startled, then appeared to be in pain.

He retreated a few steps and, when more shots came, he moved quickly to avoid the bullets. He went out the open doors and paused on the balcony, turning to Kristi's body on the couch.

His anguish was undeniable. After a moment, he jumped off the balcony and was gone.

I turned around, and the police officer from the street stood in the doorway. He wasn't such a coward after all.

His pistol still pointed to the balcony. "Are you okay?" he asked.

I stood straight. "Yes, I'm fine."

He lowered his gun. "Good, I didn't have many more silver bullets. Heh, they can't stand 'em." He was pleased with himself and eager to tell me about it, but his best friend hadn't just been killed.

I ran over to Kristi. The sight was harder to bear up close.

I didn't count, but guessed she had more than ten bite marks on her body. Her thin pink dress had been torn and bitten through, as had the black bra she wore under it, so she was practically naked. Her hair was a tangled mess and streams of dried blood covered much of her. I squeezed her limp hand.

She had truly loved being with Christopher and had spoken about him so passionately and confidently that it seemed like she belonged in his world. I hated it myself, but had begun to believe she could fit in with the Sanguans.

Yet she lay there, pale, drained, and dead; it was clear she had just been food for them. I had been foolish to think otherwise, like Kristi had been, and she had paid for it with her life. Why hadn't I stopped her from seeing him?

More Spectavi and police officers streamed into the room. They turned on the lights, fanned out, and checked the rest of the apartment—but the action was over. Two Spectavi had been killed, Kristi was dead, and it appeared many Sanguans were, as well. Christopher had fled.

What had his role been in this? He had looked surprised and very upset to find her dead, but that didn't prove anything. One horrifying possibility was that he had been there earlier, fed from her, and left her to his friends.

"Ma'am, we should get you home," one of the new Spectavi said.

I let go of Kristi's hand and checked my phone—a quarter to four. After I got up and found my knife, I looked at my friend's body one last time before making my way to the front of the apartment.

"Thank you," I said to the police officer who had shot Christopher and was enthusiastically explaining his role to a Spectavi. He nodded and returned to his conversation.

I left, and two Spectavi followed. The hallway had filled with nosy tenants who I ignored on my way to the elevator at the end of the hall.

It was still hot and muggy out, so I finally took off my fleece. A few police cars with their sirens on, as well as a few more of the Spectavi's silver SUVs, had shown up. When we reached the nearest SUV, the two Spectavi went to the front, and I got in the back seat. I gave them Todd's address, and we drove off.

"Do you know me?" I asked. The one in the passenger seat turned around, and the driver's eyes found me in his rearview mirror.

"Should we know you?" the passenger asked.

"I'm Vera," I said.

"Vera who?"

I started crying again. "I don't know. I'm sorry."

"I don't know anyone named Vera. The police officer said your name was Erin."

"It is. Erin Rose. I'm sorry." I sobbed. Kristi was dead. My best friend in my tiny world was dead.

"What happened?" Todd asked when I got to his apartment. It was five minutes after four. He had finally texted while I was on the way home, so he already knew Kristi was dead.

"They killed her," I said. "The Sanguans, Christopher, I don't know, but they killed her."

Todd held me, and I cried into his shoulder.

"It's not safe here," I said eventually. "I don't know if it's safe anywhere."

11

Grant waited for me at a table near the bar. The restaurant wasn't very crowded.

Todd begged me not to go, but I had to know if Grant played any part in what had happened to Kristi, and I needed to see his face and his eyes when I confronted him. I had my knife in my pocket, even though its uselessness had been proven on Christopher.

"Did you have anything to do with it?" I asked, as soon as I sat down.

"With what?" Grant asked.

"Kristi, my friend, she's dead."

"I'm sorry, Erin. No, I didn't. I don't kill humans when I feed, remember?" He looked genuinely sad for me, like he honestly related to my pain. It helped me block out the memory of our conversation at Fire and Ice for a moment.

"Do you know who did it?" I asked, determined to press on for Kristi.

"No, what happened to her?"

"She was killed in Georgetown by a pack of Sanguans. A

friend of hers, Christopher, showed up when it was over, but I don't know if he was involved."

"If it's the Christopher I think it is, that doesn't sound like something he would do," Grant said.

"Well, it's done, whether it was him or not, and your people did it."

Grant looked slightly offended. "I don't have 'people' like you think I do. I'm labeled a Sanguan, but I don't have allegiance to any central authority; that's the way the Spectavi work."

"Well, however your kind works, Kristi is dead because of it."

"I'm sorry. I truly am," Grant said.

As quickly as he assumed who Christopher was, I suspected Grant did have a hunch as to who had done it, even if Grant hadn't been involved. Of course, I couldn't really be sure that he hadn't been. The only thing I knew for certain about Grant was that some part of him craved my blood.

A waitress came by, and I ordered a Diet Coke so at least one of us would be paying for something.

"I'm leaving D.C., Grant. I can't help you and James. I can't go to Eure. It's too dangerous here."

"Do you think it will be safer anywhere else?"

"I don't know, maybe. Maybe I'm cursed in this city. Or maybe I'll stay out of cities altogether." Todd and I had decided to go west, possibly to San Francisco. We hadn't settled on an exact location, but we were both set on leaving.

"You don't want to know what Edmond did to you?"

I shook my head. "I'm not Vera; I'm sorry. I don't know why you're so convinced that I am."

"It is you. Look at the photo again." Grant took it out and put it on the table.

When I picked it up, I recognized William immediately. From the back, Edmond had the same big build as in person. And there was the girl.

It was a girl with long brown hair like mine. Her face appeared similar to mine, and she did seem to have green eyes.

"I don't know. How can you be so sure?" I stared at the picture.

"It's you, or who you were. It all makes sense. Edmond had a brilliant, young, female human scientist who worked with him on secret projects. We know that. This girl had long brown hair, like you. You can see she had green eyes, like you. She looks tall, like you. And she looks just like you. Suddenly, a year and a half to two years ago, as best we can tell, *poof*, she disappears. And then you show up with no memory from a little over a year and a half ago, and James verifies that you aren't lying. It all adds up."

I didn't know what to say.

Grant continued more forcefully. "Erin, when James said you had no memory of your past, he meant it. It's a blank slate, exactly like you think it is. Doesn't that sound like something only an old, powerful vampire could do? Edmond is one of the oldest."

"I've spoken to Spectavi a few times. If I was one of their star scientists, why wouldn't they have recognized me? Or at least had a clue about who I might have been?"

Grant relaxed in his chair. "I don't know. There are a lot of Spectavi; maybe you never met those you talked to, or maybe Edmond told them to lie."

Again, at a simple question, their story fell apart.

"I met Edmond at my office, too," I said. "I shook his hand, and William's. They didn't even flinch at the sight of me."

"That doesn't mean anything. Don't you think they could hide their reactions from you?"

"Like you could hide yours from me?" Once more, I was keenly aware of why I had come and who I sat across from.

Grant shook his head. "I had nothing to do with Kristi, I swear. And you may not believe me that you were Vera, but Edmond is killing old Sanguans for no reason. You could help us regardless."

"You keep saying that, that there's no reason for what's happening. Don't you drink from young women against their will? Isn't that a reason?"

"It's my nature. I'm a vampire, and I have to hunt someone. Those I feed on heal and their blood is regenerated."

"Why not stick to those who want you to do it?"

"I usually do, but ultimately, I'm driven to hunt who I hunt."

"Driven by what? What drives you to prey on young women like me?"

"I can't explain it completely. The same force that keeps me alive and gives me my strength is a hunger that I have to feed."

"Have you fed today?"

"No, but I will later. You don't have to be scared, I promise."

Maybe I didn't, but I wouldn't be around much longer to find out. "What about synthetic blood? Why don't you drink that?"

"Some Sanguans have switched, and they seem happy to join the Spectavi when they do. It's not for me though. I don't trust the Spectavi." Grant looked as thoughtful as he had when describing Francis to me at Night. "I had a friend who switched, and she was different after she did. I might frighten you, but I like who I am. I don't want to change, and I don't want to be killed because I won't."

He looked sincere, but fortunately or unfortunately, he had become a monster to me, and I couldn't seem to let it go.

"I have to go," I said. "Thank you for your help with Snake and for showing my picture around, but I can't help you or James. I don't think I'm Vera, but even if I was, I'm not anymore. I have a new life ahead of me, and it starts away from here." I left three dollars and got up from my chair.

Grant got up, too. "Good luck, Erin. I'm sorry you're going. You could have been a big help to us, but after what you've been through, it is certainly your right to choose as you wish. Be safe."

"Thanks." I didn't hesitate to walk away.

I looked around for Snake as soon as I got outside the bar, curious if Grant would still kill him if he hurt me, or if I had just lost that protection.

But it shouldn't matter. I would take a cab to Todd's and, once out west, Snake, along with everything else, would be behind me.

———————————

"Todd?" I called into his apartment when I got back from seeing Grant. Todd didn't answer. He hadn't said he was going out and hadn't left a voicemail, but it was only twelve thirty, so he had plenty of time.

I found a note on the kitchen table:

Had to run to work, be back soon—Todd

I sat on his couch and checked my email, but found nothing new. I lived with Todd, and Kristi wasn't going to be sending me any more messages. My life was so small; losing her hurt so much. It wasn't fair. My *whole life* wasn't fair.

Picturing her body on the couch, I cried softly. My once vibrant friend looked so pale and lifeless, her clothes had been torn to shreds, and there were so many bite marks. They must have sucked her dry. And she had called me while it was happening! It had to have been slow and terrible for her.

Why had I brought her to Night in the first place? I remembered when she had talked about living forever as a vampire, and I felt like a fool for entertaining the idea with her. We were helpless mortals, and she hadn't lived long at all.

Todd came through the apartment door. Thank goodness. I needed him.

"Hey," I said. He stopped on his way to the bedroom and seemed confused. "Todd, are you okay?"

He turned to me. "Who are you? What are you doing here?"

"What?"

"What are you doing in my apartment?"

I stood up. "Todd, it's Erin. What's going on?" I wiped tears from my face with both hands and sniffled as I stopped crying.

"Erin? I don't know anyone named Erin." He went into the bedroom and came out with his laptop.

"Todd, what's wrong with you?"

"How do you know me?" It didn't look like he was joking.

"I live here, Todd. We're dating. It's me, Erin Rose!"

He looked different, more serious and focused than normal. "I'm sorry, there must be some mistake; I don't know an Erin Rose."

I walked over and put my hand around his arm. His muscles felt harder and more defined than they should have.

He brushed my hand away. "What are you doing?"

His cheeks looked firm, and his strong chin was more pronounced than I remembered.

"Please open your mouth," I said quietly. He did, and I saw fangs. "Oh, my God."

"I won't hurt you," he said.

His two fangs were just a little longer than his teeth would have been, but they were sharp and unmistakable. "You're a vampire."

"Yes."

I stepped back. "How did it happen? Are you a Sanguan?"

"No. I swore to God that I would never drink human blood to stay alive," he said. "The Sanguans are animals."

"Why don't you know me?"

"I'm sorry, but I don't." He reached for the door handle. "I won't be back tonight, so you may stay here if you wish, but please don't be here when I return tomorrow."

What was going on? The Spectavi had done it, presumably, but I couldn't fathom why. A few hours beforehand we had stood right there and talked. And swearing to God didn't sound like Todd at all.

I ran out after him. "Todd, wait!"

I caught up to him at the closed elevator doors. "Why don't you know me? It's Erin. We were going to move away together. It's what you wanted. It's what we *both* wanted."

"I'm sorry I can't help you. Do you need me to call someone for you? Is there someone that can come get you? I can pay for a cab if you'd like."

"No, Todd, no."

"Then please leave me alone." He turned to wait for the elevator.

I cried again and started to walk away. I turned back, and he stared at the elevators. I ran the rest of the way to his apartment.

12

My door closed behind me, and I dropped a full bag of my things from Todd's. I felt numb standing in my kitchen, looking out at the packed boxes in my barren apartment.

In the last two nights, my life had been ripped away from me again. Unlike before, I knew exactly what I was missing, and who. Instead of nothingness, memory after memory of two people filled my mind, and at that moment, missing them seemed worse.

Kristi had been my best friend. We didn't talk all the time about every little thing, but she knew my secrets, and I trusted her. The list of people who fit that description had started and ended with her, at least until I began dating Todd.

Todd, I had let myself get closer to than anyone I had ever known. He had shown me what my life could be if it wasn't a constant struggle to find out about my past. I never thought it would happen, but with Todd, I had become ready to leave my past behind. I might have already been in love with him, even if I hadn't seriously considered it before.

And we were supposed to be leaving in just a few days.

Instead of our vacation, we were going to move out of D.C. right away. While it wouldn't have helped Kristi, being *so close* to leaving made everything hurt so much more.

Whatever had happened to Todd, there was no way he had done it to himself voluntarily. I couldn't imagine it.

I found the nearest box, knelt down, and started unpacking. I was tired of crying and didn't know what else to do.

———————————

My keycard still worked at my office door. I hadn't slept and still wore my jeans from the night before.

Other secretaries and younger staff members worked diligently at their desks. I went to Todd's office first, but found it empty as I expected it to be in the middle of the day. Mr. Oliver's was also empty, as were all of the managers' offices.

"Erin, do you know where everyone is?" A young man named Scott got up and followed me to my desk.

"I don't know, but I don't think it's safe here anymore," I said.

"What do you mean?"

"I'd leave before nightfall. I don't know what's going on, and I don't trust our new owners."

I collected a few things I had at my desk while Scott watched—my headphones, a pack of gum, and medicine from my drawer. They all fit in my pockets. I left my coffee cup because I didn't feel like carrying it.

I turned to Scott. "Tell whoever you can. Leave before

the sun goes down. Don't come back, and call your boss during the day. If he'll talk to you then, it might be safe."

"I don't understand."

"Vampires. They might all be vampires now. Unless you want to be one too, I wouldn't come back here."

"Oh, my God." He looked sick. He finally got it.

"Maybe I'm wrong, but maybe I'm not. Bye, Scott."

I left and headed back to my apartment.

———————————

Later, on a cool, clear evening, my t-shirt and fleece barely kept me warm enough. I waited for Grant to pick me up outside my apartment and take me to meet James. I had texted Grant during the day saying that I needed to talk to them both immediately. I didn't say why, and he hadn't asked.

I had spent the whole day thinking about what my pathetic life had come to and what I had done to deserve it. It seemed a cruel joke that I was alone again, just like before. I almost couldn't believe it.

As far as I knew, I was only twenty-two years old, yet somehow there hadn't already been enough tragedy in my life when my memory was erased, so Kristi's death and Todd's transformation had to be piled on top of it. I had tried to start over, but it had only led to more pain. I contemplated the possibility that I could never be happy and should just stop trying.

I asked God why it had all happened to me.

After hours of misery and anger, I let myself accept that the situation wasn't exactly the same as before, in part because I knew more about vampires. I knew Grant, James, and Zhilan, and had even met Edmond and William.

Of course, I hated them all. The Sanguans had killed Kristi, and the Spectavi had taken Todd.

I considered the photograph of Vera anew. I didn't understand why none of the Spectavi recognized me, but since Todd didn't either, something had to be going on.

Or maybe there didn't. Perhaps Todd had simply left me, and that was some other girl with brown hair in the picture. I couldn't know anything for sure, no matter how hard I thought about it.

Grant's motorcycle pulled up because, instead of starting a new chapter in my life out west, I was more desperate for answers than ever. If there was anything to find out, I had to try. He stopped in front of me with the engine running.

"Let's go. I'll explain when I see James," I said.

I put my leg over the bike. He handed me a black helmet with a dark-tinted visor and thick leather gloves. The helmet fit snuggly over my head, but my hair stayed loose outside it. I held him around his waist over his leather jacket, and we drove off.

When we were ten or fifteen miles outside the city, we had gone far enough, apparently. We pulled up to a house in a development off the highway with its porch light on. It appeared new, was of moderate size, and the yard was neat. When we went in, I looked everywhere for photos of a family that Sanguans had just devoured.

I didn't find any, and the house was mostly empty. The walls were off-white, and some furniture dotted the hardwood floors, but not as much as if the place had truly been lived in.

Two vampires wearing black with guns remained at the front door after we passed. James sat in the kitchen at a rectangular table with Zhilan, who wore a navy dress, to his right. Two other vampires in black stood at the rear of the room.

James got up from his chair. "Erin, I'm glad you've come back. Please, have a seat."

He wore a white dress shirt like last time and a silver tie. His light gray suit coat lay folded on the countertop behind him. I had told myself I could handle seeing him, but instead of sitting, I glanced at Zhilan. Her bright and youthful face nodded reassuringly, and I looked back to James. If he attacked me again, or any of them did, even if I lived, it would be the end of our association.

I took a chair on the long side, across from him. He sat back down, and Grant sat on the short side to my right.

"Can we get you anything? Water, wine, something to eat?" James asked me.

"I'm fine."

"Good," he said. "So what brings you back to us?"

"My friend was killed two nights ago. Her name was Kristi. Did you have anything to do with it?"

"No," he answered calmly.

"It was Sanguans," I said.

"Yes, it was. But there are many of us. We aren't

governed the way Edmond controls the Spectavi. I told you we don't kill when we feed on humans. I hope you will believe me when I tell you that none of us would kill an innocent human like Kristi."

"Well, these Sanguans did. Who were they?"

"There were many attacks that night. Many Spectavi were killed." James paused for a moment. "Unfortunately, more Sanguans were killed in the process. It sounds like something a vampire named Alexander would have organized, though it was foolish."

"What about Christopher? Do you know a vampire named Christopher?"

"Yes, but there is more than one."

"This one went to clubs and was seeing my friend regularly. He showed up where she had been killed. Would he have used her as bait for the attack?" I loathed even suggesting that Kristi could have been treated that way.

"I think I know the Christopher you mean. I don't know, Erin. Perhaps. He could have, but I don't have an answer for you."

I looked down and away from James. Talking to him wasn't as terrifying as I had feared upon arrival. Out of the corner of my eye, I glimpsed a hint of somberness in Zhilan's expression. It was the subtlest change.

"I'm sorry about your friend," James said. "She was a casualty of this war, it seems." He got up from his chair and walked to his suit coat. "You could help us, though." James returned with the photo of Vera and slid it near me on the table as he sat down.

I wasn't up to that yet. "If Alexander kills humans, and you disapprove, why don't you do anything to stop him?"

"I don't like Alexander's methods, and I'm different from him in more ways than you understand. Grant, Zhilan, and many other Sanguans are, too. Nevertheless, right now we all share a common enemy," James responded. "Why did you want to see me?"

He left me far from convinced, but, as usual, James had explained himself logically. "I was dating a man…" My own story was so illogical that I had to stop and collect the pieces. "Todd… and he came home last night and was a vampire— a Spectavi. And… and he didn't know me at all. I've been dating him for months and had just moved in with him. We worked together for months more than that, and he suddenly didn't remember me."

"I see. I'm sorry," James said, straight-faced. Zhilan became more noticeably sympathetic. Grant's face stayed steady.

"I don't know what's going on," I said and did look down at the picture. "Todd wouldn't have chosen to be a vampire. Could it have to do with this girl, Vera? Or me? I don't have any other ideas."

"It could indeed," James said. "I don't understand it all, but I'm even more convinced that girl is you, and that something strange is going on with the Spectavi." He leaned back in his chair and appeared pensive.

I looked right at James. "Todd said something else, too. He swore to God that he wouldn't drink human blood. He never spoke of God like that before to me. It wasn't like him at all. Are the Spectavi all so religious?"

"Most are Catholic, yes." James spoke absently, still appearing to be deep in thought.

"Why? Is God part of your war?"

James stayed leaned back, but he once again focused on our conversation. "The story of how we came to exist, if it's true, says that the first vampires were tricked by the Devil. He appeared to them and offered them superhuman strength and speed, and the ability to live forever. He said he could give it all to them, but the price was a terrible hunger that they would have to continuously feed. They agreed before knowing the hunger had to be fed with human blood. Once they found out, they didn't forsake the Devil, but instead vowed to take their vengeance out on God and His humans for what had happened to them. Edmond was one of the first to fight back against them, and he is very pious."

"But if he's a vampire, the Devil's evil is in him, too," I said.

"Yes, if the story is true, that is. And as I told you before, many of us did not choose to become vampires. Edmond may not have, and he remains devoted to God. Many Sanguans are, as well."

"And the rest follow Satan," I said matter-of-factly.

"I don't. I don't think Grant or Zhilan do, but that is their choice. I don't follow anyone but myself."

But Satan was inside them all, compelling them to drink human blood. There were rumors as to what had started it all, and the devil played a role in many of them, yet I had never heard it from an old vampire like James. It made sense, but it was terrible. It meant Satan was winning.

On the other hand, perhaps the synthetic blood was not merely an option, but God's solution. It wouldn't rid the world of vampires, but it kept them from taking human life. The Spectavi could have been winning the war for God after all, and yet, I sat in a kitchen full of Sanguans, wondering if they could help me figure out what had happened to both Todd and myself.

I turned to Zhilan. "Why don't you drink synthetic blood?"

Her sadness changed to pride when she answered, "I will not swear allegiance to the Spectavi to get it."

"Fine, that makes sense, but why ally yourself with Alexander if he's so cruel?"

Grant spoke up for the first time. "It's a war, Erin."

I turned back to Zhilan when she spoke again. "I hate Alexander, but we would be worse off without him right now."

James said, "Erin, perhaps you're right, and a vampire like Alexander shouldn't exist. Perhaps. But why shouldn't I be allowed to live? Humans fascinate me.

"I watched as the world shrunk with the laying of the first transatlantic telegraph cable and the invention of the telephone. I drove one of Henry Ford's first cars, and then I could explore this vast country more quickly. After that, there were airplanes, then computers, then networks of computers, and then cell phones. I've watched this incredible transformation, and I want to keep watching... in peace. I want to be around to see what comes next.

"I have the gifts to do so, but two hundred years ago, I

wouldn't follow Edmond and kill my own kind, and now I won't join him and drink synthetic blood, so I'm labeled a Sanguan and marked for death. I want no part in this war. In the past, I could stay neutral, but now I'm forced to stay hidden and oppose Edmond."

I imagined the world in the nineteenth century, and the changes James had lived through. But I couldn't dwell on that. "You said last time we spoke that Edmond and Vera were close. What did you mean?"

"There were rumors that she was his human companion. Edmond has had others over the centuries, but not many," James said. "If he drank repeatedly from the same spot, he could have given you that scar."

"I thought he didn't drink human blood," I said.

"He would have the world believe that, yes, but it wouldn't be hard for him to cover up drinking real blood."

"How old is he?"

"Around fifteen hundred years old."

"And he's not the oldest?"

"No."

"Who was?"

"If the legend is true, two sisters from France, where Edmond is from," James said.

My eyes grew wide. "Twins?"

"Yes, how did you know… your dreams. I do think they are the same twins."

James knew because he had drunk from me. My focus strayed and I spoke a little more softly. "But they're young and beautiful. They aren't vampires." I pictured their fair skin and light hair and them singing with the church choir. "What happened to them?"

"No one knows. Most think they're dead. And yet… if you dream about them, perhaps not," James said. "Erin, you must help us. Don't you see? Something is going on with the Spectavi, and you are the key to it."

"Maybe." But what else could I do? I was actually with my only 'friends' in the whole world. They claimed not to kill humans, but aside from the fact that they hadn't killed me yet, I really didn't have much to base trust in them on. Even so, the alternative of leaving them behind and starting over at vampire clubs on my own sounded awful. Plus, it might all have been staring me right in the face already. I picked up the photograph. Was I Vera?

The twins came to mind. If James's story was true, and I dreamt about the first vampires, I couldn't understand why they looked so cheerful. They were always out in the sun and seemed like the last people who would make a deal with the devil.

"All right," I said. "What do you want me to do?"

I wasn't doing it to help those at the table. I refused to be a pawn of the Sanguans, the creatures of Satan who had allied themselves with Kristi's killers. I would do it for me. Desperation drove me, like it had driven me to that meeting, but I found the faintest hope in James's theory that everything could all somehow be related.

———

The plan to get close to Edmond was almost comically simple. James thought that if I applied to work at Eure headquarters, and I had been Vera, Edmond would make sure I got the job and ended up near him. James said that Edmond had loved his few human companions very deeply. No matter why Vera had left, Edmond would jump at the chance to be close to her, or me, again.

As simple as that sounded, there was risk as well. Even if it worked out like James assumed it would, there was no telling exactly how Edmond would react. He could make sure to meet me, but if we parted on bad terms, he might not be happy when he did. He could turn me away quickly, or kill me. James didn't consider either a likely outcome, and neither did Grant or Zhilan. Of course, they couldn't be certain of anything.

When it was over, Zhilan was my way out. The reason they had so little information about Vera was that, when humans worked at Eure's headquarters, they couldn't leave the premises unless they quit or were fired, and we didn't think Edmond would let me quit.

It was a frightening proposition, taking such a chance and being captive there, but I wasn't really safe outside Eure, either. No human truly was; I was proof of that. At least at Eure I would be surrounded by Spectavi, not Sanguans.

After forty-five days living there and collecting whatever information I could, Zhilan would break me out. They didn't say how, just that she would come for me.

I lobbied for twenty or thirty days, instead, arguing that I'd know quickly if something was going on there that shouldn't be. But they convinced me that with only one shot, we had to be sure I learned as much as possible. James sounded pretty desperate, actually.

Unfortunately, because Eure would surely be monitoring my internet and phone use, I couldn't contact anyone on the outside while there. I made Zhilan swear she'd come for me, and then made James and Grant do the same if she failed. They all did. Those vampires really were all I had in the world, and my freedom would depend on them.

Back at my apartment later that night, I sat at my computer. I still hadn't slept, but had to apply for a job before I did. If I was going to try to infiltrate Eure, I wanted to get started right away.

Discouragingly, I didn't see many openings at their headquarters. I found one for a lab technician, but no matter what anyone said about Vera, I was no scientist. Another that didn't fit was for a software developer. They said they accepted resumes at all times and would match people up as positions became available, so that seemed to be my best hope, even if it took a while for them to get back to me.

I read over my resume and added a few lines about Snap Safe. I had memorized the lies on it for my last job interview, and it all seemed good enough. I left my current position as 'present' so I wouldn't have to explain that my boss had probably become a vampire or been killed, and I had quit.

Poor Mr. Oliver. He had a family: a wife, kids, and grandkids. What happened to Todd was bad enough. He also had a family, but no one depended on him. I had emailed and called Mr. Oliver, but received no response. Hopefully, I was wrong, but an office full of empty managers' desks left me pessimistic.

That was a growing reason why I pushed myself to go

through with our plan. Aside from my own mystery and Todd's, if Mr. Oliver and others had been forced to become Spectavi, something very wrong was going on.

I submitted my resume and went to wash my face. I finally had to go to bed. Eure's website said they would respond only if they chose to interview me. If they didn't contact me, I'd have to find some other way to get Edmond's attention.

I changed out of my jeans at long last and got into bed.

———————————

I rolled over under my covers the next day and found my phone on my nightstand. There was a new email from Eure asking me to come in that night. They had an opening for an administrative assistant in their court system that I might be a good match for.

13

Ms. Dubois showed me to my room. "Get some rest. Work starts at nine o'clock." Then she left.

I had had no idea what I had gotten myself into going to Eure. I had expected it to be a huge corporation where I would be one of hundreds of employees. Even with my name possibly flagged, I assumed I would still have a chance to blend in with the other people around me. I had been very wrong.

During the interview, I learned I would be one of about thirty humans on a campus of something like a thousand vampires. While the vampires weren't all there all the time, they did all have coffins to sleep in during the days they were. All of the human jobs were highly sought after positions, and it seemed extremely unlikely I would have gotten mine without the name 'Erin Rose' on my resume.

The job paid well—almost twice as much as my last job—though I wasn't particularly concerned with the money. I had to work on the vampires' schedule completely, instead of just overlapping a little like before. Work began at nine p.m. and went until four thirty in the morning. I had until five thirty a.m. to be back in the designated 'human' area of the complex, which included a cafeteria, library, and a gym with a pool. I wasn't allowed outside during the day.

It was Monday morning, my watch said seven minutes after four, and after not getting much sleep the last few days, I struggled to stay awake in spite of the bright overhead lighting.

The watch was thin, silver-colored, and locked on my wrist. I wasn't at all pleased when they had put it on me, but it was far more subtle than the collar, and no satanic symbols covered it, either. Swiping it near doors would get me in places I had access to. Presumably, they would also use it to track me, so the watch was going to make it hard to snoop around.

The interview process had been short. I had taken a cab to Virginia to meet with Ms. Dubois, a vampire who was my new boss, and after about thirty minutes, she offered me the job. She gave no hint of knowing me, but must have been instructed to hire me. There was no way I had been that great in my interview or that my resume was that perfect.

Earlier that first night, I had been measured for clothing, then spent a few hours signing payroll forms, confidentiality agreements, and a contract that Eure had the option to renew after a year. Vampire staff members took everything I had brought with me and told me that all I needed would be supplied. Work attire was a business suit, and I wore what amounted to pajamas currently: loose black pants, sneakers, a white t-shirt, and a black zippered sweatshirt with a hood.

I explored my room. The walls were bright white, and it

was set up like a narrow studio apartment. A sliding door in the back led to a bathroom. There was a full sized bed to the right and a flat-screen TV on the wall across from it. A simple dark brown cross hung next to the TV.

Past the bed was a small couch and a small, black high table with two chairs. Seeing a laptop on the table was a relief. They had taken my phone, and I would have gone crazy without some way to get online, even with them monitoring my activity. The kitchen consisted of only a small fridge—currently empty—a sink, and a microwave. It appeared to be made for leftovers, snacks, and nothing else.

I slid open the closet door near the entrance to the bathroom. Hanging up, I found two identical black business suits with skirts and two lightweight white shirts to go under them, along with one pair of black dress pants and a black belt. There was also a heavy black coat, a black umbrella, a black leather briefcase, and a small white dresser.

In the two dresser drawers, I found black and white underwear, white socks, one black t-shirt, one white t-shirt, black athletic pants, a black and white athletic top, and a black one-piece bathing suit. I knelt and saw two pairs of black leather pumps with thin heels and a pair of black flats.

Along with my current outfit, that was going to be it for a while.

I sat down on my bed, took off my sneakers and sweatshirt, and tried to force my watch over my wrist, but it didn't come close. The reality of my situation sank in and was unsettling. I didn't see any way to leave before Zhilan came for me.

I touched the pressure-sensitive light switch next to me and got under the covers. The lights turned off automatically at noon, and stayed off until seven thirty, but I couldn't stay awake any longer. A nightlight in the bathroom remained on.

The bed felt very firm against my weary body, and the sheets seemed brand new, almost sterile, like the whole room. None of the furniture was mine, nor was the laptop or the clothes. Just like when I had woken up with no memory in that empty apartment, I was alone in a new world.

I started to feel sick, so I closed my eyes and thought of Todd. I missed him. I replayed the scene in my head when he had come home and said he didn't know me. It didn't make any sense. Could he have possibly chosen to become a vampire and blocked me out of his mind?

I pushed that night aside and recalled happier times we had spent together—the baseball game, dates we went on, and tender moments in his apartment.

My watch alarm beeped at seven thirty, and the overhead lights in my room came on all at once. I grabbed the watch with my other hand to shut it off.

I had slept enough, but not well, so it took me a while to get going. I had woken up every few hours because it should have been day for me, and I had gone to bed so 'early.' While awake, I had considered exploring the human areas of the complex, but chose to save that for the next night. The laptop was easier to investigate, and it seemed I could get online without restriction.

The shower was on the small side, like everything else, but the water did help me wake up finally. After I had blow-dried my hair, I put my wet towel in a basket next to my closet. I had been told that my laundry would be picked up and replaced while I was out of my room each night.

While getting dressed, I smiled genuinely for the first time since arriving at Eure. I hated wearing business suits so much that my dislike for that one comforted me. Everything else seemed new and foreign, but that I knew. The shoes were comfortable, but the heels were higher than I had realized before going to bed. I wondered if everyone wore the same uniform, or if mine was because I worked in court.

I put on some of the neutral-toned makeup I found in my bathroom and left my hair down. While I was confident my cross tattoo would be well received, waiting one night to get a feel for the place before showing it off seemed prudent.

At eight thirty-five, I left my room carrying my briefcase. Ms. Dubois had shown me the court building, only a ten-minute walk away, but I was ready and didn't want to be late on my first night.

The purpose of the court was not entirely clear. Ms. Dubois had said Sanguans were tried there, which made some sense. But Francis had received no trial before he was killed… Or perhaps he had, and had escaped. Perhaps he had been on the run in the sports car that night.

Outside my room, the hallway's high ceilings had no shortage of long fluorescent lights. The walls were bare white with no windows. Even more than my room, the air had a cool, filtered feel to it. There was no one else around, and my walking was the only sound I heard. To my surprise, I passed no other bedrooms. The whole place was very empty and very strange.

At the end of the hall, I came to an elevator. My room was only on the third floor, but I couldn't find any stairs, so I waited for it. The doors opened, and it was empty. Momentary relief was followed by disappointment to still be alone.

On the ground floor, I walked down the hall in the other direction to the front of the building and finally saw another person. A young woman with blond hair stood staring at the door until she heard me and turned to watch me approach. She was a little shorter than me and wore the exact same outfit I did.

She smiled when I got close. "I'm Jennifer."

We shook hands. "I'm Erin."

"You're new here?"

"Yes, it's my first day."

"Well, in that case, welcome. Who do you work for?"

I had assumed she'd ask where I worked, not who I worked for, but it seemed like a trivial difference. "Ms. Dubois."

"Oh, she's nice. She can be strict, but she's a good boss. I work for Mr. Roberts." She checked her watch, which was the same as mine. "Just another minute."

"Until what?"

"Until the door unlocks, and we can go outside. There

won't be any light, but in another month or so the sun will give us a little for a few minutes, even though it will have already set."

"Oh, right." I hadn't been told they locked us in. It did make sense, though, that the vampires wouldn't want humans snooping around while they slept.

I noticed a camera on the ceiling and more down the hallway. One of the few credible details I had come across about Eure, was that a small human military force guarded the campus during the day. I suspected they watched the cameras while the vampires couldn't.

A boy came down the hall from the other direction I had.

"Hi, Gavin," Jennifer said when he reached us. "This is Erin."

"Hey, Jennifer, nice to meet you, Erin," he replied. Gavin wore a black suit and white shirt—that seemed to be standard. He also had on a blue tie.

Gavin was pale, and his medium-length black hair was a bit of a mess. He was cute. When we shook hands, his grip wasn't as strong as his size suggested.

"Gavin works for Victoria," Jennifer said.

He grinned. Then, without another word, Jennifer opened the door and headed out into the night.

"After you," Gavin said, so I went, and he followed. Within a few steps, we had gone our separate ways, headed for our jobs, whatever theirs were.

It was dark, like Jennifer had said it would be, but still warm out. I thought again about what an odd little world I would be living in for the next forty-four nights.

I walked alone on a concrete sidewalk next to a two-way street lined with bright lampposts. Most of the campus was set up that way as far as I had been able to tell. I passed white office buildings on both sides before coming to the one Ms. Dubois had shown me. I went up a staircase and across a large concrete patio to a set of opaque glass doors at its entrance.

An electronic reader on the wall had the blue Spectavi cross in the corner. I waved my watch in front of the reader, and the doors unlocked with a loud *click*.

Inside, I found myself standing in a large, well lit, empty lobby. Unlike the outside of the building, which could have been any white office building, the inside had a bluish-gray marble floor and columns on the walls that led up to a high ceiling.

Ms. Dubois hadn't shown me more than the outside. It was already five minutes until nine and, to start on time, I had to figure out where to go.

I tried a set of big doors on my left, but they were locked. There was no reader on the wall for my watch. There was a smaller set of doors across the room, so I tried them next. They didn't open either and, again, had no reader. I looked around and saw no other doors. Jennifer had said Ms. Dubois could be strict, but I couldn't think of anything else to try.

I sat down on a bench against the same wall as the big set of doors and waited. Nine o'clock came and went. I tried both sets of doors again. They remained locked, so I sat back down, worried that I had gone to the wrong building.

At ten minutes after, I almost left to search other nearby buildings when finally the big doors flew open next to me. I stood as Ms. Dubois came through them.

"Follow me, Erin, and get your hair out of your face," she said in her high-pitched voice. She reached into her leather briefcase and handed me a black band, then turned and went back through the doors. I held my briefcase under my arm and pulled my hair into a ponytail while walking behind her into the courtroom.

Ms. Dubois's suit looked nicer than mine, and she wore black and gold jewelry. She was very short and would have been downright tiny next to me if it weren't for her shoes. While she looked young, her very light skin made me confident I had met another very old vampire.

"Sit there." She pointed to a desk in the front of the room and off to the left. I sat down in one of two wooden chairs, which put the judge's bench to my left. The firm seat was immediately uncomfortable.

Ms. Dubois went to a side door across the room and waited at it, perfectly still with her arms at her sides. I was warm while I sat, presumably from the walk over or from adrenaline as I went through things for the first time.

The desk was wooden, like the rest of the furniture in the courtroom. There were two pens in front of me to the left, one black and one blue, and that was it. The wooden furniture all had a glossy finish, including the five rows of benches for spectators. The room's ceiling was very high, like the lobby's had been.

The judge came in wearing a black robe, followed by two

other vampires dressed like all the other Spectavi I had seen in combat, minus the goggles. They had both rifles and pistols. Two more vampire guards arrived and shut the doors behind them.

The judge and Ms. Dubois spoke quietly while glancing over at me occasionally. The judge nodded and then rose to his bench. He had white hair, skin not quite as light as Ms. Dubois, and looked old. Like James, he must have been old when he became a vampire.

Ms. Dubois came back and sat down next to me. She took a stack of papers from her briefcase and placed them in front of me. "These are today's cases. I'll show you how to fill them out, and then you can do it on your own."

I picked up the papers and started to leaf through them. There were about twenty-five forms, each with carbon-copy yellow and pink pages attached to them. Ms. Dubois pushed my hands and the papers back down onto the table. She seemed to have tried to do it gently, but the little vampire was so strong that she didn't completely succeed.

"Don't look ahead, Erin."

"Oh, sorry." The front page remained visible and was definitely a U.S. Government form, which gave a clue as to why the court existed. A stack of forms copied in triplicate made perfect sense for the government. The Spectavi must have needed the court and paperwork to comply with some kind of federal oversight.

Through a door next to the one the judge had used, a guard led a vampire into the courtroom. He was shackled at the wrists, ankles, and neck in chains and followed by another guard whose rifle was trained on him. The prisoner looked weak and sickly. His skin had a grayish tint, and I guessed he had been starved. His arms and neck appeared burned from where the chains looped around them. The chains must have been silver, not steel—or perhaps a combination of the two.

The prisoner was led to a chair facing the judge and forced to sit. From the floor in front of the chair, a metal ring snapped over the chain between his feet, locking him down.

His details on the form in front of me read:

Name: Liam Kent
Age: 16
Type: Sanguan
Crime: Murder. Two men outside a convenience store
Date: April 21
Time: 11:45 PM
Location: 1200 Prince St. Arlington, TX

The judge spoke, "Liam Kent, you are accused of killing two innocent men in Texas. How do you plead?"

"Not guilty," Liam responded.

"On what grounds?" the judge asked.

"On the grounds that I was hungry," Liam said. The judge's expression didn't change. "And the first one tasted so good that I had to try the other."

"Liam Kent, you are found guilty of this crime against humanity, and you are sentenced to death, to be carried out within one week's time."

The judge slammed down his gavel. The device in the floor unlocked the Sanguan, and the guards led him away. He looked enraged, but didn't argue. He must have known what was coming.

Ms. Dubois showed me how to fill out the form. The top in blue was the plea, the verdict, the judge's name, and the sentence. At the bottom, in black, I wrote the current date and my name, then signed in a box that said 'human witness.' The guard on my side of the room walked over, took the form, and placed it on a small table in front of him.

Another vampire came in shackled the same way and was led to the same chair as the last. The ring from the floor locked him in place. The next form read:

Name: Craig White
Age: 49
Type: Sanguan
Crime: Murder. A husband, wife, and their two children in their home
Date: April 18
Time: 9:30 PM
Location: 538 Dale St. Annapolis, MD

The vampire looked young, so the age must have been his vampire age.

The judge spoke, "Craig White, you are accused of killing a family in their home in Maryland. How do you plead?"

"Not guilty," Craig said.

"On what grounds?" the judge asked.

"I didn't do it. It's a lie. I've never been to Annapolis."

"Do you have any evidence to support your claim?" the judge asked.

"I was in Washington, D.C. that night. I didn't do this! I follow your laws!" After a moment, he continued more calmly, "I feed on humans, but I haven't killed one in over a decade."

"Craig White, you are found guilty of this crime against humanity, and you are sentenced to death, to be carried out within one week's time."

Craig appeared more shocked than Liam had been. The judge swung his gavel, the floor released the Sanguan, and I put my pen to the paper in front of me. Craig took a few steps away from the chair before lunging at the judge.

The judge didn't flinch, and Craig never got close. It happened too fast for me to make out completely, but I heard gunshots, and Craig lay on the floor, bloody and motionless. His body was full of silver bullets.

Ms. Dubois turned to me. "It's so much quicker when they do that. The humans make us wait almost a week to kill them, as if there would ever be some kind of appeal."

My hand shook as I held the blue pen to the paper.

"Come now, fill out your form," Ms. Dubois prodded.

I did, slowly at first, and then more quickly when the next Sanguan came through the door.

14

At a quarter to five, I was back in my room, starving. I should have guessed that my seven-and-a-half-hour work night didn't include a break for lunch. Ms. Dubois left me alone at one point for twenty minutes, and a new judge took over halfway through the night, but aside from a ten-minute break every hour and a half or so, I sat there, sweating in the muggy courtroom, doing the paperwork.

For a while, I had glanced at the doorway frequently, wondering if Edmond might suddenly show up to see me. He never did and, by the end of the night, I stopped checking so often.

I sat on my firm bed and took off my shoes, finally, and then my suit coat. My feet hurt, and my back was sore from sitting in the wooden chair all night. I took my hair out of the rubber band Ms. Dubois had given me and lay down. I closed my eyes and could have slept. I could have used a shower, too.

But I was hungry and needed to get out of my room and explore. However, before any of that, I had to do something else. I got up, brought my laptop to my bed, and opened the web browser to search for the first address I could recall from court. Links to stories about the Sanguan's murder filled the page of results. I clicked through to the top link, and the article described the murder just as it had been in court—except in much more gruesome detail.

I searched for a few more that I had tried hard to remember, and all of the reports matched the charges. In every case, at least one witness put the accused vampire at the scene of the crime. In most cases, many witnesses gave statements.

There had been around thirty cases, and all but two of the vampires had pleaded 'not guilty.' Almost all of them had no real defense. Most screamed at the judge about the injustice of the law they had been accused of breaking. Some presented their cases elegantly, but it was the same injustice of the law they fought against—they never actually denied committing the crimes.

A handful did deny committing them, and those cases I paid closest attention to. Like Grant, James, and Zhilan, most of them claimed they didn't kill humans when they fed and, with no jury in the court, I wanted to be sure the judges ruled fairly. Every case I investigated checked out. Link after link, the stories all matched the court proceedings.

The judges had found all of the Sanguans guilty and sentenced them to death, and I had signed my name as human witness to each. It was emotional to sign at first, but after ten or so, it had gotten easier. The crimes were so terrible.

I put on the black athletic pants, my white t-shirt, and

sneakers and carried my hooded sweatshirt. It was the most comfortable outfit I could think of to wear to the cafeteria. Everything was free, and my watch unlocked my door, yet it still felt strange leaving my room with no wallet or key.

I headed down the hall in the opposite direction from my morning walk, down an elevator, and down another long hallway after that. My entire walk was a solitary one again— just me, tall white walls, and no windows.

When I got to the glass wall of the cafeteria, I counted ten people eating, split up over two large tables. Most wore their suits from work, but one boy had changed into more comfortable clothes, so at least I wasn't breaking any rules. My watch said it was close to six o'clock.

I saw no cooks or staff of any kind, but hot food had been prepared and laid out buffet-style against the rear wall. Others took what they needed, so I did the same and filled my plate with mashed potatoes, grilled chicken, and corn. It probably looked like I was getting enough for two, but I didn't care.

Chocolate cake made its way onto my tray, and later, I'd go back for fruit and cereal to save as snacks for in my room or at work.

There were plenty of empty smaller tables, so I sat alone at the end of one. I had to try to meet people eventually, but couldn't bring myself to at that moment.

The food tasted delicious. The chicken was juicy, and the corn especially crisp. As exhausted as I was, eating energized me a little right away.

I had finished half of the heap on my tray when Jennifer

and Gavin arrived together. They saw me, and Jennifer waved, then they both went to get their meals. When they had, Gavin sat down at another table, and Jennifer came over to me.

"Come join us, Erin," she said.

I just wanted to eat. "Maybe next time? I'm really tired and won't be here very long."

Jennifer frowned, then smiled. "I'll sit here." She sat down across from me, and there was no escaping her. She still wore her business suit and had about a quarter of the food I had started with.

"How was your first day?" she asked.

"Tiring," I said. "Lots of cases."

"Yes, the Sanguans are awful. I've watched some cases. All the people they kill..." Her voice trailed off, and she looked very sad.

"It is awful." I tried to count the cases where there had been more than one victim. They added up to so many lives lost.

Jennifer's face brightened. "I like your cross!"

I smiled. "Oh, thanks."

"You must be very religious. Have you seen our church yet?"

"No, not yet."

"Well, you will on Sunday. It's incredible."

Apparently, I would be going to church on Sunday. At least the conversation was yielding useful information.

"What do you do here?" I asked.

"I work for Mr. Roberts."

"Right, but what do you do for Mr. Roberts?" It didn't seem like she intended to make things difficult, but she was nonetheless.

"He's a scientist, and I work with him. I help him mix chemicals for pharmaceuticals mostly."

Well, that wasn't so hard, I thought, but all I said was, "Interesting." I wondered if Mr. Roberts would know anything about Vera. If they were both scientists, they might have worked together.

Jennifer grew very eager. "I hope he likes my work. I hope I get to work with him forever."

"Forever?"

She blushed. "Well, maybe not *forever*, but if he makes me a Spectavi, for a very long time at least."

"You want to be a vampire?" I asked.

"Yes, of course. We all do. Don't you?"

"I'm... maybe, I'm still thinking about it." Surely James wouldn't have sent me to become one of his enemies.

"I understand. It's not easy to choose to leave humanity behind, and then you have to be selected. I have a good feeling about you though, Erin Rose."

Phew. I had been very worried until she had used the words 'choose' and 'selected.' I found myself surrounded by aspiring vampires, yet I wasn't one of them.

Jennifer and I chatted a little more as we ate. I learned that she was the daughter of a senator from Kansas and was twenty-three. It had always been her dream to work at Eure, and only after her mother had been elected was she able to get the job. She was thrilled to be there finally and seemed very sweet.

The chocolate cake was excellent, and it was almost seven o'clock when we finished. I would never sleep through the day if I didn't stay awake a little longer, so I went to go look around.

———————

My exploration was informative, but less revealing than I had hoped. I found the gym and pool both to be very modern and clean and spoke to people at each. I came across a bar and a small church for humans that I hadn't known about, but I didn't think it was the one Jennifer had mentioned.

The whole setup felt surreal. Everything was self-service, and everyone I met was between twenty and thirty years old. They all seemed to take their jobs very seriously, and then once the vampires went to sleep for the day, there was nothing to do but hang out, work out, have a drink, or go to church and pray.

I also learned that I was one of the rare people to get a job there by applying. Everyone else came from a powerful or rich family, or was a genius in their field. For humans, the campus served as one big training ground for future Spectavi vampires. As Jennifer had alluded to, not all would make the cut, so the jobs were an important test.

Most would become vampires after a few years, though. I didn't fit in, so I kept my motivations to myself.

I managed to stay up until ten before going back to my room, and to bed.

"Vera," the one on the left said.
"Vera," the one on the right echoed.
I only saw their faces.
"Vera," they repeated in unison.
They became serious for the first time.
"Erin." They sounded angry. "Erin!"

My watch alarm went off, my lights came on, and I violently sat up in bed. They had never spoken to me before. Had they called me Vera before calling me Erin? I wished I had a notepad to draw their faces, but there wasn't any paper in my room.

I closed my eyes. I could still picture them and recall their words. I had to find out more about them somehow.

Unfortunately, it was after seven thirty, and I had to get ready for work. I took the same shower as the night before, dried my hair again, and put on the same outfit, though it was actually the other of my two suits. My feet hurt as soon as I stood up in the other pair of identical shoes, but I figured I would get used to them eventually. I didn't really have a choice.

The same makeup was all I had, and I put my hair up so Ms. Dubois wouldn't have to remind me.

I ate a bowl of cereal quickly before heading out with more food in my briefcase. I had forty-three nights to go.

Jennifer, Gavin, and I met by the door again downstairs, and we talked before going our separate ways when it was unlocked. I learned that Gavin's father was a general in the Army. It had taken some work, but Gavin had been able to convince him that he could serve his country far longer as a Spectavi than as a mortal. What a strange conversation that must have been to have with a parent.

Ms. Dubois had told me to be at work by nine o'clock every night, and that court would open between then and nine-thirty. My watch said nine-twenty when she came through the doors. The only difference in her appearance was a change in jewelry.

The warm, heavy air of the courtroom hit me as soon as I walked in. I sat down in my chair, beads of sweat formed all over me, and my back ached right away. Ms. Dubois gave me another stack of forms, the judge came in, and the cases began. Just like the night before, I listened to stories of vicious murders and families torn apart.

In one case, a Sanguan murdered five whole families on a single night in a remote town in North Dakota before, by sheer luck, a passing driver heard a scream and called the police. It took the Spectavi until nearly dawn to catch the killer.

In another case, three Sanguans—two females and one male—who had slaughtered twenty-four people at a wedding reception at the University of Florida were brought in together. They had killed the groom, but intentionally left the bride alive to be alone without him. When they pleaded 'not guilty,' Ms. Dubois looked upset for the first time. I had to hold back tears myself by the time I got to sign my name, and I knew we both wished the Sanguans could have been killed immediately. A week would have to be soon enough.

After work, I went to my room to change. My clothes were gross from sitting in the incessant heat, and I wanted to be comfortable.

First, though, so I wouldn't forget the details, I searched again for a few of the names and addresses of those who had denied their crimes. They had looked no less sincere when claiming not to kill humans than Grant and James had, yet when the results came back, and I headed to the same websites as before to read the reports, all of those Sanguans had lied. I recalled Grant's admitted inability to control his urges to hunt, and then what he had hoped to do to me. After shuddering at those thoughts, I had a notion that perhaps my 'friends' were merely better at not being caught killing than those in court.

I mulled over that possibility for a few moments before checking my closet. Everything I had worn had been cleaned and replaced as promised.

At around six in the morning, I ate dinner with Jennifer and a few other people I had met the night before. Some of them went to the bar after that, but I went to the gym to run instead. After spending all night sitting, I had to do something active.

I tried to snoop around, but the human areas seemed completely locked down after sunrise. The people I talked to had stories about vampires, like close calls with Sanguans before they came to Eure, and friends who had been in relationships with vampires that hadn't ended as badly as Kristi's.

While everyone was very pleasant, none of it seemed

important. Nobody would discuss the details of their jobs, and none of them had heard of anyone named Vera. I didn't meet any other vampires.

The following night went almost exactly the same—more paperwork and more awful Sanguans. A pack of vampires terrorized an outdoor concert in Arizona, two bartenders were brutally killed in Kansas, and a single Sanguan was responsible for more than a hundred murders before being caught.

It drained me to sit through, and I still hadn't adjusted to working all night and sleeping all day, but with the clock ticking before Zhilan was to come for me, I decided to see what I could find outside the courtroom. After the last case, I had almost an hour before I had to be back with the humans.

The building with my bedroom was to the left, so I went right. I passed one building that had black-tinted windows I couldn't see through and waved to a boy walking the other way. The next building had the same tinted windows and I figured they probably all did. I would have to get inside to investigate.

I walked up to the second building and tried my watch, but nothing happened. I tested the doors, but they remained locked. I tried my watch again, and a Spectavi guard opened one of the doors.

"Can I help you, Erin?" he said. He must have gotten my name from my watch.

"Uh, no, sorry, wrong building, I guess." I quickly walked away. Investigating wasn't going to be easy.

I started back toward the courthouse. At the building before it, a vampire held a door open and appeared to be having a conversation with someone on the inside. I sensed an opportunity and jogged to the door.

"Thanks!" I said, sliding past the vampire holding the door.

An alarm sounded, and a red light began flashing. I jumped back out the door.

"Sorry!" I said. "Wrong building!"

———————————

Edmond hadn't found me yet, if he even intended to, so I spent the next few days working and trying to figure out how I could possibly investigate anything at Eure beyond the courtroom. I had very little time, for one thing, and it seemed like anywhere I wasn't supposed to be, my watch would either keep me out or give me away once inside.

My actual work was more of the same. Sanguans from all over the country were brought in, starved, shackled, and at gunpoint. I heard about their terrible crimes, and then guards led them away. Listening to it every night was horrible.

I grew more used to the chair, so my body didn't ache as much all the time, but I wasn't getting used to the heat in the courtroom. I expected it, but still sweat uncomfortably on and off over the course of each night. It must not have bothered the Spectavi.

It wasn't until after work on Friday that I found out the only night we got off was Sunday, when we instead had mandatory church for a few hours. I worked that Saturday just like any other night.

I replayed memories of Kristi and Todd when alone in my room each day before falling asleep. Kristi was gone forever, but I still hoped to learn something about what had happened to Todd. My lack of progress grew increasingly frustrating.

I had a nightmare about a court case on Friday and woke up disturbed that the Sanguans' wickedness reached me even in my room. I dreamt about the twins again on Saturday. Like the last time, I was almost sure they called me both Vera and Erin.

15

As I put my arm through my suit coat sleeve on Sunday, I realized that I had become so used to the routine that my dread for the outfit had lessened significantly. I was getting more used to the time schedule as well, but did find myself wanting to see and feel the bright sun after almost a week without it. I let the impossible idea go before long and focused on the fact that Mass would be a welcome break from my typical wretched nights.

I met Jennifer and Gavin at our usual door at nine forty.

"Are you all right, Gavin?" I asked. His skin looked even paler than normal compared to the black of his suit, and I guessed he might be sick.

"Yeah, fine," he said. "Why?"

"Oh, no reason, I guess." Prying further seemed rude.

We went in the opposite direction of my building, so I finally saw a little more of the campus. Unfortunately, there wasn't much different about it.

"It's just building after building of tinted windows, isn't it?" I asked.

"Pretty much," Gavin said.

"There's Edmond's house, and Victoria's, and others. There's a big one some of them share," Jennifer offered.

"Victoria has her own house?" I asked.

"Yes," Gavin said.

"Do we ever get to see Edmond and Victoria?" I asked.

"Yes!" Jennifer said excitedly. "We will at church tonight!"

We walked until we came around the corner of a building, and I stopped in my tracks.

The church was smaller than expected, but more ornate. It was light tan stone and had a wide front, with three arched entranceways. The pillars beside each entranceway had statues of men carved in them, and the arches were decorated with many smaller carvings. Above the middle arch was a small rose window.

"Impressive, isn't it?" Jennifer stopped walking soon after I did, while Gavin continued on. "The real one's even bigger."

"The real one?" I asked.

"Yes, in Chartres. In France. Edmond modeled this after that one. He did have the original built, after all."

"There's more to this?"

"Yes, Erin, this is only the entrance! The rest is down the stairs. Come on!"

I followed her under the center arch and down a granite staircase, quickly at first to catch up with her, and then more slowly after getting close. As eager as I had become, I didn't want to cause a commotion. We continued down, and eventually I understood why it had taken so long.

The interior was unlike any building I had ever been in,

let alone any building below ground. Massive stone columns held up the high arched ceiling of a long hall. On each side ran a narrower hallway, but the main one dominated the vast space. It must have been two or three hundred feet long and perhaps a hundred feet tall. It was so long that I couldn't see the altar up front in detail, though the massive crucifix that hung from the ceiling was impossible to miss.

Hundreds of chairs had been set up, and some were already filled. I had never seen so many vampires in one place.

"This is close to a full-sized replica," Jennifer whispered at the bottom of the stairs.

"It's incredible."

"I know. Come on, we shouldn't be late."

She pulled my sleeve until I started walking with her. I was in awe of everything—the room, the carvings on the stone walls, and the majestic blues and purples in the illuminated stained glass windows. Then there were all the vampires. Some sat and some talked in pairs and small groups. A few glanced at us while we made our way up the aisle between rows of chairs.

Did any of them know me, or Vera?

It surprised me that we kept going, but Jennifer led the way, and I followed. The people sat in the front three rows to the left side of the aisle. We went all the way to the front row where there were only two empty chairs left on the end at the aisle.

"The second row is fine. Someone else can sit here," I said, trying to come up with any reason I wouldn't want to sit there.

"It's okay, Erin. Come on, have a seat." Jennifer sat down, leaving me on the aisle. "I love coming to Mass here."

I nodded, understanding what she meant. I didn't attend Mass often because I thought it enough to follow the teachings and ideals of the Bible on my own. I had the cross on my neck as a constant reminder of God, as well. That place was different. I had no doubt I would enjoy a few hours in that magnificent cathedral the next five Sundays.

We sat for a few minutes waiting, and I took in the room some more. The altar was right in front of me and actually looked plainer than the rest of the church. The huge crucifix I had seen from afar was too near to be fully appreciated. It must have been thirty feet tall, at least. The image of Christ dominated the church from anywhere in it and certainly from so close. Knowing what I did about Satan and the vampires, I wondered what Jesus thought of the Spectavi beneath him in that room.

I felt tiny. Between the giant crucifix and the cavernous space, even the old and powerful vampires behind me seemed insignificant.

Everyone stood, so I did the same. Soft music started, and I located a small group of vampires playing off to the far right. I turned around to watch the procession down the aisle, but the room was so long that I couldn't see much. Few other people or vampires had turned as I did, so I returned to facing forward.

Eventually, a young vampire with tan skin carrying a cross reached the altar, stopped in front of it, and bowed. He proceeded to sit at the rear of the altar. Next came a female vampire.

I could only see her back, but she was very tall, at least six feet, with a big frame and very light skin. She wore a long black leather dress with a slit on the side facing me, and high-heeled sandals. The dress's back was only a thin strip from her waist to her neck and, with her long black hair in one braid, it left most of her white back exposed. Her athletic body looked perfectly toned.

A red cross dangled from a black chain wrapped around her wrist, completing her powerful look, though it was far from my idea of appropriate church attire.

She bowed slightly, and sat in the front row, across from me, one seat in from the aisle.

Edmond approached the altar wearing a respectful black business suit. He bowed and took the seat next to the female vampire, who was presumably Victoria.

I didn't know if it was good luck or bad that Edmond sat directly across from me. I hadn't learned anything going to work every day, except that the Sanguans were truly awful, so maybe being near him would lead to something.

The priest came to the altar. He was another white-skinned Spectavi, but he must have been quite young when made into a vampire.

I looked at Edmond, curious if he knew me as Vera and had seen me in the cathedral before. If so, the next question was how he'd react to seeing me there again.

16

The real Chartres Cathedral seemed even more impressive than the one I had just sat through Mass in, though only slightly. That the one at Eure had been carved into the ground boggled my mind. I had pictures of the cathedral in France up on my laptop.

The service had been compelling. The priest was eloquent and spoke passionately about doing good for humans, and specifically about preserving their right to be free of Satan's influence through the Sanguans. He created a convincing combination of the Bible and the reality of a world with vampires in it.

I doubted the Church of Rome would approve the entirety of the message, but it made sense to me, and it made sense to the people and Spectavi around me. Jennifer was visibly emotional while the priest spoke. Edmond appeared more reserved, but after he received the Eucharist, he had stood and stared up at the huge crucifix for many seconds. I had wondered what he was thinking.

Edmond never noticed me, or ignored me if he had. Like when I had seen him at my old office, it had been hugely disappointing. That he hadn't sought me out over the last week, either, as James had predicted he would, was very discouraging as well.

I clicked through pictures of Chartres Cathedral, which I had read Edmond had commissioned to be built in his hometown in the late twelfth century, and considered again the priest's words. They must have been directed at the Spectavi, as encouragement for their choice to drink synthetic blood and defend humanity's interest in the world. Even so, they had hit home for me.

I still hoped to do so many things with my life, and to experience much more than the last year and a half had allowed. I yearned to be free personally of Satan's work done by the Sanguans. They were responsible for much of the pain in my life, and possibly more than I could remember.

I decided that when I left Eure, I would move far away from Washington, D.C. and start anew. It might not solve all my problems, but it sounded like the right first step.

Three knocks came at my door. That had never happened before. I had taken off my suit coat after church, but deemed the rest of my outfit presentable enough for whoever it might be, so I went to the door in my bare feet. I opened it to find Edmond standing there, wearing his suit from church.

"Hello there, Erin." His chiseled face was inviting and kind like it had been in my old office, but I stepped back anyway; I couldn't help it.

"Hello, Mr. Duchart." I looked up at him. He was taller than I remembered, probably because he wasn't standing next to William. He appeared just as powerfully built though, and just as pale. Fifteen hundred years old, James had said.

I wished I had put on my coat before going to the door, and felt very short without my shoes.

He smiled. "Call me Edmond, please. May I come in?"

"Of course, yes, please come in," I stammered. I didn't know what my hair looked like, but couldn't run to check.

Edmond walked over to my small kitchen table and seemed to be waiting for something.

"Please, have a seat," I said. He did, and I took the seat across from him. I couldn't believe what was happening.

Over the course of his long life, he had been a Frenchman in the Dark Ages, a warrior in countless battles, and was currently one of the most important businessmen in the world, and he sat at my little table. I made sure to sit up straight.

"I like to meet all of my new employees after they've settled in. I trust you have?"

"Yes, but, well, we've already met." I paused to check his reaction. He didn't flinch, so I went on. "At Snap Safe Software, Todd Lowe's company."

"Ah yes, I remember now. How is Todd? Have you heard from him since you've been here?"

"Well, no." Did he not know? "I thought you might have heard from him more recently actually."

"Eure is a big corporation." Edmond tried to be polite when pointing out what should have been obvious to me. "While I do monitor our divisions as closely as I can, I can't watch them all as much as I would like to."

It felt wrong to keep pressing him on it, but I knew it might be my only chance. "He became a vampire. A Spectavi. It was shocking. I came home one night, and it had happened. He didn't even remember me. I thought you might know what had happened. It was so unexpected. We were planning on moving away together." I still struggled to talk about it.

Edmond looked sympathetic. "I'm sorry to hear that. Is that why you came to Eure?"

"Something like that," I said.

"Erin, in my long life, I've seen people hide many secrets from the ones they loved. In business, I've seen founders who sell companies, plan to leave, and then regret their decisions. They sometimes try to undo the sale or else come back to the company in any way they can. Todd must have changed his mind about things. If he had other plans with you, perhaps becoming a vampire was his way out of them."

I had known it would be hard for Todd to leave his company behind. Maybe I had underestimated how hard it would be. Of course, I would have stayed with him in D.C. if that was what he'd wanted.

"He didn't even like the new direction Eure was taking his company," I said. "And Mr. Oliver, my boss? I haven't heard from him since that night either."

"Mr. Oliver, he was an older man if I recall?" Edmond asked.

I nodded.

"I don't know for sure, but he might have begun to feel

very mortal. His old age could have been creeping up on him. Not everyone can become a Spectavi, but we do offer the chance to some senior managers when we acquire a company."

It was possible, but I hadn't seen any signs of it coming.

"I can tell how hard these events have been on you, and I'm sorry for the pain you've had to endure."

I tried to look appreciative, but found myself focused down on the table more than on Edmond. I assumed he was only talking about the events surrounding Todd and Mr. Oliver.

Edmond changed the subject. "How do you like working with Ms. Dubois? She isn't being too hard on you, is she?"

"No, not at all. The work is fine, it's just… well, it's horrible the crimes the Sanguans commit."

"Yes, it is. That's why your job is not an easy one. The Sanguans are ruthless creatures. They've left the path of God and let Satan dominate their actions."

I took the chance to be very direct. "Isn't Satan's evil inside all vampires, the Spectavi included?"

Edmond waited a moment, then said, "Erin, you speak to me much more freely than most humans."

"Maybe it's because we've met before." I meant at Snap Safe again, but Edmond's eyes hinted at something else.

"Maybe it is," he agreed confidently. I was no longer sure I had seen anything at all.

Edmond turned to the brown cross on my wall. "A trick of Satan allows my life to be so long. But Satan, the deceiver, is the one who is truly tricked, for every night I live for God's glory. I will see the world rid of murderous Sanguans, and now that my people can survive on synthetic blood, no more humans will die so that vampires can live."

I glanced at the cross, and then back at Edmond. "How did it start? Who did Satan trick first?"

He turned back to me. "Two sisters, twins. They were very beautiful."

"You knew them?"

"Yes. I knew them in France when I was young, a very long time ago."

He didn't know I had heard the story before. I hoped to hear something new. "What happened?"

Edmond looked puzzled. "Why do you ask about this?"

My instinct was to come up with a quick lie to satisfy him. But, out of nowhere, I meant it when asking, "I see the Sanguans in court, and I wonder what drives them to do what they do. Where did the evil come from?"

Edmond nodded, and thought for another moment before he spoke. "The sisters got very ill. Conditions in France were bad like they were in all of Europe, and disease was very common. Sometimes populations of villages and towns would be cut in half, or worse, when a new sickness broke out.

"The twins had it worse than anyone. They were fair and beautiful and full of life, and were devoted to the Lord's teachings. When they were a little younger than you are now, their father had them engaged to good men. Then, just days before they were to be married, they woke up feverish and weak. They stayed in bed, and the next morning their skin had become light gray and marked with boils all over. Their weddings were put on hold and, when the sisters didn't recover quickly, their grooms-to-be left them."

"That's awful," I said.

"It was awful, and the men weren't as worthy as all had thought, but the next three years were even worse. Every day the sisters prayed to Jesus, yet their condition never improved. They didn't die though, they suffered. They suffered while all the people around them left for fear of contracting whatever kept hold over them. For three years, they were sick and almost completely alone. Day after day they lay in bed on death's door, but death never came for them.

"One day, even such devout followers of the Lord couldn't take it anymore. God hadn't answered their prayers, so they asked the Devil if he would.

"That night, Satan appeared to the twins and offered them either a quick death, or life and the power to take revenge on those that had abandoned them. The sisters chose life, and they were healed of their sickness, but awoke to an incredible hunger. Finally able to get out of bed and move freely, they ate and drank, yet their hunger wasn't satisfied.

"They left their home on the outskirts of town and found an old friend who had ignored them while they were ill. The sisters wanted their revenge, but they had no weapons, so they killed the man with their bare hands. For the first time, they knew the great strength the Devil had given them."

Edmond seemed as captivated by his story as I was, even

though he must have told it many times before.

"The man was dead, and the twins were still hungry. They continued into town and found a group of people sharing a meal together. They killed one, and then another, and to mock those still alive who had been eating, they chewed on the flesh of the newly dead. Their blood satisfied the sisters' hunger, but only for a short time. They kept killing and eating their dead, and in the process learned that it was human blood that satisfied them, not skin or meat, and then they were vampires."

"My God," I whispered.

"Yes, the Devil played his evilest trick on the twin sisters."

"And that same hunger is what drives vampires still?"

"Yes, though it was the worst for them because they were the first."

"What happened to them?"

"They found peace, eventually," Edmond replied.

So James's story was right, if incomplete. Vampires were truly creatures of the Devil. The twins' sickness had been tragic, but they had asked Satan for his help, inviting his deception.

Still, how could they be held at fault after what they had been through? At least they had finally found peace. However fair they once were, as they appeared in my dreams, they had become something hideous.

I glanced at the cross again. "What happens to the Sanguans who are tried in court?"

"They are held for almost a week, according to the law in

this country, and then they are killed." Compared to the story about the twins, Edmond spoke much more matter-of-factly.

"How are they killed?"

"Lethal injection for some—silver," he said. "The silver is pure; the Sanguans are not."

The Spectavi hated silver just as much, but that didn't make Edmond wrong.

He continued, "Cremation for most, though. It's faster and cheaper. The sun is a limitless resource for us in this matter." It was sound business rational. "And some meet their end another way altogether. Would you like to see?"

"How?"

"You will see. Come with me, please." He got up from his chair.

I couldn't say no to that. I stood and began to put my suit coat on.

"You'll be more comfortable in pants and a t-shirt, I'm sure. I know the wardrobe here is a little limited, but you aren't going to work now. I'll wait outside."

I changed into my black pants, a white t-shirt, and sneakers and fixed my hair quickly. Carrying my hooded sweatshirt, I followed Edmond away from my room. I still felt underdressed, but he had been right, I was much more comfortable.

After a fifteen-minute walk, Edmond pointed out Victoria's house. Edmond's home was within view and larger, but Victoria's impressed me as well.

Hers was built from big, nearly black stones and had plain, round columns at the entrance. I counted twenty windows across the front, split over two levels. The windows were narrow, but tall and had steel bars over them. It looked more like a prison than a home.

We climbed stone steps up to what must have been a heavy wooden door. Edmond opened it with ease.

While we hadn't spoken much, walking with him had been an engrossing experience. It was a cool and very dark night, yet I felt perfectly safe at his side. I tried to think of some way to bring up Vera, but couldn't. For one thing, I had to be sure to see where Edmond was taking me. At the same time, I found myself unexpectedly at ease being with him and wasn't eager to disrupt the sensation. In a world full of horrible monsters, I walked with one of the most powerful creatures of all, and he didn't seem like a monster to me.

Inside, Victoria's home was dark and seemed very old. The wood floor creaked where we stepped and a light coating of dust covered the sparse antique furniture. The air was still, and the whole place didn't seem lived in at all. No one else appeared to be around.

Noises came from out back, and we headed toward them, down more stone steps and across a short dirt path to a wooden fence that stood about fifty feet high. Banks of lights sat atop it, and I heard the sound of metal colliding with metal as we approached. Occasionally, I heard screams.

We passed a guard, went through a gate, and up and out to a set of bleachers overlooking a brown dirt space enclosed by the fence. Victoria was fighting a Sanguan. Two others lay dead on the ground near her. Someone else sat on one of the benches in front of us wearing black, but I couldn't tell who from their back. I followed Edmond to a boxed-off section with six black chairs, in the middle of the bleachers.

Edmond gestured for me to sit, and I chose the middle chair on the left. I sank a little into the soft leather, and the chair's high back also made it more appealing than the benches.

Edmond sat down next to me. "Victoria likes the practice."

It was hard for me to make out all the action below because it happened so fast, but it was easier than the night at the bus stop. Unlike then, neither pouring rain nor glass separated me from the battle.

Victoria wore a tight black sleeveless top and a short, loose skirt while she fought. They appeared to be leather like her dress at church had been, and again contrasted her white skin sharply. Her hair was pulled together behind her into one long, tight braid.

Victoria stopped and held a long, thin sword with both hands over her head. The sword had to be heavy, but even a human woman of her size and strength could probably have managed it. Of course, as a vampire, it probably felt weightless in her hands.

She must have swung it, because the Sanguan who had charged her lay in front of her, cut in half. I recoiled in my chair.

"She is a powerful weapon for Christ against the Sanguans," Edmond said without turning to me.

Blood spilled out of the cut body and over Victoria's bare

feet. Holding the sword above her vanquished enemy, she looked in our direction, and her hair, which had been whipping around her head, came to rest. The person sitting on the bleachers also turned to us, and I saw that it was Gavin. He looked pale and almost lifeless as he slowly faced forward.

Victoria brought her attention back to the arena. She walked out of the blood, moved to the center, and placed her sword on the ground. Guards who had been standing against the fence ran in and took the dead bodies away.

"She practices against the condemned from court?" I asked.

"Yes, some," Edmond said. "We tell them that if they can cut her skin in battle, they will be freed. It was actually Phillip II's idea originally."

"How often do they succeed?"

"In more than seven hundred years of these battles, never."

Three fresh Sanguans with weapons charged out from below where we sat—two males and one female. With no weapon, Victoria moved quickly between them. I heard the clangs of metal hitting metal and soon saw why.

Victoria held an axe that one of the Sanguans had used to attack. From where his head had been, blood squirted out of his prostrate body. His clothes were tattered, and his wrists burned from where he had worn the silver chains.

The others fought on, Victoria with her axe and the Sanguans with swords. The female had picked up the sword Victoria had used earlier, and wielded two. The Sanguans should have had the advantage with their longer weapons, but Victoria was too fast for them.

Victoria danced between them as they fought. The Sanguans snarled like wild beasts, while Victoria remained calm and collected with her long hair swinging behind her as she moved. I heard more than I saw, but got a little better at catching some details. Victoria blocked their repeated attacks with ease.

It was clear that she had been intentionally defensive because she suddenly lunged and swung her axe, and the male was cut in two.

I flinched again when blood gushed from his body, then leaned forward in my chair. I recognized the remaining Sanguan from court. She had killed a public school basketball coach in front of her team at practice while the children watched. She had pleaded not guilty and cursed the judge while being dragged away.

The Sanguan attacked with her two swords. Victoria danced around her to avoid some of her thrusts and parried others with her axe. She might have slowed down for Gavin and me to comprehend because her movements became clearer.

The Sanguan stopped. She breathed heavily and must have known she wasn't getting anywhere against Victoria.

Nevertheless, a new rage overcame the wild vampire. She roared with a wide-open mouth and swung her swords faster than before.

Victoria came at her, and their battle once again became hard for me to make out in detail, though I continued to hear its fury.

The Sanguan's left arm fell to the ground and then her right did the same. She stood still and, like a frightened animal, looked around to the guards at the fence. They aimed their guns at her in response. She had nowhere to run.

The ancient Spectavi warrior swung her axe and took the Sanguan's head off, leaving the body to slump to the ground. Victoria waited a moment, motionless. I hadn't reacted when that Sanguan was killed. She had gotten what she deserved.

Victoria dropped her axe softly and, from under her top, pulled out her red cross on its black chain. She kissed the cross, pushed the necklace back where it had been, and walked out of sight below where we sat. Gavin got up and left the bleachers, presumably to follow her. She trained him; that was their work together. When he became a Spectavi, he'd be a warrior like her.

"It's satisfying to see them pay for the crimes they've committed, isn't it?" Edmond asked.

"Yes," I agreed.

"We can come watch again another night, if you'd like, but I think she's done for tonight. I will walk you back to your room."

17

I was glad Victoria was Spectavi. Over the following week in court, I grew more and more depressed as each Sanguan atrocity rolled into the next. The repetition of it was only broken up by cases that affected me even more deeply— often ones where young couples had been killed, or worse, when one person had been killed, leaving the other alone. At least once a night, I cried softly or came close, looking at the creature chained in front of me, hearing about the terrible things they had done.

I went back to my room after work and searched online for more details of those crimes, to read more about the victims and the lives they would never get to live.

Those Sanguans, especially, I imagined Victoria fighting and killing. And since they wouldn't all make it to the arena, thinking of them being cremated in the sun was similarly comforting.

The next time I dreamt of the twins, I woke up wondering if Victoria had played a role in killing them.

Every night, Ms. Dubois opened the court by nine thirty and sat with me. She left me alone for a little longer some nights, and that change, along with Gavin watching once—possibly scouting opponents for Victoria—were the only deviations from the routine.

The constant heat and thick air of the courtroom added to my eagerness for the end of work to come, although when it did, and I mustered the energy to attempt sneaking into a few more buildings, the same thing always happened: I was denied entrance or else set off an alarm because of my watch.

One night, I sat outside the court building until five thirty, thinking I might snoop around then.

While I enjoyed seeing the first light of dawn over the horizon, not only did I fail to stay out for the day, I wasn't even out late enough to see the sun. By five thirty-one, I had been picked up and was riding in a silver SUV being driven to my room.

Someone must have noticed the same person breaking the rules over and over, so I stopped. I tried to use a knife and fork from my kitchen to get my watch off, but nothing ever came close to working. Zhilan would come before long, and I had run out of ideas.

The second Mass impressed me just as much as the first. Edmond arrived with Victoria again, and it was exciting to see him for the first time since the previous Sunday. During the service, I thought about the twins and their story. I took pride in being surrounded by vampires who had chosen to live on synthetic blood, and in doing so had overcome the evil Satan had brought into the world. The priest at Eure assured them that God blessed their souls even as Spectavi.

I was in my room after church and hoped Edmond would come by again. I should have sought to talk to him more about his war against the Sanguans, so that I might learn something new for James, Grant, and Zhilan. But in my heart, that allegiance was dying. James's expectation that Edmond would jump at the chance to be close to me had been wrong, and I found it hard to believe their claim of respect for human life. Based on what I had seen in court, they were most likely using me. And if not, and they had told the truth about how they fed, James had attacked me, Grant admitted to attacking women against their will, and they had all allied themselves with Kristi's killers. That best-case scenario didn't sound much better than the scum who came through court each night.

Instead, I wanted to talk to Edmond for myself. Even though I didn't have high hopes, I could ask him about Vera. Aside from that, learning about his long life and his battle against Satan across the centuries would be fascinating. I had read plenty of history on my own, but Edmond could tell me what he had lived through and done in his own words, and that would be much more valuable.

I sat at my laptop reading the news to pass the time.

The war against the Sanguans seemed to be going well. Human politicians in the United States lined up to take credit for having set up or deepened the relationship with Eure and the Spectavi. Edmond was quoted in a few articles, along with many other vampires I had never heard of. In spite of that success, I came across plenty of articles detailing illegal vampire attacks and assumed some of those Sanguans would be in court soon.

Then an article title caught my eye:

New Camera Software Coming to D.C.

I clicked through and read it. It was the software from Snap Safe, and Eure planned to implement it just like Todd had described. They were doing so in close cooperation with the federal government, in spite of the fact that many local residents were upset about it. Most shocking was Todd's quote. "We're excited about the rich set of data this new software will provide here in Washington and in other major cities after that. People everywhere will be safer because of it."

That data was exactly what Todd had feared collecting, and I couldn't imagine why he trusted the government all of a sudden.

The article was a week old, so I searched for more recent ones. I found another similar to the one I had read and eventually one from a bigger newspaper:

New Team Brings Camera Software to Eure, D.C.

The article had a picture of Todd, Mr. Oliver, and his wife! There was a podium on a stage, and to one side there appeared to be humans, probably politicians. On the other side sat Todd, a female vampire I didn't recognize, Mr. Oliver, and his wife. The article said that the entire team that had developed the software was Spectavi, and listed Mrs. Oliver as one of them.

Edmond had been right after all. Mr. Oliver had become a vampire, and his wife had joined him. They must have chosen to live together as Spectavi instead of growing any older. It was shocking, but I couldn't blame them for the choice.

They appeared happy in the picture and would never have to watch the other age, get sick, or die. They would never be alone, without their companion. I just wished Mr. Oliver had told me of his plans.

And then there was Todd, who smiled widely in the picture. I could hardly look at him. He really had moved on and was full speed ahead with Eure.

I still couldn't believe he had been blatantly lying to me about his disapproval for what they planned to do with his software, but he must have changed his mind abruptly at some point. The vampire next to Todd looked very pretty, and I wondered if she had anything to do with it.

I bookmarked the article and searched for more. I found some, but the same picture kept showing up.

After that, I *really* wished Edmond would knock at my door. I would tell him he was right. Everything he said had been right.

Edmond never came to my room that night, and the next week of work seemed to drag on forever. I had something new to think about in the sweltering courtroom, and it was something terrible. Todd was really gone and, worse, he had abandoned me. I should have been mad at him for the cowardly way he had done it, but the finality of the situation upset me too much to care about those details.

Todd was excited on stage, forging ahead with his software, and I remained trapped at Eure where I had come to investigate what had happened to him. But it hadn't been Edmond's doing at all. Todd simply couldn't leave his company behind, and he might even have left me for a vampire.

In retrospect, I needn't have gone to Eure to find out in the first place—I would have seen it in the news eventually. The next thirty days before my rescue were going to be brutal.

The only good news I got during the week was that I might have a chance to see Edmond on Saturday at a big event called the Renatus Ritual, where some of the humans became Spectavi. The event took place twice a year, and Gavin was going to be among the reborn, but not Jennifer. I had been a little nervous until Ms. Dubois assured me that I wouldn't be.

I did have to attend Renatus with Ms. Dubois. Jennifer told me that all the people went with their bosses, and it was an important opportunity for each pair to spend time outside work together. If they were going to make you a vampire one day, they had to be sure they really wanted to. In my case, based on our very infrequent conversations to date, I simply couldn't imagine spending the entire time with Ms. Dubois. I hoped to be able to slip away and talk to Edmond.

I slept badly the whole week. I had become used to the time schedule, but woke up frequently after having nightmares about the twins, the Sanguans from court, or both.

In my dreams, the twins seemed healthy and human, but they were getting more aggressive, calling out to me directly at times as Erin or Vera. I looked forward to asking Edmond about the dreams when I finally saw him.

Once awake, thinking about Todd made it hard to fall back asleep. He and I had such a good time together, and he had thrown it all away. I thought he had really liked me, but obviously he hadn't.

But what did I really know about dating? I had so little experience that I must have been wrong about his feelings for me. My mistake had probably been getting my hopes up in the first place.

I stood in my white towel and held the dress that had appeared in my closet while I worked the night before. It was long, light gray, satin—as Jennifer had said all of the human girls' dresses would be—and a little plain, but nicer than I had expected.

Three knocks came at my door, like when Edmond had visited before. Could it be him? It shouldn't have been Ms. Dubois; we were supposed to meet outside the church later.

"I'll be right there." I hung up the dress. I was still wet, but quickly threw on black pants, a bra, and a white t-shirt, in an effort to look somewhat presentable in case it was Edmond.

I ran to the door and opened it, to find Edmond wearing a tuxedo, holding a long black garment bag.

"Hello, Erin. I'm sorry to bother you, but something has

come up, and Ms. Dubois won't be able to make it tonight. You shouldn't go alone, and I hoped you would accompany me instead."

"Okay," I said, stunned.

"And I thought you might like this better than that drab gray dress they have you all wear. This one will match your eyes I think." He handed me the bag.

"Oh, thank you."

"I'll meet you outside the church at eleven thirty," he said and then walked off.

I shut the door, rushed to my closet to hang the bag, and unzipped it.

The dress was long and formal like the gray one, but more elegant. The shoulder straps were thin and the back very low. The bottom was loose and fancier than the gray dress, and the emerald green satin shined even in my dark closest. I had never worn anything like it.

I found matching high-heeled sandals in the bottom of the bag, along with a small box containing pearl earrings. I didn't know how he could have gotten everything on short notice and been so sure it would fit, but remembered that they had measured me for all my clothes on my first night. Plus, how hard could it have been for someone like Edmond to make happen?

A part of me still hoped to get dressed up like that to go out somewhere with Todd in California, not to meet a vampire at a ceremony where people would be turned into Spectavi.

But Todd was gone, or at least had moved on, and I had to move on, too.

And Edmond was no vampire I had met on the street or in some club. He led the Spectavi, was over fifteen hundred years old, and wanted to see *me* in that dress that night. I felt flattered.

The dress was gorgeous, and it did match my eyes perfectly. My back was bare where the dress plunged low, but I put my hair up in a bun anyway. I couldn't ignore how much of my body was exposed, but I'd be surrounded by Spectavi, and I didn't want to disappoint Edmond.

I headed out of my room and down the elevator to meet Jennifer, determined to make the most of my night with him.

18

"Wow, where did you get that dress?" Jennifer asked, standing at the door where we always met. Gavin wouldn't be joining us because he had to prepare for the ceremony.

I couldn't help a wide smile. "Edmond gave it to me to wear."

"Edmond?"

"Yes. Ms. Dubois can't make it, and he didn't want me to have to go alone." I managed to look a little concerned.

"I hope she's okay."

"Me, too." I didn't really care, not that I hoped for anything bad to have happened to her.

Jennifer looked down at her light gray dress. "I hope Mr. Roberts thinks I look nice tonight."

The relationship of boss to employee was so different there, but of course, it had to be. "You look great! I'm sure he will." She really did, so I did my best to be convincing.

Outside, in the warm night air, the walk to the cathedral took longer than normal in our dresses. We were both too nervous for idle chitchat.

As we got close, it hit me that one thing I hadn't been

nervous about was walking alone with Jennifer. After what had happened to Kristi, and what I witnessed in court each night, I would never again walk so free of worry outside of Eure after sunset. Two young women in formal dresses would be tempting prey for Sanguans.

The thought left my mind upon seeing how brightly lit the entrance at the top of the staircase was. To one side stood a large mass of light gray—all the humans who weren't involved in the ceremony, with the women in the same style dress Jennifer wore and the men in suits of the same color, with slightly darker ties. On the other side, vampires in black tuxedoes and colorful outfits walked by and down the stairs.

A few people turned as we got close, and they noticed my emerald green dress. After some initial embarrassment, I became more confident when explaining to them that I was waiting for Edmond and that he had given it to me. I saw a handful of jealous looks, but for the most part, people were supportive and told me what a tremendous honor it was.

We fidgeted while we waited, and no one seemed to be having conversations of substance. Nerves were high with all that was at stake.

One by one the vampire bosses arrived, some on foot, and others out of the back seats of fancy cars. They brought their human companions down to the church, and our group shrank.

I smiled next to Jennifer when Mr. Roberts arrived and told her she looked wonderful. He gave her a black and silver bracelet, and she looked happier than I had ever seen her as they headed off together.

Eventually, only three of us remained, and we ran out of things to discuss, so we just stood silently, waiting for our vampires. Alicia's came, so it was only Derrick and me left until his showed up in a black limousine.

I stood alone at the top of the stairs watching other vampires walk past me, some by themselves, and some in couples. Edmond wouldn't abandon me, would he?

Finally a long limousine pulled up, the longest I had seen all night. It had to be him.

Instead, Victoria came out of the back door and shut it behind her. Her long, black satin dress clung to her powerful, almost perfectly white body. Her black chain with its red cross was wrapped around her wrist. Victoria had the same calm demeanor as always, and for the first time I realized how pretty she was. I guessed she hadn't been many years older than I was when becoming a vampire.

She glanced at me, and her presence weighed heavily on my mind. The sensation ended when she passed and went down the stairs.

Her limo drove away, and another just like it pulled up. *Please let it be Edmond.* The back door opened, and it was. He wore the same tuxedo as before and carried a small box with him.

"Erin, you look beautiful."

"Thank you," I said. "And thanks for the dress."

"You're welcome. I brought something else for you. It isn't much."

He handed me the box, and I opened it to find a narrow cross on a silver chain. I assumed it must be white gold or steel. I didn't think he'd give me silver.

"It's platinum," Edmond explained.

I took it out of the box and held it in front of me.

"It's beautiful, Edmond, thank you."

I undid the clasp and brought it behind my neck. Edmond moved behind me and put his hands over mine. His fingers were solid stone, and I couldn't imagine how they could work with something so small, but his touch was gentle, and he had no trouble with the clasp.

When I turned to him, the cross hung above where the dress covered my chest.

"Wonderful." Edmond held out his arm, and I took it with my hand. It was so firm that it felt like holding a statue and not a living being.

We headed for the staircase, and I pictured what my new platinum cross must look like compared to my black tattoo. One covered the mark of a vampire, and the other was a gift from one.

Edmond was patient while I walked carefully down the stairs. I focused completely on not falling, so I didn't see the scene in the church until we neared the bottom.

And then, what a sight it was.

Below the massive crucifix that hung from the high ceiling of the great hall, a crowd of vivid color and elegance mingled happily. The chairs for Mass had been removed, and red, blue, and yellow banners hung from the tall columns. More light shone through the stained glass windows than normal and, in that brightness, the light gray the other humans wore stood out as drab compared to the vampires' outfits.

It was truly a grand gala and, like many things at Eure, it was like nothing I had ever experienced in the short life I could remember.

The cathedral was crowded. I had seen as many vampires at Mass on Sundays, but then, aside from Victoria, they were conservative in their appearance.

In front of me, some of the Spectavi's faces were made-up dramatically, and many wore outfits other than western dresses and tuxedos. Instead, some wore the clothes of what I assumed were their native lands, from countries all over the world. The result was an extremely wide variety of styles and colors.

Edmond walked me into the room, and we started talking to other vampires almost immediately. A small orchestra played soft music from the same spot they did at Mass, and vampire waiters brought around drinks. Edmond handed me a glass of wine and said it was a Bordeaux from a great vintage in 1961. He didn't drink anything, but told me that the other glasses were the synthetic blood that the Spectavi drank regularly. The wine was the first alcohol I had at Eure, and I enjoyed it, but found it softer tasting and thinner than what I normally drank.

We made our way to the front of the hall and had short conversations with many vampires as we went.

"Denis, this is Erin," Edmond said to a lean vampire with black hair.

"Erin, it is a pleasure to meet you." Denis took my hand and kissed it gently. "You look lovely."

"Thanks," I said shyly.

"Erin, Denis is an old friend from France."

"Very old," Denis said. "And still very upset with you, Edmond."

"Oh, let it go. It was hundreds of years ago," Edmond said.

Denis was calm, but concerned when he explained, "Erin, I hate to bring up something so... unpleasant, but Edmond here didn't lift a finger while Joan of Arc was condemned and killed. I'll never forgive him."

"No, you won't!" Edmond said with a big smile and shook Denis's hand. "It's good to see you, Denis."

"You as well, Edmond, as always," Denis said.

Edmond turned me away from him. "It was a very complicated situation."

We met a female vampire who was almost as big as Victoria. She had a similar impressive physique, and her skin must have been very dark when she had been human.

Edmond introduced me. "Imani, this is Erin."

"Nice to meet you, Erin. What a splendid dress," Imani said.

"Thank you."

"Edmond, when are you coming to Africa again?" she asked.

"Soon, a few months maybe," he responded.

Imani wagged her finger at him. "Well you'd better be sure you do."

When we left her, Edmond explained that Imani was an important vampire in Africa.

All of the vampires we met complimented me on my

dress, and some did on my new necklace, too. I tried to thank them graciously, but the attention was unusual for me, and I couldn't help being in awe of them, especially the older ones, so I wasn't sure how I did.

After the introductions, for the most part, the vampires spoke with Edmond exclusively. I didn't mind. I found it exciting just meeting them and getting glimpses into their long lives, so I sipped my wine and listened.

None of them hinted at having met me already. Surely if I had been Vera and attended the same event before, someone would have recognized me. It was unexpected, but each time we left a group of vampires and Vera hadn't come up, a moment of relief came over me.

As we moved from group to group, I saw a wider variation in skin color than with Edmond, Victoria, Ms. Dubois, William, and the judges, who were all very old and had either very light or almost totally white skin. That night, I moved among gradients of color, from the almost human-looking skin of very new Spectavi, to the many shades of others like Denis and Imani, before ultimately getting to the whites of the ancients. I saw it on Sundays a little, but the hall was darker then. Mostly young Sanguans came through court. Finally, the full spectrum was evident.

Eventually, we reached the front and, while Edmond engaged in a comparison of the military strategies of Charlemagne and Napoleon with soldiers who had fought in their armies, I noticed ten white beds arranged in front of the altar with large vats of red liquid behind them.

The medical equipment set up beside them—small

machines, tubes, and trays next to each bed—reminded me of the night's true purpose. Renatus. Rebirth. I didn't expect it to be pleasant, however it worked.

I went back to the conversations with Edmond, and we moved around the room some more, but stayed close to the front. I saw Victoria and smiled at her, but she didn't react. I wasn't sure if she had seen me.

William did smile when he saw me and said hello before leaving to prepare for the ceremony. Jennifer waved to me, and I waved back. She didn't want to leave Mr. Roberts's side, and I didn't want to leave Edmond's.

I hadn't had any time alone with Edmond to ask my questions, but was enjoying myself too much to mind. I'd get to them later.

Before long, the music stopped, and everyone quickly ended their conversations and turned to the front of the room. Edmond walked to near where he normally sat at Mass and made sure I followed close behind and stood next to him.

The priest from Mass came to the front, behind all the beds, and said a short prayer. When he had finished, the ten humans who would become Spectavi walked in from the left side of the church, followed by William, who wore a white lab coat. The humans wore white gowns and had wrappings on their right wrists.

The humans each lay down on a bed and, one by one, William connected a clear plastic tube to their already prepared wrists. Except for the others in the crowd shuffling in place, the church was quiet.

After the last wrist, William went to the front next to the priest and held a tablet computer in his hand. Each person's vampire made their way out of the crowd and stood over their human's bed. Gavin appeared very eager looking up at Victoria, who remained emotionless. Her old blood would no doubt make him a strong vampire.

When they were all in place, Edmond took a step forward; all eyes fixed on him.

"Friends, we are here tonight to welcome new allies in our war against the Sanguans. Jesus tells us that no one can see the Kingdom of God unless they are born again. Those before you have chosen to be reborn so that they may live for God and fight for Him for all time, and they have proven their worth to do so among us."

He turned and spoke to the people on the beds. "We thank you for your sacrifice and for the work you will do in God's name."

Those that had glasses raised them for a second, then took a sip. I followed as soon as I saw what was happening, and then Edmond stepped back next to me.

William touched his tablet, and the machines next to the humans began to hum quietly. The clear tubes coming out of each wrist filled with their red blood. I moved closer to Edmond.

"They must be drained of most of their blood first," he whispered.

The people stayed calm while the machines sucked their blood from their bodies. Some closed their eyes, and others left them open. I watched Gavin mostly, and his were open.

It seemed to take minutes, and I don't know if I could have watched it if I weren't with Edmond.

Finally, the tubes became clear again, and the machines stopped. The cavernous room was silent; no one fidgeted. The humans lay completely motionless.

Victoria brought her wrist to her mouth first and bit it, and then the other vampires did the same. She moved her wrist above Gavin's mouth, and a few drops of her blood dripped into it. Gavin came alive, lifted his mouth to her wrist, and sucked on her open wound for more.

The other vampire and human pairs did the same, but I couldn't watch anymore. I turned my head into Edmond's chest and closed my eyes. It was like lying against solid rock.

"They have to drink first, and Satan will enter their bodies before we will master Him, and then they will be left with His power, but not His thirst."

I looked back, and the people continued to drink, most furiously. Some had grabbed the arms of their vampires, and the vampires' physical exertions to stay still and let them keep drinking suggested the process was taking its toll. Except Victoria. She didn't react at all while Gavin drank. I turned toward Edmond again.

"Look now, Erin," he said after a few more seconds.

The humans, or new vampires, had stopped drinking. Most seemed angry and restless. Their eyes were wide, and their chests rose and fell rapidly. Gavin reminded me of an animal ready to pounce.

"The hunger a new vampire feels is a powerful force, especially for ones made by vampires as old as these. It would dominate their will for some time if we could not help them," Edmond said.

I almost turned away again when the tubes running to their wrists refilled with a lighter red, from the machine side. When the synthetic blood hit Gavin's wrist, he started to slow his breathing. It took a few moments, but gradually he and the others calmed down completely.

The old vampires disconnected the tubes from the new vampires, and the new ones sat up. The priest walked past them, leaving the way he had entered. The old vampires led the new ones away, and William followed behind.

"What will happen to them now?" I asked Edmond.

"After Mass tomorrow, most will leave here with their mentors and learn their new roles at Eure and in the war," he said.

I nodded. Vampires again surrounded Edmond, and the conversations picked back up. While recovering from what I had just seen, I didn't pay as much attention as before. I held Edmond's arm while we moved from group to group and I started growing tired from my lack of good sleep, or the wine, or both.

Edmond must have sensed it because after we left a conversation, he didn't move us to another, and instead asked, "Are you feeling all right?"

"I am. This is wonderful. I'm just a little tired."

"We can leave if you'd like. The ceremony is over."

"No, no, that's all right." I smiled. I still had things to ask him and was in no rush to go back to my room and be alone.

We mingled among the crowd. I got another glass of wine and kept listening and meeting new vampires. Edmond was friendly and moved between them like a politician who needed their continued support, as well as a business leader who ran their company. His role at Eure and in the war must have required the combination, but Edmond was supremely confident and clearly up to the task.

All of the vampires we met were beautiful or at least very attractive. I realized that, except for Snake, who was disfigured, every vampire I had ever seen up close was pleasing to look at, even the Sanguans in court when they weren't acting wildly. I hadn't let myself see it before, after what had happened to me, but I saw it that night. I recalled Todd's features, which had subtly changed the night he became a vampire, and came to the conclusion that the process must refine one's appearance.

Satan certainly did give his agents a great deal in return for corrupting them. Of course, those who had his gifts without his malice filled the cathedral. It was very impressive.

Eventually, the church began to empty. I came across Jennifer again, still glowing at Mr. Roberts's side, and waved goodbye when she left. I was glad she had a good night and thought that she might be part of the next ceremony or the one after that. It scared me, but it seemed to be what she truly wanted.

"You look tired, Erin, shall we go?" Edmond asked. We stood at the base of the long staircase at the front of the hall.

"Sure, but... can I ask you something first?"

"Please," Edmond answered.

"The twins you mentioned last time we spoke, how did you defeat them if they were so powerful?"

"Why do you ask about the twins again?"

"I dream about twins sometimes, and I think they're the ones you told me about. They're part of the reason I'm not sleeping well. If they're dead, I wonder why I dream about them." It felt good to tell someone else, to hear my secret out loud.

"They aren't dead, Erin. I've been able to give them peace, but so far I have not been able to heal them, though I keep trying." Edmond looked up to the massive crucifix, and then back to me. "Would you like to see them?"

"They're alive? Here?"

"They do not walk the night, but they are alive, resting here," he said.

I nodded. I couldn't believe it. After so many dreams, the twins were close, and I would see them soon.

We spoke to a few more groups on the way out and said quick goodbyes to a few others, but I paid much less attention than before. I could think of nothing but the twins.

We got out of the limousine at Edmond's home, which was big and stone, like Victoria's, but much more inviting. It was white, with large ornate columns at the entrance and had a domed roof. The inside had lighter walls and well-lit rooms filled with brighter furniture than Victoria's. No bars covered the windows, and I imagined what it would be like with bright sun shining through them.

Like at Victoria's, the wood floor creaked while we walked, but at Edmond's the sound evoked senses of history and formality, not decay and darkness. The building was really more of a palace than merely a home.

Edmond led me through most of the ground floor. He took pride in showing me the priceless furniture, art, and artifacts he had collected over his long life. I politely gave him my attention knowing the twins were mere moments away.

He placed his hand on my bare back and guided me while we went from room to room. After some initial apprehension at his touch, I calmed down. I didn't fear Edmond. I felt privileged to see the ancient texts and religious icons he had on display, as well as the medieval standards he had fought under.

We walked through a dining room, toward a steel door and two guards. The guards stood aside as Edmond entered numbers into a keypad.

Overhead lights came on when Edmond opened the door, and we started down metal steps against a wall overlooking the basement. The walls were tall and lined with steel, and three coffins sat in the middle of an otherwise empty room. Judging by their size, I estimated the space was eighty or a hundred feet long, and about half that wide. The air was cool and very clean.

Wires and plastic tubes, less than an inch thick, ran from two of the coffins and went into a room with a large clear window facing us. It must have been a control center, because computers and vats of red liquid filled it.

Edmond waited at the bottom of the staircase, but I took another step forward onto the steel floor. The three coffins sat a few feet apart from each other and a few feet off the floor on small stands, hidden from view underneath them. From where we came in, the one with nothing attached to it was on the far left and looked old and wooden. The other two were identical and steel. All three had large crosses on the lids.

I turned to Edmond. "I can feel them."

"They are powerful, but they are at peace," he said.

Heaviness weighed on my mind, but it did so gently. I didn't think I could have handled it otherwise.

"What are their names?"

"Ariane is in the middle, and Caterine is on the right."

I walked to them, and the weight on my mind grew as I approached. I ran my hand over Ariane's coffin, and my reflection was perfect in its shiny steel lid. I braced for a violent reaction, but none came. They were at peace as Edmond had said.

I turned to him again, and asked, "Who's the third coffin for?"

"It is mine. The wood is from my home in Chartres," he said. "I left the twins once before, when they were sick, and I shouldn't have. I won't leave them again."

I nodded and pointed at the tubes coming from the two coffins. "And this is synthetic blood?"

"Yes, it lets them rest, finally. Without it, their hunger

would overwhelm them, and Satan would make them do terrible things. Unfortunately, it is not yet a cure."

I went back to Edmond who was still on the last step of the staircase. "Who was Vera?" I asked, looking up at him. "Her name is in my dreams, too."

Edmond's eyes met mine. "Vera was a nun who visited Caterine and Ariane and tried to help them when they were sick. She prayed for them and visited them longer than anyone else, but her prayers went unanswered."

As Edmond finished his sad tale, a measure of satisfaction washed over me, and it took a conscious effort not to smile. Not only hadn't I been Vera, but my dreams made sense, too. I still didn't know why they came to me, but at least they meant something. James's information was wrong. He didn't even have the right name for the girl in the picture.

Edmond took my hand and led me upstairs. He rode with me in his limousine and brought me back to my room a few hours before sunrise.

19

Caterine and Ariane woke me from my sleep once that day. When they did, I imagined Vera tending to the sick sisters in France. It made sense finally.

I got into my business suit and was excited to see Edmond at church the following night. I still wore the cross necklace he had given me. He sat next to Victoria as usual and smiled when he noticed me. The new vampires sat in the front row to Victoria's right and then processed out behind the priest as the Mass was ending.

The service had a lighter mood and served in large part as the end of Renatus. After it was over, I went up to Edmond. I couldn't help myself.

"I hope you slept better, with some of your questions answered?" he asked.

"I did, a little, thank you," I said.

Victoria walked between us silently. She might have glanced at me, but I could never be sure with her.

Edmond spoke again. "I have work to do, Erin, but I hope I'll see you soon. I will come by on Tuesday after work if that is okay with you."

I told him that, of course, it would be. I felt so safe with him. Being at Eure, surrounded by Spectavi, helped that feeling, but it was Edmond most of all. He had answered some of my questions, and he seemed to like me, even if I didn't really know why.

I briefly considered the possibility that Edmond had lied about Vera, but it just didn't seem reasonable. I had been introduced to at least a hundred vampires at Renatus, and none even hinted at having seen me before. It was irrational to think they were all lying.

Aside from that, Edmond's devotion to God was unquestionable. It guided his work at Eure and with the Spectavi, and he never could have done something as sinful as what had been done to me.

It was possible that James's information was not only inaccurate, but that he had fabricated it intentionally. He took a name that Edmond would know and gave it to a girl in a picture that looked like me. I had been too eager to trust James and scolded myself for it after what he had done to me. I considered myself very fortunate for how things had worked out.

I had twenty-four nights left and hoped to get to spend time with Edmond on many of them.

I met Jennifer in the cafeteria after leaving the church, and we took turns gushing about our nights while we ate. She had a great time with Mr. Roberts, as I had thought, and said she had felt like a princess in her dress at his side.

When she said it, I understood I had felt like that, too, that I had been Edmond's princess, or his young queen. It hadn't occurred to me then because the night had been unlike anything I had ever experienced. Most girls my age had already had school dances or proms when they were younger, but not me. That had been my first fancy gala. Edmond was surely king among the Spectavi, and I had owned his attention for a night.

I spent the rest of the night thinking about Edmond and the twins. When the time was right, I'd ask him if he knew how my past could have been stolen. I wasn't in a hurry to bring it up; I enjoyed thinking about the future significantly more.

Work the next night went as it always did. After the excitement of the weekend, I dreaded going back to it, but as usual, Ms. Dubois came through the doors and opened the court. I asked where she had been on Saturday, and she simply replied that she had been away on business.

Once again, I sat warm and uncomfortable while the Sanguans came and went. I hated that room, but signed each form as expected. I thought about Edmond a lot and ignored most of the proceedings in front of me until it came time for my next signature. While I wished he were meeting me that night, instead of the one after it, at least I knew when he would be.

A young-looking Sanguan that reminded me of Zhilan entered the court. She was small, had a youthful face, and ultimately a similar calm demeanor. She didn't fight while being led away.

Zhilan was supposed to be coming for me in twenty-three nights. For a while, I had worried what would happen if she failed, leaving me captive. I wondered if James or Grant would really come themselves as they had promised, and if they were even capable of it. They had been so confident in Zhilan when laying out our plan.

I started to think that I didn't want her to come. Surely if I left with her, Edmond would never trust me again.

I probably should have gone for a run after work, but went to bed early instead so that the next night would come as soon as possible. I slept well for a change, until waking up around six in the evening. Unable to sleep anymore, I went online to see what was going on in the world outside of Eure.

After quickly catching up on other news, I focused on vampires. I found plenty more Sanguan murders and searched for a court case from the night before where the Sanguan swore his innocence over and over. As expected, he had been lying.

I found another article about Todd and his software. A new picture showed Todd and the same female vampire that had been with him before, giving an interview. She had long blond hair, and her low-cut shirt didn't seem at all appropriate. There had to be something between them, and he must have left me for her.

I hated Todd so much.

Work seemed to take forever that night, but eventually it was four thirty, the last case was done, and I could leave the depressing courthouse. I signed the form and ran outside. Edmond waited there with a wide smile. I returned it with my own, and he put out his arms for a hug. I relaxed against his stone embrace.

We drove to his home and sat outside in the backyard on a blanket overlooking a small lake. It was warm, so our suit coats lay next to us. I drank a glass of wine, while Edmond had nothing, again. With only an hour before sunrise, I got a big question out of the way.

"Why do you like spending time with me? Why not one of the others who are so set on being a Spectavi one day?"

"You're not?" Edmond asked.

"Well, I don't think so. I don't know, maybe," I said, a little worried.

"It is your choice," he said. "I like you because you aren't sure what you want. I can tell you're searching for answers, and that your future is uncertain."

Good, it was my choice.

Edmond went on. "The other humans who come through here are all set in their goals and, believe me, it's a good thing. We need more leaders in our fight against the Sanguans. God needs them, and they will fight for Him.

"The others had the money or connections to get their jobs here, and most will achieve their goal of becoming a Spectavi. You applied on your own. Your background is a fine one, but it's not from the elite of society like the others.

"Erin, your strength comes from within you and is real. I look at you and can't help but see it. Most of them were born into privileged lives. I find humans like you much more interesting."

"Thanks," I said softly. No one had ever complimented me like that. Even if the details of my background were fake, the gist of it was right on. It didn't seem like the time to tell him it was a lie. I would have other chances.

Edmond leaned closer. "And I think you're very beautiful."

I must have blushed. I hoped he'd kiss me. He might have been working through a similar thought, because we were both quiet for a moment before we resumed talking.

Every few nights, I would be with Edmond for an hour before sunrise, and I spent even longer with him on Sundays. He was usually finishing up some work when we met, but once he put it down, he would give me his full attention. Some nights we talked at his home and others we watched Victoria fight and train Gavin.

Sometimes the Sanguans injured him in battle, but never her. His wounds healed before my eyes or, if they were bad, would heal before I saw him next. Edmond explained that was why Victoria always cut the heads off of her victims, or else cut their bodies completely in half.

I learned that Victoria was German, and Edmond had met her when she was one of the few women to take up arms during the Third Crusade. He described her as a great warrior even as a human and went into such fine detail that, while there didn't seem to be then, there must have been a romantic relationship between them at one point.

I visited the twins sometimes, as well. My nightmares about them were becoming more frequent, and I hoped to learn something about why by being near them. I said prayers over their coffins and imagined them resting below the steel lids. The first time Edmond left me alone with them to take a call for work, I had been nervous, but they remained peaceful. My nightmares didn't stop, but I did think the sisters were less angry and aggressive the more I prayed.

I learned more about Eure from Edmond. The massive, global company was seemingly involved in every industry imaginable. When one line of business performed poorly, whatever caused it meant another probably performed better than expected. That arrangement, combined with their hoard of cash accumulated over the centuries, meant the company was financially very stable.

Some of his colleagues would rather Eure's main office still have been in France, but after the World Wars of the last century, Edmond steadfastly defended his decision to move. He much preferred the security of being located in the United States.

The campus was unique among the company's locations. More Spectavi were made other places, but the ones that came from their headquarters would be the leaders in the company and the war. Greater numbers of people worked in more normal conditions at other Eure sites. Edmond traveled to them sometimes, but hadn't much recently. He had seen the world many times over and preferred to conduct business on video conferences when he could.

One night, I asked about the software Todd's company had developed. Edmond said he wasn't intimately involved, but expected the new software to be used in Washington,

D.C. as planned. I asked if he worried about people's privacy, and he argued that it was a small price to pay for increased safety from Sanguans.

During that discussion, I recalled Kristi's murder. If the cameras had been used that way back then, I wondered if she might still have been alive.

I cherished the safety I had found at Eure and agreed that using the cameras made sense in the city.

Another night, I asked about Francis and if Edmond had known what crime he had committed. He said he hadn't known Francis, but asked if I believed there was any way he was innocent. I didn't.

Edmond never kissed me as I hoped he would, though sometimes I thought he wanted to. Perhaps he was afraid of being tempted to bite me if he did. I assumed the synthetic blood would keep him from craving my blood, but maybe he wasn't sure. More than once, I imagined what his bite would feel like.

I also recognized that he might not have been interested in me that way. He was fifteen hundred years old, led the Spectavi, and ran a global company, and I was merely a young human. He could have been with so many other people or vampires who had more to offer him than I. If time with him was all I could get, I wouldn't complain.

I paid even less attention at work than before. I just didn't care about the Sanguans who came through the courtroom. Instead, I spent the hours thinking about my upcoming nights with Edmond and the approaching night when Zhilan was supposed to come for me.

20

In a change from the seasonally warm, humid nights, it rained lightly and was cool after work. I had two nights until Zhilan was supposed to take me away and had decided to tell Edmond the truth. If I didn't, and Zhilan came for me, I would have to explain it then anyway. If I made something up, Edmond could drink from me and discover the lie. I'd rather he hear the truth from me before it came to that.

Besides, the truth was that I had come to investigate, and to be rescued, but instead hoped to stay with him and the Spectavi. I'd also tell him about my past, finally, and ask if he could help me figure out what had happened.

For a while, I dreaded having to explain those things to Edmond, but, certain in my desire to stay, I had become excited to do so. There would be no more secrets between us.

It had been a night of particularly gruesome cases and, eager to get away from it, I stepped out onto the concrete into the rain even though Edmond's limo still approached from far down the street. I had forgotten my umbrella, but wasn't worried. Eure would dry my suit or just give me a new one. I welcomed the cooler air after being inside the courtroom all night.

Before I knew what had happened, a hand held my mouth closed, and I flashed back to Snake at Night. Like then, I tried to break free, but like then a vampire held me.

How could it be happening to me again? And how could it be happening to me at Eure?

Emotions I hadn't felt in weeks rushed to me. What would the Sanguan do? I couldn't fight back. Where would I be dragged to this time? Would my fingers be snapped like twigs again, or would it be worse?

The creature that held me brought their face near mine. I recognized Zhilan's green eyes. *Thank God.*

She pulled down her mask to reveal her face. When I relaxed after recognizing her, she let me go and stepped back. She wore a black outfit that covered her completely and held a short black sword in one of her gloved hands. Fresh blood dripped from the tip of the blade.

"Come, Erin, it's time to go."

"You're early!"

"James has been killed; Grant is in trouble. I'm sorry, I had to come now or else I might never have been able to."

I looked past Zhilan to Edmond's slowly moving limousine down on the street. He must have seen us.

I stepped back from her. "I can't go. I'm sorry."

"What?"

I shook my head. "I'm sorry. I have to stay. It's not like you said. There's nothing wrong with the Spectavi. I'm not Vera."

Zhilan grasped my arm tightly. "Erin, they're lying. You were Vera; you must believe me. They killed James! They're going to kill Grant."

She let me push her hand away. "They must have deserved it," I said plainly. Even so, Zhilan need not suffer. I couldn't go back to the life that she would take me to, but she had kept her word and come for me. "Edmond is coming. You have to go."

Her attention shifted to the arriving limousine. If Edmond had seen me talking, he had never sped up because of it. I wondered if he had called guards, or if Edmond would fight her himself.

"Edmond." She pulled her hood off her head.

He got out of the limo and stood by its rear door.

"Come here, Erin," he said calmly.

In an effort to keep the peace, I walked down the steps instead of running. I stood next to him with my briefcase at my side, and he put his arm around my shoulders. He shared my lack of concern for the drizzle that rained down on us.

We stood there watching each other, Zhilan on higher ground with her sword, and Edmond with no weapon I could see, waiting for who knows what. I had seen Victoria begin fights with no weapon, but Zhilan was no common foe if she had been able to get to me there.

Edmond turned his head to the right and, by the time mine followed, the battle was in front of me. Gavin had appeared from down the street and met Zhilan's sword with his own. He was similarly dressed, but in light gray and with no hood or mask. An alarm siren went off from somewhere behind us.

Gavin was taller than Zhilan, as most she fought must have been, and he yelled repeatedly as he swung his silver-colored sword. Those yells accompanied the sounds of their metal blades cutting through the air and colliding.

As best my human eyes could tell, Gavin attacked constantly, and Zhilan successfully repelled him. She occasionally struck out offensively, but didn't seem in a hurry to do so. Zhilan parried and moved, parried and moved, and continued over and over while her opponent came at her. And then she must have found what she had been waiting for.

She let out a loud cry, and Gavin was on the concrete below her sword, bleeding significantly from his side. Gavin's sword was on the ground and the arm that held it pinned under Zhilan's foot. He didn't move and appeared afraid as she raised her blade, holding it with both hands.

Instead of ending him, she swung to her side and was driven back against the weight of Victoria's sword. They paused to size each other up, and Gavin sped down the street with blood gushing out of him. Three silver SUVs pulled up on both sides of Edmond's limo, but the Spectavi remained inside them.

Victoria wore a dark red leather skirt and matching top that didn't cover her white midsection. As usual when she fought, her hair was in a braid behind her. She held a sword longer and brighter than any I had seen her wield in the arena. Zhilan was tiny compared to Victoria's huge frame, and concern filled the smaller vampire's eyes. I didn't want her to die, but I wasn't going to try to stop it. I feared Victoria, too.

They rushed toward each other, and Zhilan yelled occasionally as they fought. Victoria didn't, but when they stopped, I saw more determination in Victoria's eyes than her usual utter calmness. She didn't underestimate her opponent.

Zhilan was just too small, so she tried to expand the area where they fought to gain an edge. She danced around like Victoria usually did in the arena, attacking when she could.

Unfortunately for Zhilan, despite her efforts, the smaller warrior didn't have a quickness advantage over the much larger one. Victoria's powerful body and mighty sword kept up with Zhilan wherever she moved. Victoria was incredible.

Blood hit the ground, and a tear in Zhilan's clothing revealed skin on her arm. Another formed over her thigh, and she stopped, kneeling on one leg. In that position, she had to strain tremendously to repel a ferocious blow from Victoria's great sword.

Zhilan managed it, barely, and then flipped back away from Victoria and leapt up to the side of the building. She held herself there and looked down at me. Victoria remained where she had been and stood straight, holding her sword in one hand down at her side.

After a few seconds, Zhilan moved along the side of the building, then over it, and was out of sight.

Victoria walked toward Edmond, who still had his arm around me. She took her red cross from under her top and kissed it as she came close.

"You won't chase her?" I asked. I had never spoken to Victoria before.

She addressed Edmond. "The sun will rise soon." As she passed, she added, "Be careful, Edmond."

The rain didn't seem to bother her while she walked at human speed in the same direction that Gavin had gone. The SUVs drove away.

Edmond opened the limousine door, and I got in and started sliding on the leather seat toward the other end. Edmond sat down quickly, shut the door, and grabbed my thigh to keep me from moving away. I let go of my briefcase, and he pulled me closer until my leg was against his solid stone one.

"I'm so sorry," I said frantically. "I was going to tell you. I didn't want to go with her." He must have been so angry with me.

He took his hand off my leg and ran it over my damp hair. "It's all right, Erin."

With his hand there, he kissed me high on my cheek, very gently. Then he kissed lower on it, then again on the side of my chin.

I had been longing for those kisses. I didn't expect them after keeping my secrets from him, and I melted as they hit my still-wet face.

"Now I know," Edmond whispered. I closed my eyes, and he kept moving down until he kissed below the chain of the necklace he had given me. I expected him to keep going lower, but instead he next kissed near my scar.

I flinched, and he must have let me because he could have held my head perfectly still in his iron grip. My eyes remained closed.

"Don't worry," he said. "I swore I would never take another human life to feed, and I swear I won't take yours."

James had forced his bite on me, and Snake would have if he could have. But Edmond was different. He would protect me from those vampires I couldn't fight on my own. For the first time in such a savage world, I could be completely safe.

"You suffer needlessly, Erin. Let me help you be at peace," he whispered.

I leaned slightly, and he finished bringing me closer. His fangs touched my skin, with only an instant of pain.

My blood ran into his mouth, and I was no longer in the limousine, or at Eure, or in Virginia. I was nowhere. My body grew warmer until I almost couldn't stand it, and then, all pleasure. I felt my blood move inside me as he sucked it out. I couldn't sense his touch or fangs anymore and only felt my own body. From the top of my head, out to my fingers, and down to my toes, I felt more than I had ever felt in my entire life—bliss.

As he drank and I got even hotter, a vast array of joyous emotions flowed through me, each singularly exquisite. I strove to recognize them all, in order to experience them fully, but then, in a moment of spectacular delight, they merged and became indistinguishable from one another as the glorious sum of all the emotion.

It might have gone on for a few seconds, or it might have been a minute or more, I didn't know. Time didn't matter, except that I wanted the feelings to go on.

Then I had returned to the limousine. My body was still very hot, and Edmond held me.

"You were not Vera," he said. "You were not that girl in the photograph."

I knew it. And Edmond knew my mind completely. He knew all that I could remember, including the Sanguans I had plotted with. He knew my dreams about the twins, and all my fears and how my past had been taken from me.

I moved my head against his chest, and he held me there. I cried. Edmond understood the pain and emptiness thrust upon me by some monster.

He knew my anguish when Kristi had been murdered, and when Todd left me. He had learned how much I feared the world of vampires outside Eure's campus.

"I will find out what I can about what happened to you, Erin."

I had a vague sense of time again, and he held me for minutes before he spoke to the driver through an intercom and we drove away.

When we reached my building, Edmond said, "It's nearly dawn, and you need rest."

He opened his arms, and I leaned back from him. I made myself stop crying and, when facing away from him, wiped my nose with my suit sleeve. After opening the door, I turned back and did my best to smile, but must have still been a mess.

"I'll see you after work," he said.

I reluctantly shut the door and went inside.

I composed myself on the way to my room and realized I had become very tired. I felt weak, too. My briefcase was heavier than it should have been.

Once in my room, I took off my wet clothes, put them in the basket, and saw myself in the bathroom mirror. Blood ran down from the black cross on my neck, and I should have been upset. The girl that stared back at me should have been furious to have had her scar opened once again, but I wasn't. I felt right, finally. My unrelenting fear and anger and pain had been vanquished by Edmond's bite, and it felt so right.

I washed off the blood, got dressed, and got into bed.

I wished Edmond were there with me. He had been correct; aside from that wish, I was at peace.

21

It took me longer than normal to get ready the next night. Even though I had slept soundly for one of the few times in weeks, and for almost fourteen hours, I moved very slowly.

I skipped the cafeteria, but still didn't get to the courthouse until after nine for the first time. Thankfully, it was in time for Ms. Dubois's arrival.

I sat down in the courtroom, Ms. Dubois took her seat and handed me the paperwork for the night. She squinted at me. "What's that on your neck, Erin?"

My hand went to my tattoo. The bite must still have been red.

"It, um…" I stammered. What could I say?

Ms. Dubois was stern. "William is trying to clean that up for you, I'm assuming? It can be very challenging to remove a scar like that."

"Yes… Yes, he is. He just started," I said.

She nodded. "Good, then. I hope he is successful."

Did she know what had happened and was trying to help me? It didn't sound like her. She had never done anything nice for me. But she had never been especially mean either, not really. She just asked me to do my work, be on time, and look professional.

Perhaps she honestly believed what she had said about William helping me.

I uncovered my cross and stared at the two dots of blood on my hand.

The first Sanguan came through the door. I wiped my hand on my skirt and turned to listen to the judge.

The first few cases kept my attention, but once the adrenaline from the tense moment with Ms. Dubois wore off, my own thoughts distracted me.

I had let Edmond bite me and had even wanted him to.

I had really liked Todd and would have moved away with him, but it was only a hope that we could have had a normal life together. Having seen what I had seen, all the horrible things the Sanguans did and the lives they destroyed, it had been a foolish hope. Even if Todd hadn't left me, he couldn't have kept us safe from them. And he claimed not to know me anymore.

But Edmond did. He knew me completely, and I was safe with him.

The courtroom didn't feel as warm after what I had felt with Edmond and, with that thought, I became even more eager for work to end.

Outside the courthouse, Edmond took my hand and held it while we rode in the limousine to his home. We smiled at each other, but didn't talk. Surely we both looked forward to the same thing.

He led me up a staircase in his house that I had never been up before and into a dimly lit room with a large wooden bed that was covered in white. A large cross that matched the wood of the bed hung opposite it on the wall. A small lamp on the far side of the bed provided the light.

Edmond sat on the bed, and I sat beside him on the thick comforter. He pulled my suit coat off while I slid my arms out of the sleeves. He placed it next to me, then took off his coat and laid it on top. He loosened his tie, added it to our pile, and opened the top button of his shirt.

Edmond reached behind me and undid my hair and, when it fell, he moved it so it hung over the front of my left shoulder. He brought his mouth to the other side of my neck.

His fangs sunk into the still-fresh wound, and there was no pain at all before the joy and heat grew in unison, more slowly than before. I opened my mouth to make a sound— but don't remember hearing anything if one came out. The feelings of my body commanded my full attention. I could feel everything, everywhere and, when it seemed impossible, somehow I felt more.

Since we had parted the night before, I had yearned to be with him again, and finally, I was. It was really happening. Then I couldn't form such complete thoughts as my mind became overwhelmed with pleasure. He slowly drank and drank, and I grew hotter and hotter. The feelings and emotions started pouring out into my body from deeper within me in waves at the same slow pace. One crashed through me, and then another, moments later.

It went on and on, from deeper and deeper. Wave after wave hit me.

And then he was done.

I opened my eyes. He lay on the bed face up, and I rested on his rock-hard chest with his heavy arm around me. I was sweating all over, making it hard to be certain, but his body also seemed warm. His shirt was soaked where I lay, so I started to move away, but he stopped me. He could move me as he pleased, yet he always did so gently. I would never resist him anyway.

My right shoe had fallen off, so I used that foot to get my left off, as I closed my eyes and put my head back down. I was so tired of the constant, hopeless search for my past. With Edmond, I wouldn't have to be alone in the Sanguan-infested world any longer.

Our bodies cooled down for a few minutes, until I picked up my head, and asked, "Why do you drink from me?" The question had interrupted my tranquility when it came to me.

"Do you not enjoy it?" he asked.

"Yes, I do. But why don't you drink synthetic blood like your followers?"

"I don't have to feed often like most of them do, and I have learned to control the demon inside me. I know I won't take your life." He paused before going on. "When I drink from you, I can feel your suffering, your happiness, your hope, and your frailty. It reminds me of when I was human long ago."

I pulled myself up his body and moved my neck toward him. For what he had given me, I wanted to give him what he sought in return. His fangs were inside me again, and my body grew hot. The first drops of blood left me, and I became lost in ecstasy.

I sat very still most of the time at work after that. The temperature in the room didn't bother me, nor did my chair. It took me longer to fill out the forms than it used to. Edmond drinking from me each night was making me weak and tired, but I didn't care.

I never had the energy to go to the gym and went to the cafeteria when no one else would be there. I had my lie about the fresh bite mark on my neck, but didn't want to have to come up with more lies about my health as well. I didn't eat much anymore, anyway.

Chitchat with Jennifer didn't interest me, and I stopped meeting her at the door before work. She was very pleasant; she just wasn't important to me. Plus, she had Mr. Roberts.

I had Edmond, and all I thought about was being with him.

We spent the next few nights in the same bedroom, and then we moved to other places in his home. He had a room full of old Bibles on display. There was a study with priceless paintings, including a van Gogh. He even brought me to his office one night.

"That's a great view," I said, looking over his desk through a window out to the lake behind his home. The office setup was fairly typical, aside from the big screens for video conferencing on the wall across from the large wooden desk.

A low bookshelf was against another wall. Edmond had a big leather chair behind the desk, and two chairs in front of it. Edmond sat down in the big chair.

"Come here, please, Erin."

I couldn't fit next to him in the chair, so I slid onto his lap, and he held me there. I moved my hair to my left side and, before I had even finished, my body started getting very warm, very fast.

We only had an hour each night after work, but the following Sunday was a muggy, clear night, and we spent the entire time after Mass lying outside together near the lake. Initially, the grass bothered me, and there were bugs, but after Edmond drank from me the first time, none of that mattered.

While we stared up at the stars for hours, he drank from me briefly, over and over. It was always incredible, yet the experience seemed somehow different each time.

We watched Victoria, Gavin, and other Spectavi fight some nights. I saw many great Spectavi warriors, though none seemed a match for Victoria.

Edmond had clothes brought to his house for me to change into when we went to the arena. I relished the feeling of blue jeans the first time I wore them, and Edmond said he didn't mind me wearing them, even on nights when his business associates watched with us.

Victoria constantly instructed Gavin and occasionally stepped in to ensure he wouldn't be hurt permanently.

"No, no, no," I heard, as Edmond pulled his fangs out of me one night. The words came from a vampire sitting beside him, whose name I hadn't caught.

Gavin stumbled away from a Sanguan. I couldn't tell what had happened to him.

"He fights like a child, Edmond!" the same vampire said.

"Victoria will straighten him out," Edmond replied. "Don't worry."

"Well, while he bleeds for a while, what do you think about the launch strategy?" I wasn't sure what the other vampire referred to.

"It's good, but not great. I think as it stands it'll sell, but you can do better," Edmond said.

Victoria finished off the Sanguan in the arena.

"That's it! That would be much better," Edmond said.

But that didn't make any sense. What would be much better? What had I missed?

I never took part in the conversations and had trouble keeping up with Edmond's business or the action of the fights after he drank from me.

While we were alone together, we mostly talked about all that Edmond had seen and done over the centuries—the kings, the queens, and the popes he had known, as well as the battles he had fought with both humans and vampires. While France and Europe were his favorite topics, he had plenty to say about the rest of the world.

I had so few memories, yet for the last fifteen hundred years, he had lived through the great events of the world, and had even played a role in many of them. I loved to listen to him after he drank from me, and he seemed to enjoy telling the stories.

I no longer had nightmares about the twins, and it was a relief to sleep soundly each night. Regardless, I visited them often and prayed over their coffins as Vera had centuries before. Some nights Edmond joined me, and some nights he left me alone with them.

I was thrilled when Edmond closed the courts to take me to events on behalf of Eure or the Spectavi. He gave me elegant dresses and exquisite jewelry to wear. I wore more diamonds and gems than I had ever even seen before, and felt like a princess at his side on those nights.

One night, we went to a theater where vampires danced and did acrobatics right at the limit of what the human eye could discern. After being unable to make out most details of the battles I had witnessed, it was captivating to see the creatures moving much faster than humans, but slow enough to comprehend.

"That was wonderful, Edmond." I clapped at the end of the show.

"Yes, they are the best," Edmond said. "Would you like to meet the performers?"

"Oh, yes, please."

We walked down from our balcony seats to the backstage area.

"Timothy, this is Erin," Edmond said to one of the lead vampires.

Edmond had given me a long pink gown and a diamond choker to cover my bite mark. Timothy kissed my hand over my white glove. "Erin, it's a pleasure to meet you. What brilliant diamonds." He was a very handsome vampire. "Edmond, she's lovely."

"Erin, do you have any questions for Timothy about the performance?" Edmond asked.

I did. I wondered if it was hard to slow down for human eyes, or if it came naturally to him, but it felt rude to ask. Instead, all I said was, "No, thank you."

It was so exciting to meet the performers, even though I couldn't bring myself to say much while we did.

Edmond took me to a dinner in honor of a woman whose husband had been killed by a Sanguan. She and her family had fought off the vampire and eventually identified him so he could be arrested. I remembered the case from court. The Sanguan had maintained his innocence, even while clawing at the floor to resist being dragged away.

Edmond spoke from the podium in front of the room, "We're winning, and we're winning because of the close cooperation with the Spectavi that this administration has pushed for."

Everyone in the room clapped, including the Vice President of the United States.

Edmond continued, "Sanguan criminals are being wiped out faster than ever before. Their numbers are dwindling and closer cooperation with the federal government will ensure that even the most powerful Sanguans won't be able to hide from us. Our cities will be safe again."

People stood and clapped, and I joined them. Edmond stood confidently at the podium. His speech was done.

When we sat back down, I smiled politely at the human couples at my table, like I always did with them. Inside, however, I pitied them because their lives together were so very fragile. Just as had happened to the woman we were honoring, every night they could be attacked and have the one they loved taken from them, or be killed themselves. Most would be powerless to fight back, and their lives would be ruined.

But I had Edmond, and other people at the dinner had their own Spectavi at their sides. It was the only sensible way to survive as a human.

Edmond hadn't uncovered anything about my past, either who I had been or how it was done. He agreed that a powerful vampire probably had something to do with it, but cautioned that plenty around the world fit that vague description. It was good he investigated for me, but I didn't even think about it most nights.

22

I loved the walk up the staircase to the white bedroom in Edmond's home. Edmond always led me up the stairs slowly, even though we were both so eager to get to the top. Sitting on the soft bed was like sitting in a cloud.

I loved to listen to Edmond explain the history of everything in each room where he drank from me. It was fascinating and relaxing at the same time.

I loved seeing moonlight reflect on the lake and then watching the water change color as the sky started to glow with dawn's light.

I loved going to Mass even more than before. The glorious services in the wondrous cathedral served as perfect preludes to the long nights I shared with Edmond.

I loved how the platinum cross Edmond had given me looked on my neck next to my black one.

The night before at Mass, I had gazed at the crucifix that hung from the ceiling and thanked God for my newfound peace and for Edmond.

"Erin!" a familiar voice called out, as guards led a Sanguan into the courtroom.

It had been about a month or two since Zhilan's rescue attempt, but I wasn't sure exactly. The nights flew by with Edmond. Grant's yell woke me from my newly typical courtroom trance.

"Erin!" Grant called again, as his weakened body fought against his silver shackles.

"This is a lie, Erin. I didn't do it." Zhilan had said he was on the run.

The form in front of me read:

Name: Grant Larsen
Age: 33
Type: Sanguan
Crime: Murder. A husband, wife, and their two children in their home
Date: August 3
Time: 10:30 PM
Location: 538 Dale St. Annapolis, MD

The ring locked him to the floor below the chair.

The judge said, "Grant Larsen, you are accused of killing a family in their home in Maryland. How do you plead?"

"Not guilty," Grant said. "Erin, I didn't do this! You know me. Please!"

"You will address me only," the judge said calmly.

I didn't enjoy seeing him like that, but he was guilty like all the rest.

"On what grounds do you plead not guilty?"

Grant looked up at the judge. "I don't kill humans when

I drink! I swear it! I didn't kill those people. Like you, I believe humanity deserves to be free from vampire rule." The judge didn't react, and Grant turned to me. I stared straight back at him with my pen to the form on my desk.

"Grant Larsen, you are found guilty of this crime against humanity, and you are sentenced to death, to be carried out within one week's time."

The device in the floor unlocked, and the Spectavi led Grant away. He resisted even more on the way out. He turned back, and yelled, "Erin, they killed James. They're after Zhilan. They hunt us for crimes we haven't committed!" And then he was gone.

Of course he had done it. Perhaps the demonic force within him drove him out of control, but he had committed that terrible crime. I thanked God it hadn't been me who had fallen victim to one of Grant's cravings, then signed his form and gave it to the guard.

"Grant is guilty, you know. James was, too," Edmond said that night, after he drank from me. My bare chest rested against his while we cooled down.

"I know," I said, without moving.

I lay in my bed later, at peace and about to sleep soundly once again, when Edmond's words came to mind.

Of course, Grant was guilty. All of the Sanguans were. Why had Edmond gone out of his way to point that one out?

It was nothing.

But it had woken me, and my mind began to turn. What were the details of his crime? A family in Maryland? Annapolis was it?

I took my laptop to bed. I had stopped searching for the details of those who claimed their innocence and knew what searching for Grant's would lead to, but maybe I owed him that much. After all, his offer to help me had eventually led me to Edmond.

There it was, a whole page of search results, like always. Grant had murdered a husband, wife, and their two children in their home. Their neighbors heard the commotion, called the police, and the Spectavi captured him.

I put my laptop back, returned to bed, and closed my eyes. My thoughts drifted to Edmond at my neck.

My eyes opened again. What was it? I had seen the proof, and Grant was guilty, just like the rest.

I pictured the screen in my mind:

...a husband, wife, and their two children in their home. Their neighbors heard the commotion, called the police, and the Spectavi captured him.

The language in the news article sounded familiar. They all did, actually. The murders were all similar, and the same websites reported on them each time, so it made sense.

I got up and opened my laptop again.

The article about Grant's murder remained open. I read the sentence over and over.

...a husband, wife, and their two children in their home. Their neighbors heard the commotion, called the police, and the Spectavi captured him.

I must have read it fifty times before copying it in its entirety and pasting the whole thing into the search engine. Pages of results came back. I clicked on the first link, scanned the text, and found:

Craig White murdered a husband, wife, and their two children in their home. Their neighbors heard the commotion, called the police, and the Spectavi captured him.

It matched exactly. My mind picked up steam and started to move with a little more energy than it had in a long time.

I took the entire paragraph after Grant's name, and it matched the same article about Craig White. I placed the two side by side and saw that the articles were almost complete copies, word for word, except for the Sanguans' names, the victims' names, and the date and time of the murders. The street addresses and the names of the witnesses were identical.

The exact same crime, in the exact same home?

My God, Grant might not have been lying. He might not be guilty.

My mind raced to recall other names from that night, but failed because I had been paying so little attention. Some first names came to me, but I couldn't come up with the matching last names. Of course, I knew where my mind had wandered instead of paying attention.

Frustrated, I stopped trying to think of names. When I did, a new idea came to me.

I went into my history of visited websites. I found a long gap of very little activity for most of the last two months, but before that, a very long list. I had been much more diligent when I first arrived.

From one of the old articles, I took a chunk of text and searched. Once again, results appeared and I compared two articles from the same source. Once again, they matched except for the names, date, and time. Again, the addresses and the witnesses' names and statements were identical.

I searched and searched and most of the cases came back the same way. In a few instances, three or four articles were obvious copies.

It would have been impossible for every one of those families to have been replaced with another of the exact same size, that was subsequently murdered in exactly the same way, and then for the witness statements to be the same, too. There was just no way.

The Sanguans in those cases had passionately claimed their innocence in front of the judge. Some had gone on at length about lives that included the arts, history, and simply experiencing all that the world had to offer. The charges were complete fabrications, they had said, and many claimed never to kill when they drank, just like Grant, James, and Zhilan.

Regardless, the judge had found them all guilty, and I had signed off on them. Yet it seemed like I shouldn't have. The Sanguans hadn't been lying.

I had been lied to. The court was a lie.

Oh, my God.

Oh, my God, oh, my God, oh, my God. I thought it again and again.

I could see Grant in court when he pleaded with me to believe him. Grant didn't crave families; that should have been my first clue. He was innocent of that crime, but would be killed for it regardless.

I remembered when Grant had told me about Francis, the historian who had made him a vampire. I replayed it in my mind and heard the love in Grant's voice and saw it on his face when he spoke of how Francis had saved him and shown him a new life. I felt his heartache when he spoke of Francis' murder.

I recalled the truth in Zhilan's eyes when she told me that James had been unjustly killed, and that she had come to rescue me while there was still time.

But I wouldn't believe her, and that time had passed.

Beyond her reach, Edmond was lying to me. Ms. Dubois and the judge had to be, as well. Did Victoria know? Probably. But most importantly, Edmond, my king among vampires and my protector from the cruel world, lied to me every night we spent together. Only an hour earlier, he had made a point to reinforce Grant's guilt.

What else had he been lying about? Had he taken Todd from me and made him forget me somehow?

What about Vera? He could have lied about her and that might really have been her in that photo. Yet no one recognized me as her, and no one knew her.

But perhaps that was the connection. Maybe Edmond had not only taken my past, but somehow made the Spectavi forget me.

Oh, my God.

It started to add up, even if I wasn't all the way there. It could have all been connected. Grant, James, and Zhilan were sure I had been Vera. They might have been right all along.

I pictured the photo. Edmond was a monster—worse than the monsters I had feared before. Tears welled up, but I held them back. The realizations were crushing, but deep inside I sensed I had cried too much at Edmond's expense already.

One day, Todd came home and had forgotten me; it hadn't made any sense. But maybe it was Edmond's doing and Todd really hadn't acted rationally. Edmond's words explained Todd's actions, but if the news stories that backed them up weren't true, Todd could have actually been a victim, and so could Mr. Oliver and his wife.

I could have been with Todd right then, starting a new life, but Edmond wouldn't allow it.

And what about the twins? I had stopped dreaming about them since Edmond had started drinking from me. They had been reaching out to me, calling me both Erin and Vera. They knew both names, so they must have known some secret.

Then Edmond had silenced them.

What if Caterine and Ariane weren't as evil as Edmond had said? They didn't look it in my dreams. James had said the Devil tricked them, but Edmond was the one who said they'd sought out the Devil. What if Edmond had lied, and the sisters were innocent?

Perhaps Edmond feared them, but couldn't kill them, so

he had captured them and held them as prisoners in his own home.

That was a lot of guessing about the twins, but they surely knew the name Vera.

I wanted to confront Edmond, call him a liar, and tell him I had figured out what he had done to me. But then what? Would he lie again with his twisted tongue to try to convince me I was wrong? More likely, he'd kill me or erase my memory again. No, I couldn't confront Edmond.

Sharing the discovery outside Eure seemed sensible, but I had no phone, and online communications would be intercepted before getting anywhere, or at least give me away. I would be left at Edmond's mercy.

I pictured the twins, trapped in their steel coffins. Nobody knew they were at Eure, or even alive for that matter. But I did. I had a pretty good idea about how to wake them, too, and then they could finally tell me about Vera.

I had to do it after work the next night. If Edmond fed off me again, he'd know the truths I had learned, and my plans, and he could do with me as he pleased. Even if he hadn't personally erased my memory, he must know who had and why.

The thought of Edmond taking my life away was unbearable, even if I wouldn't remember it. I couldn't start over again.

Recalling Edmond feeding from me made me nauseous. I couldn't deny the pleasure, but it had all been born from lies, deceit, and worse. If I had been Vera, he had fed from me before. He took my very sense of being away somehow, and I had come back to him so he could feed again. I did it unknowingly, but I hated the thought regardless.

A strong sense of embarrassment grew within me. My weakness had allowed Edmond to possess me.

I felt so ashamed and didn't know if I could have dealt with it except that my mind had started to clear. Pieces of a puzzle I had convinced myself didn't exist were finally coming together.

Vera's true story was a vital piece. Caterine and Ariane had to know it, and I had to free them so I would too.

23

I couldn't sleep thinking about all the wrongs Edmond had surely committed, and all the others he might have. While the hours slowly passed in my little room, I became enraged when considering what he had done to me as Vera, and how he had taken me back as if nothing had happened. I felt intensely humiliated to have let him. While still not completely certain, I finally came to grips with the fact that I had probably been Vera.

At times, I sat in the darkness and imagined seeing the sun. Edmond had locked me in the reality he had created at Eure, and I hadn't seen it in months. I hadn't even thought about it since he started drinking from me, but it shone overhead, waiting to warm my skin, if only I could run out to it.

Over the course of the day, I searched repeatedly for matching articles detailing Sanguan crimes. I had to confirm my conclusions about Edmond's lies. With each search came more damning evidence.

The police and the Government didn't know, didn't care, or they couldn't stop Edmond from doing as he pleased. I had no idea which, but neither of them could help me where I was.

I thought about the twins, as well. If I could have dreamt about them, I might have tried harder to sleep. Caterine and Ariane must still have been calling to me for help, and I preferred those nightmares to silence born from Edmond's deceit.

I asked God why circumstances had led me back to Edmond, and once again, why all the terrible things in my life had happened. I grew furious with Him and didn't understand Him at all.

Eventually, it occurred to me that Vera might have earned the sentence, and I was left serving it. If true, it was cruel, but maybe she had been, too.

In spite of my conflicted feelings toward God, I couldn't turn my back on Him—as before, He was all I had. I prayed that He would forgive me for being blind to Edmond's nefarious ways for so long, and that somehow I would live through the night.

In brief moments of calm, I reassured myself I was doing the right thing. While not certain of everything I had put together, there was no more time to wait and investigate further. I couldn't live with myself if I did nothing, so freeing the twins was my only choice.

When the lights came on at seven thirty, I had already dressed in my business suit and sat at my small table wide-awake. A finished stem of grapes, an empty cereal box, and my closed laptop sat in front of me. I had stopped searching hours before.

I wanted to leave the necklace Edmond had given me behind. Pure as it appeared, it was rotten, and I didn't want it near my own cross any longer. Unfortunately, Edmond would notice, so I would have to wear it for one more night.

I picked up my briefcase, glanced at the cross on the wall, and left my room. I marched to the cafeteria to get a big breakfast and snacks for later. It would be much more than I normally ate, especially recently, but might help get some energy back in my body.

Jennifer was eating and saw me walk by with my food. "Erin! You're up early today."

I had hoped to avoid other people and stay focused on my new path. I didn't want any distractions. But intentionally brushing her off could raise suspicions, and maybe I shouldn't anyway. Perhaps I could warn her somehow. She was such a sweet girl and had been nothing but nice to me. I sat down across from her.

"I was just up," I said.

"I haven't seen you in so long," she replied.

"I've been busy, I guess."

"Busy seeing Edmond?"

"Well, yes." I faked the tiniest smile.

"It must be so wonderful," she said.

"It's complicated; he's a complicated vampire."

"What do you mean?"

What could I tell her? "Edmond loves God very much and wants to do His will. But he has to make hard choices as the leader of the Spectavi. I don't agree with all of them." I hadn't had that line of reasoning before. It sounded almost understandable until I remembered the gravity of his crimes. It wasn't an occasional innocent victim of war; he had killed hundreds, if not thousands, of Sanguans unjustly. He had destroyed my life, and who knew the real story of the twins?

"But you love him, don't you? I love Mr. Roberts." Jennifer appeared to be so happy.

I failed to smile that time. "Of course."

"Good! Well, I have to get ready for work. Hopefully I'll see you soon." She got up to leave.

I noticed the bracelet from Mr. Roberts on her wrist. "Jennifer," I said, and she stopped. "You seem so happy here, living your dream." I took a second to find the right words. "Just remember to be strong, be smart, and be yourself. Whether you become a vampire or stay a human, don't give up your individuality for anyone."

She looked confused. "I won't." She walked away.

I checked my watch and got to eating. The knife on my tray was the same as the blunt one I had stolen from my room, so I stuck with the one already in my briefcase. It wasn't much, but it would do what I needed it to later that night.

––––––––––––––

I got to the courtroom and sat down outside the big doors as usual. As soon as I let go of my briefcase, Ms. Dubois came through the doors. It wasn't the night to be late, and I had just made it. Sweat covered me before I reached the uncomfortable wooden chair, and I didn't expect to cool down at all.

It was hard for me to sign the forms. All of the vampires pleaded not guilty, and I couldn't trust myself to know which meant it and which didn't. I wouldn't judge them as I had in my mind before.

Many were guilty, and they were truly fiendish creatures, but at least some weren't. Some followed society's laws and drank from humans consensually.

Then there were those like Grant who, while innocent of the charges they faced, were guilty of forcing their bite on unwilling people. The thought remained unsettling, but no longer disgusted me as it had. Compared to murderous Sanguans, Grant's crimes seemed trivial. I came to the same conclusion comparing him to Edmond. With all the vampires Edmond had killed unjustly and what he had done to me, Edmond was far worse than Grant.

James seemed deserving of a similar opinion, even considering he had drunk from me. He had always acted logically and had shown the discipline he claimed to possess by stopping before taking my life. I felt bad about losing my faith in James, but understood that my faith wouldn't have kept him alive and leaving with Zhilan wouldn't have led to the opportunity to finally learn some of Edmond's secrets.

I also didn't believe Spectavi corruption ended with their leader. At least a few more had to be involved and possibly many, many more. It scared me—especially considering Grant's admitted lack of control in picking prey—but it seemed correct to conclude that there was much more to fear in the depraved world than Sanguans like Grant, James, and Zhilan.

I would have tried to save Grant if it were possible. Since it wasn't, I took solace in the hope that, just as Grant had wished for something good to come of Francis's death, something good would come of his own.

Sitting in court over the long night, it was very difficult to sign off on the Sanguans who passionately claimed to be innocent of their charges. They told stories of peaceful lives that I had been blinded to in the past, only thinking of the gruesome murders on the paper at my desk. I looked out at them with sympathetic eyes for the first time. Grant had been right there, and I wished at least he had seen those more sympathetic eyes before they took him away.

Form after form, I forced myself to sign. It was one more night's worth, and it would be the last night's worth.

I ate an apple during one break, and raisins and more dry cereal during another. I couldn't tell if it helped, but figured it couldn't hurt. As the night went on, I considered my warning to Jennifer. My fog had lifted, leaving the knowledge that, over the last few months, Edmond had driven me to become feeble and subservient.

He had me placed in the hot, depressing courtroom to watch case after case, hour after hour, night after night. I tried to stay objective at first, but didn't know how anyone could have resisted being overwhelmed by the evil constantly presented in that place.

Somehow though, I should have found the strength to do precisely that.

Edmond seemed so wise, offering answers to all of my questions, and an escape from my dreaded loneliness. But in truth, those answers and my loneliness had been his strings, used to pull me as he pleased, because he was a puppet master, with me as his puppet.

He dressed me in elegant gowns and fine jewelry. We went to dinners, shows, and exclusive parties. It had been like something out of a fairytale, and I had lapped it all up. All of a sudden, I wondered if I had worn those dresses before, when I had been Vera. He always seemed to have a new one for me to wear that fit just right.

Ahh! I wanted to scream out into the courtroom. I had acted like such a fool!

Rage built inside me, and I struggled to sit still while counting down the minutes until four thirty.

If I had been Vera, what happened to me then was not my fault. It had happened before I was Erin Rose. I couldn't have saved Kristi, and if Todd had been taken from me, it was likely Edmond's doing. But I had let myself become weak and dependent on Edmond. I hung on his arm and hardly spoke while he dragged me from event to event. I went to him every night without fail and without question.

I submitted to his bite. It was literally inhuman, it felt so good. And it did give me peace, but it had done so by dulling my senses to everything else around me. I went to him for more each time as if going back for some drug I couldn't live without. He had gotten me hooked, but I should never have let him in the first place.

I wondered how long he would have kept me like that, under his control. Would he have let me stay his puppet for years or for a lifetime? Could he have made me a vampire and controlled me for many lifetimes?

I was furious at myself, but determined to let that anger drive me.

Finally, the last Sanguan was found guilty, and the judge's gavel brought me back to what lay in front of me. The vampire sulked out of the room, and I signed my last form. I left the blue and black pens, said goodbye to Ms. Dubois, took my briefcase, and walked out to meet Edmond. It was a warm, humid night with a clear sky and no breeze. We were going to watch Victoria fight.

Edmond's limousine stopped, and I got in. He looked up from a tablet computer and ran his fingers through the loose end of my ponytail. I smiled. I had to get away from him before he bit me again.

"Do you mind if we stop at your house so I can change out of this suit?" I asked.

"Of course." He told the driver we would be stopping and returned to reading his tablet.

It was going to work. I experienced a new nervousness. There wasn't much else to the plan, and it would work.

Soon I could know so many truths, but soon I might be found out and killed, possibly even before getting any answers at all. I forced myself to stay calm.

We stopped in front of Edmond's palatial home. I grabbed my briefcase and opened the limo door.

Edmond glanced up from his reading. "Don't be long."

"I won't." He had given me an excuse to run from the limo.

Inside, I went straight for the basement door. The two guards were there as always and, as always, I didn't talk to them.

1-1-9-4-1-2-5-0, I entered the combination I had seen Edmond enter so many times before—the starting and ending years of the construction of his cathedral in France. Edmond's trust that he had complete control over me was going to be his undoing.

The door closed behind me, and I walked down the metal stairs. The room was cool, and the three coffins were arranged as always: Edmond's, then Ariane's and Caterine's.

I stepped off the last stair, and the twins' power weighed on my mind. Soon they would be free. I wondered how they would react and if I would still dream about them. I considered the possibility that Edmond had told the truth about them. What would such evil be like in the world outside his basement?

But Edmond had become all lies to me.

I neared the coffins and heard my shoes against the steel floor over the hum of the machines that pumped blood to and from the bodies. The first time Edmond had left me alone with the twins, I had been scared, but that was a different fear. I had never paid so much attention to the sounds I made down there.

I reached into my briefcase and moved a red apple aside to find the small knife. I put the briefcase down and stood over the coffins with the knife in my hand.

A few tubes ran to each coffin, along with other cords and cables. Two tubes from each were blood red—one in and one out, presumably.

Who first? Did it matter?

I brought the knife to one of the red tubes coming from Ariane. *Please, God, forgive me for what I am about to do if I'm wrong.*

I held the plastic tube tight with my left hand and, with my right, pushed the knife against it. It moved slowly at first, but the knife made progress, and then slid through the rest of the tube more easily. Blood poured out onto me and the floor.

My heart racing, I cut the other red tube, and then Caterine's tubes the same way. I dropped the knife and pulled the cables and cords from each coffin with both hands. I took a few steps back and wiped the synthetic blood from my hands onto my already stained clothes. A thin pool of it had formed below me, but had stopped growing. I didn't want to be far from the coffins, so I stood there in the blood.

I kept standing there because I didn't know what to do next. That was as far as my plan had gone. With the machines off, there was no sound except my breathing.

I checked my watch repeatedly, as well as the door above me. Minutes passed and nothing happened. I debated trying to open the coffins, but was afraid.

Three minutes.

The room remained still. What if this had been a bad idea? I couldn't undo it at that point. And what if my conclusions were wrong about Edmond? I knew what I had seen when I searched online, but maybe there was another explanation. I shifted my shoes in the puddle of fake blood.

Five minutes.

I said another prayer that I had made the right choice. I checked the door again and wondered if I had given the plan enough thought. Edmond would surely come looking for me eventually. How long until he did?

Six minutes.

Maybe I had to do something more to wake them. I walked to Ariane's coffin and put my hand on its shiny lid like I had many times before. I slid my fingers along the edge. *Thunk*—something moved against the wall of the coffin.

Edmond burst through the door at the top of the staircase. He jumped down and lifted me by my shoulders to push me against the far wall.

"What have you done?" he screamed. He shouted to the guards standing at the top of the staircase, "Get William! Get Victoria!"

An alarm sounded upstairs.

"You lied to me!" I screamed back. "You lied about it all!"

I expected him to slam me against the steel wall, but instead he let me go and took a small step back.

"I love you," Edmond pleaded. "And I loved you then. I did it because I loved you!"

"I *was* Vera! You're a monster!"

"They drove you mad, Vera!" He pointed at the coffins. "You tried to help them with different mixtures of synthetic blood, but you couldn't. They wouldn't leave you alone, and you kept trying, but nothing worked. Sometimes it hurt them, and they lashed out at your mind. You wouldn't let me help you find peace from them."

"I wouldn't let you feed off me anymore, so you erased what I knew and who I was, then you sent me away?"

"You wouldn't become a vampire, and I wouldn't force you to. I loved the human that you were. But I couldn't stand seeing you in pain. Caterine and Ariane are my curse to bear; they should never have been yours. I wanted you to have a chance at a normal life, so I did what I did."

How could he have loved me and done that to me?

The alarm continued to sound while Edmond turned to the coffins and then back to me. "When you came back to me, I thought it was a gift from God. I thought we'd been given a second chance together, and you were at peace with me here this time, Vera. Why did you do this?"

"To know the truth! The courts are a lie, and I had to know what else was."

"The Sanguans? You know what they've done, the damnable creatures that they are. They would enslave humanity if I didn't stop them!"

"Some, maybe, but not all. Some want to live in peace. And some didn't choose to become vampires. It's not for you to judge them as you see fit." When I said that, I understood more clearly what Edmond had made himself into. "You're not God."

I gasped as Ariane's coffin lid opened, and her white arm appeared. Edmond turned around and held me back with one arm. Caterine lifted her lid. The twins sat up, rolled their necks, then pulled tubes out of their opposite wrists. Fresh skin filled in the holes the tubes had gone into.

They leapt out of their coffins and toward us. Edmond

moved forward to keep more space between them and me.

The twins appeared as they had in my dreams. Each was dressed in a white sheet with a gold band holding it close to their waist. Their skin looked almost pure white, like Edmond's, and they stood nearly as tall as him. They were thin, and I wouldn't have been able to tell them apart except that Ariane's long blond hair was a few inches shorter. They both smiled, and I stared at two beautiful angels.

"Don't hurt her, my sisters, please," Edmond said.

They were his sisters?

"Vera? No, why would we hurt Vera, who finally set us free?" Caterine looked at me. "Or are you Erin now? Which do you prefer?"

I didn't answer. Her eyes were bright red, like her sister's. Their smiles faded, and I didn't think they were angels anymore.

"How long were you going to keep us locked up here, Edmond?" Caterine asked.

"As long as it took to help you, to heal you from what Satan did to you," Edmond said.

Ariane spoke for the first time. "Satan? I don't think so. It was his gift, yes, but our brother did this, Edmond, you know that. But we are glad he did; you know that, too."

Edmond shook his head. "You wouldn't say that if you were yourselves. Nicolas did it out of his love for you, but he made mistakes." Edmond looked up and yelled, "God, why do you not forgive him and end this?"

Ariane appeared angry. "Love? Like what you did to Vera out of love? It wasn't *love* that drove you or Nicolas to do what you've done."

Caterine added calmly, "Don't you see, Edmond? If God could end this, he would have by now."

"You can't end it, either!" Ariane screamed. She pinned Edmond against the steel wall to my left, though I hadn't seen them move. She held his arms out from his body. He clutched a gun in his right hand, but hadn't been able to use it.

As old as he was, Edmond must have possessed incredible strength. For fifteen hundred years, he had helped direct the course of history, fighting in great battles and wars along the way. Yet he strained against his sister and couldn't break free. With all her awful might, she continued to push against him to keep him there.

Then Caterine was perched on Edmond's shoulders and took his head with both of her hands.

"No, Caterine!" he screamed.

She twisted his head to the side. Edmond couldn't get free. His head turned farther than it should have gone.

"God have mercy on them!" he cried.

Ariane let his arms go and drove her knees into his chest. She joined her sister in pulling, and Edmond's head ripped from his body, which fell to the floor. Blood ran down from his head and spurted out of his body.

The twins seemed tired from the effort, but they had done it. "Goodbye, brother," Ariane said over the sounding alarm. She walked over and placed his head in the coffin she had been in. "I only wish you were alive to know what centuries in here feels like." She slammed the lid down.

Caterine picked up Edmond's body and took it to his

own coffin. "You can lie here again like you did, mocking us with your freedom." She put the body in and brought the lid down over it. "Never again."

The sisters exchanged glances, then walked toward me. I hadn't moved. I might have been able to run while they held Edmond, but not anymore.

Their eyes burned red, and it was hard to look past the fire and see the twins' beauty.

They kept coming, and it became impossible to resist their great beauty, in spite of their eyes.

But they were monsters. The fusion of extremes seemed unnatural and wrong. I didn't think such creatures should exist on Earth.

Their power preceded them and became like pressure crushing my mind from all sides as they advanced. I pushed my body back against the wall to get away from it, but there was nowhere to go. Step after step, the pressure grew.

What would they do after finishing with me? I had let loose the manifestations of Satan's evil upon the world. Would God forgive me when He judged me?

Their bodies almost touched mine when they stopped in front of me. Ariane ran her hand over the scar on my neck and opened her mouth to reveal her sharp fangs.

Caterine's red eyes blazed. "Thank you, Vera."

"Yes, thank you, Vera." Ariane stared at my neck. Her touch was stone, but gentle like Edmond's had been. I dreaded what her bite would be like.

The door at the top of the stairs flew open, and William took a few steps down. Spectavi guards in gray crowded behind him. The sisters both snarled up at them.

William turned and fled with the other Spectavi following him.

Caterine and Ariane looked back at me in unison, smiled, and then sped off after him. I was alone and free from the sisters' force on my mind.

I slid down against the wall to the floor and surveyed the scene in front of me while the alarm blared overhead. Edmond was dead. His coffin and Ariane's lay closed with his body and head split between them. Caterine's coffin was still open.

I had let them out into the world. I kept thinking it over and over. Edmond was a villain, but he had kept his sisters away from humanity, and I had let them out.

I asked the Lord to forgive me.

I reminded myself that I wouldn't have set them free if Edmond hadn't done what he had done to me. I needed to know the truth, and Edmond had left me with no other choice.

At long last, I knew I had been Vera and that Edmond had robbed me of that life. Maybe he thought he had loved me, but what he had done to me made it hard to believe he had really known what love was.

Edmond was guilty, even if I was, too.

My watch said it would soon be five o'clock. I hoped they would forget about me down there and leave me to watch my first sunrise in months. If not, I would do everything I could to get out of that place to see the next day's.

I wondered what was going on up there, and if setting

the twins free had made it easier or harder for me to leave Eure. Once I did, I had to figure out what to do with the other truth I had learned, that Sanguans were being unjustly convicted and killed.

I undid the clasp of my necklace and examined the cross for a moment before putting it in my suit pocket. I would keep it as a reminder of how blind I had let myself be to Edmond's lies.

My attention turned to the doorway again; Victoria looked down at me. She descended the staircase slowly, and I stood up. She appeared emotionless as ever and wore the black leather she often fought in. She had flat sandals on her feet and two swords crossed behind her back—two swords for the two sisters she had come prepared to fight. But she was too late.

Victoria stepped off the last stair and then was across the room, driving me into the wall.

"Aaaah!" I cried out. The steel had dented where my body hit, and the force of her hands broke through the bones in my left shoulder and my collarbone on the right.

Victoria punched lower and broke some of my ribs. I gasped for air with caved in lungs.

She stepped on my right foot—*crrrshhh*.

She punched me in the side of my right hip. The force sent my lower body to the left while she held my upper body still. I felt a tearing in my back—*tsss... snap*! I couldn't feel my legs or feet.

She let me go, and I crashed to the floor, then fell to my right and couldn't stop myself from continuing down until the side of my face smacked steel.

"You stupid little girl," she called down to me.

I struggled to breathe, in agony everywhere I could still feel.

She stepped on my left hand very slowly, and I watched it crumble beneath her foot. She picked me up by the neck and held my head at her eye level. I could move my arms a little, but only struggled for a few seconds before giving up as Victoria ignored me.

"How could you do this, Vera? I told Edmond not to send you away and then told him not to take you back, but I didn't expect *this*." She finally showed anger, before quickly calming down and continuing. "Still, I am sorry to have to do this." She ran a finger over my scar. "I helped give you this, you know. I raised you with Edmond and, when you were little, you used to beg me to drink from you. You were cute once."

I should have been more horrified, but was in too much pain to care.

"You were my greatest human pupil, Vera, and William couldn't keep up with you in his lab. You were a rare human, worthy of our time and attention. But look what Edmond has reduced you to. You're nothing now. You've followed him around like a trained dog since you came back. You sat silent in my arena while he fed on you like you were a piece of meat. It was pathetic to watch."

She pulled my limp body toward her and spoke softly in to my ear. "I mourned for Vera, but I will not mourn for Erin Rose."

Her fangs were on my neck and inside me. My body grew

hot as she sucked my blood. It was wonderful; it was horrible! My mind pleaded for her to stop, but when she didn't, I kept feeling the pleasure everywhere, even in my legs that had been numb.

She sucked harder and faster than Edmond, and she had to have been taking more blood than he ever did. My body got hotter and hotter as she went on, and I couldn't stop my emotions. I didn't care that I had set the twins free; I didn't care that my body was destroyed. All that mattered was what was happening at that moment.

Wave after wave hit me. I shouldn't have been experiencing such joy, but I couldn't help it. She kept drinking, and the waves came faster and faster. I was so hot.

I felt incredible, but was getting too hot. My ability to even consider resisting slipped away.

She drank more.

I burned.

Wonderful.

—————————

I heard the alarm going off. My head lay on the floor. I opened my eyes and saw Victoria walking away. I tried to lift my head, but couldn't, and then couldn't keep my eyes open anymore, either. I heard the alarm for a few more seconds, and then heard nothing.

24

Surrounded by darkness, I didn't know where I was or how I had gotten there. I stood on an invisible surface in the middle of black. I wore my business suit, clean and crisp as if it had just come out of my closet. My feet were bare; my shoes must have come off when Victoria attacked me.

With that thought, all that had happened rushed back to me. Edmond was dead, and his sisters set free. My body wasn't broken where I was, but I lay dead or dying in Edmond's basement. I had once been Vera.

I heard nothing except for my thoughts. I wasn't breathing and felt neither hot nor cold.

Silently, a white light flashed in one direction. It was far in the distance, but I couldn't tell how far. The light flickered and grew, then shrank, then grew again. I took a step toward it, and the light seemed to stabilize. It had been a hard step to take. I took another, and it was just as hard, but the next one got easier. So did the one after that.

Each step became easier and it felt good to be getting closer to the light. I kept walking and getting happier. When I had almost reached the light, I stopped to examine it.

The light was brilliant and perfect where it filled the black void. It seemed to be a few feet taller and wider than me, and I enjoyed looking at it. I tried to see deeper into it, but saw only pure white.

The faintest noise caught my attention, and I looked behind me. There was nothing there.

I faced the light and felt glad.

The noise came again; it sounded ever so slightly louder. Again I saw nothing and turned back to the light.

The third time it was louder, so I turned my body around to try to find its source. There was only black, but I heard it again. I took a step away from the light and felt sad to have done so.

Looking back at its brilliance, I grew happy again, but the noise captured my attention once more. A single, steady beat came from the opposite direction of the light, each one about three or four seconds apart. I took another step toward it.

It must have been my heart beating slowly, I reasoned.

I kept walking away from the light and became more upset as I did, but part of me wanted to hear my heart beating again and again.

The beats grew louder and became like a drum beat as I moved toward them, but they didn't pick up speed as expected.

Something red flickered in the void with each new beat. As I got closer, the red grew larger and the beats even louder, while the white light shrank behind me. I kept going, and the red flickering disappeared. Instead, I saw the steel-lined room in Edmond's basement, but it was very small.

Each drumbeat was like thunder, filling the void completely and still getting louder. With each step, the room became larger.

When the room was almost full-sized, I peered into it, then stopped. I realized it wasn't my heart that I heard thundering around me.

I turned back to the light to make sure I still could, then back to the room, and then did it again. I took a step toward the light.

I turned to the room and saw Edmond's coffin. On the long side facing Ariane's, a drop of red blood dripped out of the bottom edge and hit the floor with a thunderous beat. His body bled inside the coffin; there must have been a crack in the old wood.

Another drop came. The choice I had to make was clear. I already knew I would choose Heaven, or God, or whatever the pure white light led to.

Drop.

Edmond's blood meant taking Satan's power inside my body. The Devil's evil would be within me, compelling me to do his work.

Drop.

I wouldn't swear allegiance to the Spectavi and drink the synthetic blood Edmond had created. I would have to feed on humans to survive. But I could never bring myself to do that.

Drop.

I turned to the light. It looked so pure and wonderful. It

was the whitest white I had ever seen, and I had been close enough to touch it. Surely it led to Heaven, and there was no choice to make.

Drop.

But, Heaven for who? Was it for Vera or Erin? Or both?

Drop.

I imagined seeing Kristi again. I missed her. But who else would be waiting for me there? Aside from Todd, I hadn't been close to anyone, and he was potentially immortal—and could also have been another victim of Edmond's and need my help.

Drop.

I must have had a human family once, at least a mother and a father, but I didn't know them. What if I didn't like them? What if they weren't in Heaven, or what if they had abandoned me and that was how I had come to Edmond and Victoria in the first place?

Drop.

I remembered what Victoria had said about Vera, that she had been a scientist and a warrior. Could I be those things again? What else was I capable of? I knew so little about Vera, about myself. Would I discover more in Heaven?

Drop.

As Erin, I had only two years I could call my own, and there was still so much of life to experience. Would I have that chance in Heaven?

Drop.

What about Caterine and Ariane? I had let them loose

upon the world and couldn't do anything about it. But maybe that wasn't true, and I could do something. If I had been willing to die to learn the truth about them and about myself, shouldn't I be willing to do this to fight their evil?

Drop.

But then I would be like them. And I would be like all the Sanguans who had come through the court. Most did commit the horrible crimes they were accused of, and I would become one of them.

Drop.

I looked back at the light. Would I ever get this chance again? What would God think of a Sanguan who fed on His humans to live?

Drop.

Would I be able to stop myself from killing those I drank from?

Drop.

What terrible things would Satan's power drive me to do?

Drop.

I couldn't feel my legs. My head lay on the floor. I heard the alarm going off and couldn't hear the drops anymore. I was back in Edmond's basement, in my broken body, in agony. I struggled to breathe and felt weak, thirsty, and empty, but the pain was the worst of it all.

I tried to move my left arm, but it hurt too much at my shoulder, and my hand was crushed. My right side was better off, and I managed to lift myself a few inches with my arm and turn my neck. I saw Edmond's coffin thirty or forty feet away, then fell back down.

I reached my right hand out on the floor and pulled. My face scraped across steel, and my limp legs dragged behind me. I pulled again and moved a few feet more. The incredible pain in my upper body led to perverse gratefulness that I couldn't feel below my waist. Each time I moved, the pain amplified, and I expected to pass out at any moment. I wished I had chosen Heaven.

But I hadn't. I didn't really wish that and was in too much pain to consider it all over again. Amid labored breaths, I lifted my scraped face off the floor and pulled myself toward the coffins.

I pulled and made some progress, but became exhausted and rested my head on the floor. It was too hard. I would die before getting there.

My eyes closed, and darkness crept into my mind. I couldn't make it.

Drop.

I opened my eyes, picked up my head, and after taking as deep a breath as possible, pulled, and then pulled again. The pain persisted, but I had to make it, so I pulled until the drops coming from the lower edge of Edmond's coffin became clearly visible.

I pulled my crippled body through the puddle of cold synthetic blood and kept pulling until moving to the side of the coffin.

Could I really do this? Should I really do this?

I leaned under the coffin and opened my mouth with my head sideways, but missed the next drop that fell. I pulled myself a little farther and turned my face to the cracked edge.

A drop hit my cheek—hot! My skin sizzled while I stretched my tongue for the blood that ran down my face.

The next drop, I tasted—just as hot, burning the back of my throat. My eyes opened wide, and the pain in my throat disappeared. I remembered to swallow the drop after that, and it warmed the top of my chest as it ran down into me. I stayed there, and the next few warmed me farther down into my stomach. My crushed left hand tingled, then so did my right foot.

My breathing got easier, and I pushed my upper body off the floor with my right arm, making sure not to miss a drop. I leaned on my elbow and found I could move the repaired fingers in my left hand.

Each drop of the ancient blood tasted so good, and I could taste it all over my body.

While catching the drops, I brought my legs under me and knelt on my knees facing the coffin—my spine must have healed significantly.

No longer relying on my arms to prop myself up, I reached out and grabbed the coffin.

My body was heavy, but I slowly brought myself toward the source of the blood I needed. Inch by inch, my body gradually became lighter, until finally my mouth covered the edge. The next drop hit me and, when I sucked it down and kept sucking, the hot blood streamed out of the coffin more quickly.

I closed my eyes and recalled the small statue from Night that Stan had made and painted. Baphomet. I remembered how hideous it had been. It had seemed so lifelike.

At that moment it filled my mind, and it wasn't lifelike— it was life. Baphomet told me to keep drinking the healing blood, so I did.

My body grew hotter and hotter and was strong again.

I drank, and drank, and I had to have more. It felt so good. The blood was so hot. I was drinking power.

I drank and knew I wouldn't have my fragile human body anymore.

I wouldn't be a toy for vampires to play with and feed on.

I wouldn't be afraid of the world I lived in.

I would never again have my memories stolen.

The power coursed through my body. I wanted it all, and Baphomet said no one could stop me from taking it.

Thhcrnckh! I dug my teeth into the wood and sucked the blood faster and faster. I was burning hot, my heart raced, and I could feel my chest rising and falling as I breathed along with it.

From deep within me, a burst! The heat ignited into a raging inferno.

I drank more and more until the stream of blood slowed. I sucked harder and got more, but it slowed again. Then it stopped. I reached my tongue into the crack and found a little blood, and then it was all gone.

I leaned away from Edmond's coffin, and my heart continued to race while I knelt with my eyes still closed. My breathing slowed gradually, and I cooled as it did. I stretched my neck from side to side, then rolled it around. I stretched my wrists and healed fingers. I felt strong, but I didn't know how strong. I ripped off my watch with ease, threw it to my right, and heard a loud *clang* when it hit the wall, followed by a duller one when it hit the floor.

I searched my mind and found only memories I had created since the morning I woke up alone in my apartment and didn't know myself. I didn't know what Edmond had known. I didn't know anything Vera had known.

I felt for the scar on my neck. It was gone.

I opened my eyes, stood, and turned to Ariane's coffin. I saw my reflection in the lid.

My face had been perfectly healed, and my skin looked a little lighter than before, but the black cross on my neck was as dark as it had ever been. I opened my mouth and saw my fangs.

I was the vampire Erin Rose, and I was hungry.

THE END OF BOOK II

Connect Online

Thanks for reading. If you enjoyed the story, please leave a review at your favorite online retailer.

Get the latest updates about S.M. Perlow's works by signing up for his newsletter:

smperlow.com/newsletter

Find him online at:

smperlow.com

twitter.com/smperlow

facebook.com/smperlow

Works by S.M. Perlow

Vampires and the Life of Erin Rose

Novels
Choosing a Master
Alone
Lion
Hope
War

Short Stories
Alice Stood Up

—

The Grand Crucible

Novels
Golden Dragons, Gilded Age

—

Other Works

Short Stories
The Girl Who Was Always Single